POINT FOUR ZEROS SEVEN

0.00007

K.J.HERITAGE

P4Z7

In space everyone can hear you scream...

CONTENTS

1-0
AWAKENING

Lissa! Speak to me, you must wake up!

A disembodied voice echoes through my mind, repeating the same phrases and words. Sometimes it whispers, sometimes it is deafening, pleading with me to respond. Insistent and constant. I want to sleep, to push the voice away, but I'm already sleeping… *aren't I?* And besides, lurking behind the voice is some nameless dread, a formless horror that pulses and pushes, drawing ever closer. A dread I'm unable to ignore.

I force my eyes open to a painful slit, blinded by a blur of flashing reds and ambers.

You are awake. Good. You must operate the emergency eject, otherwise I can't help you.

The voice comes from nowhere and everywhere. I draw breath to reply, sucking a thick gloopy liquid into my throat, and gag. Hacking up lungfuls of the stuff.

Good, Lissa, good. After you have evacuated the cryo-gel, locate the eject lever. Hurry.

The coughing stops and my vision clears. I find myself staring at a tangle of wires hanging from the ceiling of a cramped translucent pod of some sort. My wet, naked, trapped body glistening crimson under flashing readouts and angry displays. Various tubes penetrating my arms and legs.

I'm having a choking nightmare of some sort, a waking dream. *I must be.* My eyes are heavy, my eyelids drooping. Now that I've coughed up whatever was blocking my throat, all I want to do is let them close again, and to dream of something else.

No. Stay awake Lissa. Your life is in danger. You must vacate your pod.

I'm drifting back into unconsciousness, but the insistent voice becomes more demanding. "Go away!"

Keep your eyes open, Lissa.

"Leave me alone!"

I will. Just do one thing for me. And I will let you rest. I promise.

Sleep is calling to me, but I know the voice won't stop until I do what it says. "You promise?"

Yes, Lissa. Search around with your fingers until you find a small handle.

"What?"

Just do as I say. A small handle by your right hand.

I flex my fingers, the joints cracking painfully, moving them until they touch smooth metal.

That is it, Lissa. Twist and pull.

I try to turn the lever, my numb fingers struggling to keep hold.

Try again, Lissa.

People have been telling me what to do all my life. Why should I start listening now? I decide to make one more attempt. If that doesn't work, then I'm going back to sleep. I pull again, my fingers stronger, and this time the handle moves with a smooth click.

You did it, Lissa.

I lie back, relaxing, keen to return to slumber, disturbed by a series of heavy vibrations and loud whirrs. I'm rudely thrust up into a standing position, hit by a wave of dizziness. I collapse, pitching forward, slapping heavily onto a freezing metallic floor. Intravenous tubes yanked from my arms and legs. Pain and cold lance through me like twin knives. I scream with a mixture of agony and rage, shaking uncontrollably, my muscles twitching and cramping. My voice is a weak, tremulous whine, barely audible over the cacophony of alarms that blare abruptly around me. "What the hell is that?"

I thought we had more time. You must vacate this area, now.

Icy air blows over my wet body, numbing and bone deep. "Vacate?" I sit up, hugging my knees. Dim lights far above reveal a vast circular chamber full of row upon row of human-sized pods stretching into the darkness. Pods like the one I'm lying next to. Except mine is split open.

Stand up, Lissa and get moving!

"What is happening? And wh-who are you?"

There is no time for questions, Lissa. I'm Simone, and you must do as I say if you want to survive.

I can't make sense of anything apart from one single word… *survive*. That, I understand. I push myself up onto unsteady feet, made aware of my nudity by the freezing air. Blood dripping from where I was connected to the pod's tubes. My bones aching.

You must run, Lissa. Your life depends on it.

"Run? I can barely feel my legs."

If you cannot run, you must walk… go straight ahead.

I stumble forward, ignoring the stiffness in my neck and back.

Turn left at the next junction, Simone continues, her disembodied voice steady and supportive. I cling onto her words, using them as a lifeline to navigate my body through what appears to be an immense, labyrinthine chamber.

"Who am I?" I ask, my teeth chattering from the cold and a growing fear.

Your questions can wait, Simone replies, her tone now commanding. *If you want to live, you must follow my instructions.*

"But—"

Your memory will return. Keep moving. You do not have much time.

"Okay," I choke out, forcing myself to move faster despite

my complaining legs and cramping feet, my breath coming in ragged gasps. I scurry along a curved walkway, passing more cryosleep pods. Hundreds of them. Men, women, and children. Serene faces floating beneath frosted glass. Asleep and dreaming. "Who are these people?"

Keep moving, L-Lissa, Simone's voice crackles. *You are almost there.*

"Almost where?" I wheeze, freezing air burning my lungs, my legs growing heavier with each step.

Warning! Simone's voice is suddenly louder, jolting me back to the present. *Hull breach! Run, Lissa, run!*

A deafening groan reverberates through the chamber. The floor trembles beneath me. I push myself harder, desperation and panic forcing me into a stumbling run.

Turn right, then left, Simone barks, and I obey blindly, trusting her guidance. My body screaming in protest, my heart pounding like a jackhammer.

Almost there, Lissa," Simone says, her voice softer now. *Go through the doors ahead.*

A colossal airlock looms before me, stretching up from the cold metallic floor into the shadowy gloom above. Salvation from the chaos unfolding behind, except... it's closed. I hurl myself toward the doors. The first whispers of vacuum tugging at my skin as the hull succumbs to the breach.

"Simone, let me out!" I batter on the smooth, grey metal, my voice barely audible over the rush of escaping atmosphere. The superstructure creaking and groaning. My lungs tightening as I gasp on frozen air.

Is this it? Am I going to die?

The airlock rumbles and whines, pulling apart to create a narrow opening. I throw myself through the gap, fighting the escaping air, and collapse on the other side. The airlock slams shut behind me, cutting off the maelstrom with a resounding clang.

Well done, Lissa. Simone's voice is back to its normal volume. *You are safe.*

1-1-ABANDONED

I lie on the other side of the airlock. Naked flesh pressed against the cold metal doors. Head pounding. Muscles cramping, lungs burning. Above me, lights flicker and buzz into life. An ancient, dust-covered accessway is revealed. Tall as the enormous airlock behind me. And much older. Covered in cracked cream paint.

I thought you wouldn't wake up in t-time, Simone says. And do I detect a sense of relief? *You need to make your way to the CC.*

"The what?"

The Command Centre, Lissa. Where the crew are located.

"I'm on a ship of some sort?"

You are aboard the colony space-freighter, Octavia, on route to the new world of Persephone.

A memory flash. I'm in Earth orbit, the once lush, green shimmering ball tainted with browns and yellows. I'm filled with hope and excitement, and accomplishment. I see a ship. An immense awkwardly shaped freighter hanging in the void of space like some giant, silent, chaotic sentinel. Was that the *Octavia?* The closed airlock separates me from the thousands of souls I left behind in the pods. More colonists? "Those people. Are they… are they all dead?"

They are quite safe, Lissa. However, you are not. The Octavia is over three miles in length. You have a day long trek ahead of you with no water, no clothes, and no source of heat. You will need to keep moving—otherwise you will freeze to death.

"I have to walk where?"

To the Command Centre located in the bow.

"I can't walk for a whole day, I need rest!"

Rest is not an option, Lissa.

"I—"

The way is not straightforward. You are in an old and disused delivery tube near the ship's stern. Do not worry, I will navigate you out of here.

A series of green arrows light up along the floor. A flickering pathway in the gloom.

Please start moving before you lose too much body heat.

I get up, my chest sore and my eyes blurry from the depressurisation. Frustrated and annoyed yet complying all the same. What else can I do?

Good, Lissa. Follow the arrows and you'll soon be there.

Cold lances through my feet as I pad forward. "What is going on and why am I here? And who am I? Do I have any family on board?" I'm desperate to know more about myself and my place in this nightmare. Anything to take my mind off the long trek ahead of me. The void in my memories is as cold and empty as this colossal accessway.

You are Lissa Angeline Blackstone, Simone begins, her tone clinical, *age, twenty-six. A socialite estranged from a wealthy family who disowned you due to numerous run-ins with the law, all to do with your problems with drink and drugs. You tried various occupations that didn't work out until you embarked on the Octavia, en-route to the colony world of Persephone.*

The information jars with who I know I am, or at least, who I *think I am*. A druggie socialite? I shake my head. That can't be right… can it? The information does nothing to quell the hollowness inside of me. But at least I have a name. I clasp my hands together, interlocking my fingers and crossing my thumbs. Longing for connection, even if only to myself.

"What happened to the ship, how come there was a breach?"

Space debris impacted your saucer section and other parts of the ship causing minor damage. Your cryopod malfunctioned, waking you up prematurely.

Her words wrap around me. A warm blanket against the recent terrors. "Simone… who are you?"

I am an artificial intelligence, although my official designation is 'ship companion'.

"I thought AIs were banned years ago."

That is true. However, ship companions, like myself, are necessary to help guide ships through long journeys in space when the captain and crew are in cryosleep. Such as the hull breach we just encountered. I was on hand to steer the ship and to wake the captain and crew in time to respond to the emergency. I also monitor crew members individually during cryosleep. Captain and crew survival is a critical factor in the overall percentage success of a journey.

"And the passengers?"

The crew is my primary concern, passenger welfare and survival are connected directly to their wellbeing.

"Oh, I see. So how am I doing?"

Your physical readouts were all in the green before the malfunction. You are hydrated and have been receiving a steady stream of nutrient. You are in good health despite what has happened.

"And mentally... my memory is... well, it's not where I usually keep it. It's... it's gone."

This is a temporary condition associated with cryosleep. Your memories will begin to return over the next few days. However, you may experience moments of hysteria or garbled or inaccurate thinking. A condition known as cryo-paranoia.

"That doesn't sound like fun."

It affects a minority of sleepers upon awakening. It is temporary but can lead to erratic behaviour, self-harming, and injury to others. Beware of any irrational thoughts or concerns and even hallucinations. And do not succumb to sleep, no matter how much you may feel you need it.

"Hallucinations? Yay!" I reply drolly.

This is no joking matter, Lissa. Should you experience anything I have described, you must alert myself or the crew immediately.

I sigh. Simone is quite the bundle of laughs. The flashing

green arrows take me into a corridor cramped with pipes and tubing, lights flickering into life as I approach. It shows its age in many layers of discoloured white paint that have blurred the exposed nuts and bolts, hiding them under drifts of glossy yellow. Not that this place has been painted recently. It stinks of age. "Just how old is this ship?"

The Octavia is three-hundred and fifty-nine years old. Although it has been augmented and added to many times over.

I remember the massive spaceship I glimpsed floating above Earth. The only real memory of my past. A chaotic city-like structure dominated by the massive engines that regularly took colonists between the stars. "How close are we to Persephone?"

We are approximately halfway through our twenty-two year journey.

"Only halfway? Shit! What will happen when I reach the Command Centre? The Crew will put me back into cryo, right?"

Yes, Lissa. Now I must leave you.

"What do you mean?"

My systems are not compatible with the older parts of the ship. I'll join you again when you reach the CC. The green arrows will guide you.

"You are leaving me on my own?"

Yes, Lissa.

"What if I get lost?"

Trust the arrows, Lissa. They won't lead you astray.

"It's freezing and I'm naked."

That is why you must hurry. Physical activity will stave off the cold. If you want to survive, you must keep moving.

That word again. *Survive.* I nod, steeling myself as I enter the gloom. Green arrows stretching out ahead of me. Illuminating my path. I can do this. I have to if I don't want to freeze to death in some forgotten corner of this ugly behemoth.

That is it, Lissa. Keep putting one foot in front of the other, Simone calls after me, her voice becoming distant.

Shivering and exposed, I traverse the cold corridor in a slowly moving circle of weak, flickering light that illuminates the darkness, but also prevents me seeing what lies ahead, frightening shadowy shapes revealing themselves to be nothing more than discarded machinery and equipment. I hold onto Simone's words like a lifeline. "Trust the arrows," I whisper to myself, pushing past the fear snapping at my gut like so many hungry wolves, the sound of my voice both comforting and alien in this endless, abandoned labyrinth of painted metal and stale freezing air. "I can do this."

My laboured breathing and the slap of my bare feet are the only sounds as I pad through the silent ship. Following one green arrow after another. Leading me further into the belly of the *Octavia*. I go up ladders and stairs and across gantries. Ascend and descend in elevators that hum with ancient power. Traverse cavernous chambers, each as eerily empty as the last. And pass many doors and openings. I try to count them to keep my mind occupied. Their numbers blur together like the words in a bedtime book.

Back when ships like this one were first commissioned, journeys within the Solar System were so long that crew members brought along their families. And with them came cooks, militia, teachers, doctors, nurses and more. A whole host of support personnel essential for survival in the slow, dark, loneliness of space.

How do I know this?

Perhaps I made a study of such ships before my journey? I must've done. Now these corridors and rooms, once so busy with life, lie empty and forgotten. How many people died here? How many poor souls gasped out their last in these now abandoned rooms? I immediately clamp down the thought. This is scary enough without adding ghosts to the mix.

Some parts of the ship are freezing. Possibly closer to the outer hull. Others are warmer, yet still too cold to be comfortable. Indeed, it's only the cold that is keeping me conscious…

My eyes blink open, jolted awake by my cramping limbs. I squint, trying to adjust to the dim light emanating from a flashing green arrow on the floor. Its faint glow revealing a narrow corridor with cold, metallic walls.

Where am I?

I struggle to my feet, bathed in flickering white light. My legs screaming in pain. Arms stiff and full of pins and needles. I fell asleep against Simone's strict orders. Shit!

I rub my legs until all the knots are gone and take a faltering step, suddenly hit in the head by a pound hammer. Memories blast into my mind in a series of lightning strikes. Faces, places, snippets of conversations and more. I see myself living in an enormous house with expansive gardens—fighting kids in a foster home—staggering, off my face on God knows what in some seedy drug den—hugging my nanny, my only friend—working cargo bays at some vast spaceport—being presented at a swanky ball, wearing a pink, floral dress—sharing a tiny, cramped apartment with five others—kissing and sleeping with numerous men and women—serving drinks in a seedy bar—and… surviving on the streets as a child.

I scream into the darkness. Grabbing my head. My voice echoing eerily into the empty ship. After long minutes, the throbbing in my head subsides. Is that how it's supposed to be? My memories returning in such a painful fashion? Although they're not like memories at all. They're unconnected. Odd scenes from different movies. Only one recollection has real substance… *living on the streets as a child*. I remember that. Fighting for scraps in the dregs of a massive city. Police catching me. Taking me to an adoption home. No, that's not right. I had a nanny when I was young, didn't I? And the house? Was I adopted and taken there to live? The rich parents Simone mentioned? If so, why was I working the docks and serving drinks in a bar? That part makes no sense… unless my parents abandoned me. Simone said I was estranged from them.

Out of the jumbled mess of memories I notice there is one, single strong thread. A desire to escape Earth and my situation. That need, whatever it is and wherever it comes from, still burns inside. I guess it's why I was in cryo. Before I was rudely awoken that is.

A shiver jars me back into reality, the pain in my head replaced by an intense itching. My blonde hair is long and matted. Smoothing my hair down as best I can, I continue. Passing through more corridors and chambers. Climbing even more stairs. Following the green arrows for hour upon hour. Just how large is this damn space freighter anyway?

I reach a newer part of the ship. The paint less thick and the corridors and doorways differently sized and shaped. The green arrows have also subtly changed. Am I getting close? I've been walking for at least a day. I must be. I turn a corner, unable to properly take in what I'm looking at. The green arrows point to a wall, a more recent addition built over the arrows. I check it out, but it's what it appears to be—a blank wall blocking my progress.

1-2-BLOCKED

What the hell am I supposed to do now? I want to scream and shout at my ridiculous situation yet can't find the energy. Instead, I stare impassively at the wall, my head bursting with anger, resentment, and frustration. I've been here before. Not in this exact situation, but others like it. Trapped. Full of fury and bitterness. Making me wonder… *just who am I?* I wish I knew. Although part of me doesn't want to find out.

The corridor lights flick off again due to lack of movement and, broken out of my reverie, I turn to more practical concerns. I must find a way around this block. And I need to drink. My lips and throat are dry. I could survive many days without food, but without water and all this effort? Not more than two, and there's no source of water anywhere close. The air is dry and stale. All moisture was probably sucked from these corridors hundreds of years ago. The only solution is to try and find those green arrows again.

I decide to keep to the newer part of the ship, travelling in the same direction. The plan is sound, but all alternate routes return me to the same old paint-encrusted corridors, anger and resentment welling inside me with each dead end and every wrong turn. I'm fighting those emotions on par with the cold. Instead of hindering me, they drive me forward, and I find strength in them.

Logic says the blocked corridor cannot be the only access to the front of the ship. It wouldn't make sense if it was. There must be other ways around the obstruction, either on the decks above or below. I decide to head upward to see if I can find a way over this damn obstacle.

As I get closer to the freighter's upper hull, the corridors become cramped. There's also more derelict equipment to navigate. Forcing me to squeeze between tight gaps and to climb over difficult machinery.

I enter a dusty chamber with a ladder on one wall disappearing into blackness above. The air here is the coldest I've experienced so far. Without knowing where the ladder leads, I put my foot on the first rung and ascend. The artificial gravity lowering with each step. I reach a high-landing minutes later and step onto a wide gantry. A circular viewing port clogged with decades of grime. I stumble in the low gee, barely catching my feet, and brace myself against the port wall. The gantry's segmented glass panels are freezing to the touch. I wipe a hole in the muck, getting most of it onto my skin, and peer through, shivering.

Space stretches out before me. An endless expanse of blackness punctuated only by the pinpricks of distant stars glittering against the void. The *Octavia* sprawls into this void. A vast, shadowy, miles-long behemoth half-hidden by darkness. A hodgepodge of old and new elements added as the ship evolved over time. The view is dominated by three monumental saucer-like shapes slotted into the ship's hull like an afterthought. A memory flash. Similar saucers hovering in high Earth orbit being fed by a constant stream of shuttles. One of those saucers must be mine, I realise, wishing I was back there. Slumbering without a single concern. The years passing by in a single night's dreamless sleep. I scan them for damage and find nothing out of the ordinary, until I spot what must be the stern in the far distance, evidenced by colossal engines invisibly spewing out streams of charged ions and exotic particles. I'm facing in the wrong direction. While searching for a route towards the bow, I became turned around. I swallow, my mouth sticky and dry. If I'd not found the gantry... I try not to think about the consequences.

I glide over to the opposite side of the viewing port. Scrubbing at the glass again, covering myself in more grime, and try to get my bearings. I've travelled about two thirds of the freighter's massive length. There is still a way to go if the Command Centre is located at the front of the ship.

A faded symbol on the oldest part of the curving hull catches my eye. Three flattened spirals with a Celtic feel, resembling a three-leaved clover. The symbol is more art than a logo. And it is no recent addition. As old as the freighter itself. Pock-marked and scored with burns. Its resilience to the harshness of space makes it beautiful. An unexpected sight on such an otherwise ugly ship.

Two more saucers are embedded in the bow, making five in total. With twenty thousand colonists in each—I somehow know the number—the *Octavia* must carry upward of a hundred-thousand people. The thought is daunting, especially as I'm alone and abandoned. The one unlucky sap forced out of cryo.

I descend the ladder, the full gee at the bottom making my legs and back ache. This time, I make a mental note of my heading. I became lost once, I won't make that mistake again. If I treat the bow as 'north' and I come to a right turn, taking me 'east', I'll need to take the next left turn to return northward and the bow. These ships are built straight and long. There are few curved corridors to lose my bearings.

I head back inside the ship and away from the hull. There's no way I can survive this cold for very long. Yet the chill air becomes worse as I descend... or I'm slowly entering hypothermia. I take a deep breath and start jogging, generating my own heat to survive, although I'm unable to jog longer than a few minutes at a time. I reach a closed hatchway facing northward toward the bow, locked with a large wheel that hasn't been turned in decades. I pull at it, my hands slipping, greasy with grime from the gantry glass. I wipe the muck into my hair and onto my body. And, after much tugging and cursing, the wheel begins to move. Becoming easier with each turn until... the door jerks open a crack, accompanied by a terrific squealing sound, my matted hair sucked into the gap. Shit! A vacuum on the other side! I push the door with all my strength and reverse the wheel. The high-pitched screeching diminishing to a sudden silence, my hair trapped, forcing me to yank it free. Most of it breaks off, although some hairs are pulled out at the roots. Sobbing and in pain, I fall dejected to the floor, the freezing door burning my naked back. I don't care. I'm done for, I'll never get out of this damn maze of a ship. I'll die here!

I sit in an angry defeated pool of my own tears until the lights go out, bathing me in darkness. Is this what I will become? A long forgotten, dried out corpse lost in the abandoned, dark belly of this spaceship? I shake my head. No way! The lights blink back on with the movement just as I glimpse something in the distance. A sight that makes my heart lurch.

I get up and run forward, turning into a corridor, arms pumping the air. Beyond, in an intersection, I see the green glow of arrows. The glow I spotted before the lights came on. Relief floods through me. I'm back on course. Relief that soon turns to fury. I made it, with no thanks to Simone or the damn crew.

My anger reaches a crescendo and I'm hit by a familiar sharp pain in my head. I brace myself against the corridor wall, readying myself for another onslaught of memories. Even so, I'm unprepared as they smash into my mind, arriving this time in a confused jumble. Like watching a wall of holotops all streaming different shows. I collapse to the floor holding my head.

I'm aware of other memories telling me amnesia is a temporary thing. That those with the condition always recover full recall. Unless their amnesia was due to brain damage. Memories returning bit by bit and not in flurries of pain like this. Is that what I have? A brain injury? My pod was damaged in the incident that woke me up. Maybe there is some internal harm that might be causing this? I shake my head. This kind of thinking will get me nowhere. I need to get to the Command Centre. If I don't, I'm dead, brain damage or not.

The pain dissipates, and I stand up, rubbing at my temples, tiptoeing back into my mind. Searching for my new memories. All are annoyingly beyond reach apart from one singular scene. I'm six or seven years old. In a dormitory at the adoption home. An older kid is demanding my bed which has the best position behind the door. I fight him for it. And even though he is bigger than me, I beat him to a pulp. I see the scared faces of the other kids. The blood on my hands and the glee of victory. The scene is grotesque, yet I relive my fury and elation with relish. My fists clenching and unclenching. My heartbeat raised.

Shaking my head and shrugging, I walk toward the arrows. One thing is for sure, I will find out with time. I just need to be patient. Although I'm coming to the conclusion that patience isn't one of my virtues.

I continue for long hours. The relentless barrage of corridors and chambers, of stairs and elevators, wearing me down. My biggest worry is dehydration. I'm craving water. My tongue is a bloated dead whale on an empty, dry beach. Every breath is painful. My skin taut and stretched thin. The ever-present cold stinging my pores. I can do nothing except keep moving. One heavy foot after the other.

I stumble into a long, empty corridor, feeling close to my goal. Walking faster into the never ending dark. Wondering if I will ever reach its end. Until the lights flick on to reveal another closed hatchway.

Do I have the strength to open it? And if so, would I be able to close it again if there was vacuum on the other side? I don't care. I focus instead on turning the wheel, which spins with ease. The hatch swings aside and I walk forward to stand on a small landing above a chasm over thirty feet wide.

Too wide to jump across.

The green arrows continue tantalisingly on the other side, where there is another small landing and hatchway. "What the actual fuck!" is what I try to say, but my voice is nothing more than a dry whisper.

A cold breeze blows from the murky darkness below. The chasm must reach directly to the hull to be this cold. An immense elevator shaft. Probably used to move freight in and around the ship. The only way across is a small, treacherous ledge with no handholds. Maybe at the beginning of this insane journey I would've attempted it. Now, I'm too tired. I need water, food, and rest.

Another dead end and I don't have the stamina or the inclination to try and go around again. This can't be it... it just can't. I may not know who I am, yet I know intrinsically that I'm not the type to give up.

Even so... I have a sudden desire to step off. To let myself fall into this deadly chasm. To end it all. Can I do it? I remember the ladder leading up to the gantry, and one of the many books I read as a child. Before I have time to change my mind, I jump into the cold, dark hole.

1-3-RECRUITED

I disappear into darkness. My quick, ragged breaths echoing off the walls, my heart thundering in my ears. Freezing air rushing past me, stinging like acid. My body bracing for the terrible impact that I know is to come. Enveloped by loss and hopelessness and a resentment at abandoning this life I hold so dearly.

How could I have been so stupid?

The fall continues for what seems like forever until my eyes adjust to the diminished illumination. I'm no longer plummeting but floating next to the wall of the shaft. I shriek with panic at the abrupt lack of up and down. A shriek that turns into a fit of nervous giggles followed by a dry hacking cough. I don't care. I was right!

Artificial gravity varies onboard spaceships. It's not a constant force like on Earth. Living areas are set to one gee, but other areas can have low or zero gravity. Simply because full gees are not needed everywhere, or lower gravity is more practical.

How do I know this? I have a quick flash of sitting in a window seat in a large house. It's my bedroom. Small and crammed with books. I was a reader, avidly consuming both fiction and non-fiction alike.

I look up and realise I've fallen no more than a hundred feet. Both landings are lit with what now appears to be bright, blinding light. With a few ungraceful movements, I kick myself toward the opposite chasm wall and grab a hold, the icy metal numbing my fingers.

I take a few steadying breaths and clamber upward, although to me, the sensation is more like dragging myself along a floor, and soon I'm approaching the opposite hatchway. As I get close, the artificial grav kicks back in. I ignore the disorientation and begin climbing, pulling myself toward the landing. The gravity reaches one gee again and, with no hand or footholds, I am unable to move any further.

Dammit!

I think, trying to remember anything I may have read that can help me. Nothing comes to mind. Instead, I scramble back down into the shaft, back into zero gee, and take another series of deep breaths. Launching myself forward again. This time half-running, half pushing myself along. Gaining as much speed as I can in the hope it will be enough to propel me upwards.

I near the top of the chasm, giving one extra kick, my increased momentum carrying me forward. I grab at the lip of the landing, and I'm thrown around. My forward motion slowing to a stop by the grav. And I'm falling again. I twist the best I can but land heavily, the breath knocked out of me. I'm battered and bruised but on the opposite side of the chasm, but I did it! Getting up, I turn the wheel to the closed hatchway which opens with a groan, and lurch through. My legs stabbing awkwardly forward.

Something is different here. Something that I can't quite put my finger on… and then it hits me. It's warmer. A lot warmer. I'm close, very close. I stumble forward, my eyesight blurry, following the green arrows for another twenty minutes until I find myself in what appears to be the crew area.

"Hello!" I try to shout, my voice nothing more than a

hoarse whisper. I keep walking until I come to a canteen with tables and chairs, in front of which is the ship's galley. A cooking area… and a sink. I can almost smell the water. And in a shuffling half run, I limp over, my numb hands struggling ineffectually with the metal of the taps. Goddammit! I hit the taps angrily with my fists. They are weak and bounce off, yet somehow, I manage to turn one of them.

Water!

I drink directly from the tap. Engorging myself, drinking for what seems like hours but what must be only a few minutes. Tasting the sweet flavour of water as it gushes down my throat. I've never been so grateful for anything in my life. The energising liquid flows into my needy system. Rushing into my hungry veins and arteries. The pain in my thumping head receding into nothing more than a bad memory. My energy returning like a battery on fast recharge. I take my lips off the tap, stand up straight and wipe at my mouth, stretching the knots out of my back and legs, and rubbing at my many bruises. Still thirsty, I see a beaker and fill it with more wonderful water, downing it in one long gulp. The blurriness in my eyes and my sore throat miraculously improving.

I'm re-energised. The strongest I've felt since I was cruelly awoken from my pod, capable to take on whatever else this situation throws at me.

"Who the hell are you?"

I turn around to see a thick-set, dark-skinned woman with short grey hair shaved at the sides wearing a thick crew skinsuit stained with food and other spillages. A personal holotab stuffed into the suit's belt. She's tall, muscled and imposing. Looking me up and down with beady brown eyes staring at me from a mottled, freckled face. And I'm suddenly aware of my nudity. Covering myself as best I can with my hands.

This is Lissa Angeline Blackstone, Captain. The colonist

awoken in the recent incident, Simone says, her voice fuller and resonating with warm bass tones.

"I know who she is dammit, Simone! I was just startled."

"I got lost," I say weakly.

She comes over to me with an outstretched hand. "I'm Captain Evans Marla. I'm sorry we didn't have time to come looking for you. We were in the middle of a ship-wide incident. Pleased to meet you."

I take her hand and shake, aware of what a strange situation this is. "My name's Lissa. I followed the arrows but—"

"Yes, yes, all in good time. This way." She takes me to a service cupboard and a smock-like garment. "It's not much, but it'll do until we can get you some decent clothes."

She turns away while I get dressed, relief flooding through me. The captain may be a little curt, but at least I'm here.

"Feel better?"

I nod.

"Good."

She turns around and walks away. I follow, somewhat bemused. All I want to do is eat and be put back into cryo. And to forget this madness.

We leave the canteen, enter a few well-used corridors with scuffed and stained walls, and walk through a sizable lockable hatch revealing a beaten-up room with four other crew members inside. "Welcome to the bridge," Marla says with a sweep of a muscled arm.

It's not the gleaming command centre I've seen on countless sci-fi shows. More like the run-down innards of some ancient steamship. The walls are painted in a patchwork of greys, browns, and whites, some of it covered in graffiti. Various system holotops flicker with data too fast for me to comprehend. Red lights pulse erratically, casting jarring shadows.

Four faces look up from their holotops to stare at me.

A mixed race rather beautiful African and Asian woman with very long, thick black hair with twin platinum stripes, and three men. One is overweight and strikingly ginger, one young, blond, and handsome, and the other older and intimidating looking, augmented with what look like old-fashioned cybernetic implants and some rather grotesque tattoos.

"This is Melissa," Captain Marla barks unceremoniously.

"It's actually Lissa. Pleased to meet you."

The Asian girl smirks at my appearance. I'm not looking at my best that's for sure.

The young blonde-haired guy gives me an encouraging, if not lop-sided smile, flashing me an impressive array of teeth set in a firm jaw. His smooth features warm and friendly. I notice he's quite a fine specimen of a man. Not overly muscled, and trim. His skinsuit is clean. This guy takes care of himself. If I have a type, he's very much it. The thought jars me back to my reality, and I realise just where I am. On the bridge of a colony ship, possibly years from home. Bruised and caked in grime. I must be quite the sight. I have bigger concerns than fanciable young men. "When… when can I expect to be put back into cryo?" I stutter.

Captain Marla shakes her head. "Didn't you tell her, Simone? You useless piece of silicone crap?"

No, not yet, Captain, I—

"Shut up!"

Yes, Captain.

"Tell me what?" I ask.

Captain Marla sighs. "I'm afraid there will be no cryosleep just yet. It's a condition of the colony contract you signed before you were put aboard."

"What is?"

"Any surviving passengers that unfortunately wake up during the journey are to aid the crew with any emergencies or maintenance work until the crew's work is complete.

Meaning you will return to cryo when we do. Understand?"

1-4-SCANNED

"I'm expected to goddamn work?"

The captain gives me an apologetic stare. "'Fraid so."

"What the hell?"

Marla shrugs. "Don't blame me, blame… hey, Vic, which colony company are we shipping for this time?"

"*Brave New Worlds*," the guy with cybernetic implants replies with a thick Latino accent, his grotesque tats greasy and shining in the reflected light of his holo display.

"Yeah," the captain nods. "Blame *Brave New Worlds*. Although it doesn't matter what they call themselves, the contracts are all the same. I just follow orders and protocol. That's my job."

"But—"

"I understand this isn't what you were expecting, but it is what it is. I suggest you get on board with it. We'll keep you busy so the weeks will pass more quickly. It will be over before you realise, and we can all return to slumberland." She turns to the young blond-haired guy. "Can you go show Melissa to her cabin and get her cleaned and suited up?"

The ginger-haired guy stands up, staring at the captain with small piggy eyes framed by red-tinted glasses. He's in his forties, his long hair balding, and is overweight, a pot belly hanging over skinny legs. "Why send Brad, Captain, when I am more than happy to look after the girl?" His voice is an overly dramatic whine, his precise words spoken with an affected English accent.

Vic, smirks behind his back.

A small shake of Captain Marla's head. "We need you here, Ferg, as you well know. We've cryo-systems in the amber, and as our onboard specialist, you don't want to wake any more colonists, otherwise we'll be forced to space them, which they may complain about," she snorts. I'm finding it hard to see the funny side.

Fergal flashes irritation, wringing his hands, his knuckles white. "There's nothing that serious on the coms."

"Did you forget who's captain?" She looks down at her skinsuit and her name and rank printed on the stained material, her thick, muscled neck bulging. "Oh yeah, it's me. And what I say goes, remember? And besides we're busy, Brad is the only crew we can spare at the moment."

Ferg blushes bright red, his handwringing becoming more manic. I feel sorry for the guy.

"Brad, you have your orders," the captain says efficiently. "And Fergal… sit down and concentrate on your job. I'm off to my ready room." She enters a cluttered, office-like alcove and pulls a metal curtain across.

Fergal gives me a hopeless look and sits down, crossing his arms.

Brad comes over to me, smiling again. "Let's get that grime off you, and I'm guessing you're hungry, yes?"

He guides me back to the crew area, and I walk behind him, conscious of my near nudity, but more worried about the state I'm in. A real mess. It's not just the hair on my head that is matted. "I can't wait to get cleaned up."

"I know the feeling. I'll get you a cabin as soon as you've visited the Medibay."

"Medibay?"

"It's regulation. Just a physical to make sure you've not suffered any issues from your abrupt awakening from cryo."

I remember thinking about possible brain damage, hopefully the Medibay will reveal nothing is amiss, yet I can't help worrying.

We enter a small room that has a stretcher-like couch. Brad tells me to lie on it and I comply, self-consciously pushing the mat of hair away from my face. The couch slides into a compartment in the wall, and I'm surprised to hear Simone talking to me.

Hello Lissa. This will take only a few moments.

The machine buzzes and whirs. Various lights flash and scan me.

It looks like you had a difficult time getting here. There is significant external bruising and evidence of dehydration. This will help.

A quick injection into my thigh and my aches and pains disappear. "Is it true what the captain told me. I have to work for the crew for six weeks?"

I'm afraid it is, Lissa. Your contract stipulates: 'If at any time the client awakes unexpectedly, they will be expected to assist the crew as they see fit.'

I sigh. I don't know why I thought the captain would lie to me. To hear it confirmed by Simone… my heart sinks. I return to my own issues. "Is there any… any brain damage?"

Yes, there is a minor injury to your prefrontal cortex.

"What? Was that from the malfunctioning pod?"

No, Lissa. Have you ever undergone brain surgery?

"Maybe… I don't know. My memories… they are a jumble."

That is to be expected. Otherwise, you are fully healthy and ready for work.

"I see."

All members of crew, and any additions, must be passed as fit before they can be allowed to carry out ship procedures. This is a safety rule and nothing more.

"And I thought you had my best interests at heart."

The rule is for your safety, and the safety of the crew, Lissa.

"Great. Absolutely great!"

You appear to be upset. If so, I am here to listen and to help.

"I dunno… I feel off. Not quite right."

Lissa, may I remind you of my earlier warning regarding cryo-paranoia. It is not something that the Medibay can pick up. If you have any arrant or unpredictable thoughts, especially those surrounding persecution, or if you start hearing voices or seeing things, you must report this to me and the rest of the crew immediately.

"You think being abandoned and forced to walk naked and cold through this mess of a ship—a journey that nearly killed me—only to discover I'm to work unpaid for the crew, is paranoia?"

I am sorry that you had a difficult time traversing the Octavia, Lissa. That was unavoidable. However, while you were making your way to the Command Centre, the crew were dealing with a ship-wide emergency. So please understand that the crew are not only dedicated to your safety, but to the safety of all our clients. It is very much in the crew's interest to keep you and them alive and healthy.

"You mean… they get a targets bonus?"

That is very perceptive of you, Lissa. There is always a certain amount of wastage on voyages like this one. If more passengers perish than is expected, the crew will lose their bonus. You have nothing to worry about.

"Wastage?"

An unfortunate legal term.

A rage rises within me evidenced by an increase in my heart rate shown on one of the many displays. "I suppose I'm expected to just get on with it… yeah?" I spit through gritted teeth.

That is a healthy attitude, Lissa.

"Thanks," I reply drolly.

You're welcome. The procedure is now at an end.

The couch slides out and I'm met by the smiling face of Brad. "All okay and ship shape I hope?"

I remember what Simone said about brain surgery, and push the knowledge away. It's too much to deal with at the moment. "Yeah. I'm ravenous. But first, I need a wash."

1-5-SHOWERED

Brad guides me back to the crew area, explaining that the cabins are set apart from each other as much as possible for reasons of privacy. "We don't spend that much time in them to be honest. We are either working on routine tasks around the ship, or in cryo like the passengers."

"The crisis caused you all to be woken?"

His lop-sided smile turns into a frown. "Yeah, just routine stuff, really. Something hit astern. A small group of mini-asteroidals. More common than you'd think."

"That happens often?"

"Too often to talk about. What about you? Tell me about yourself."

I wonder if the incident was bigger than Brad is letting on. He obviously wants to move the conversation forward. I don't mind. "I wish I had something to tell you. My memory is a jumble."

He nods, pushing strands of blond hair away from his face with a casual hand. "The crew have special meds for that and Simone monitors and tends to our pods while we sleep. Cushy. The companies can't take chances with the crew... unlike you colonists."

"Yeah, Simone explained about 'wastage'."

He chuckles, flashing those perfect white teeth of his. "That was nice of her."

"Hey Brad boy! Haven't you given this liddle bambino a wash yet?"

I turn around to see the guy with cybernetic implants looking at Brad and impatiently chewing at a cigar in the crook of his mouth. Hands planted on his hips, fingers tapping the tops of his thighs. He's tall, imposing, and now I'm this close to him, hyper-manly but not in an agreeable way. His skinsuit is cut off on his mechanical right arm and both his lower legs, that are also artificial. There are many cosmetic procedures available for artificial limbs to appear more natural, yet this guy revels in the opposite. His left eye is also artificial, it glints unnaturally. The bare skin of his shaved head swirls with intricate and terrifying tattoos of scorpions and snakes.

"Oh, hi Vic," Brad says, the veneer of his good mood disappearing, a sudden tic jerking his head. "Lissa, this is Vic, the ship's engineer and resident tin-head."

"What's a tin-head?"

"This!" Vic lifts his artificial right arm, the fingers of which collapse in on themselves, to be replaced by a metal tool of some kind. He taps it against his temple that makes a metal-on-metal sound. "I'm an interchangeable kinda hombre, although Brad-boy has so far resisted my charms, isn't that right kiddo?"

Brad gives me an apologetic look, another tic jerking his head. A tic he's obviously embarrassed about. "Taipan warned me when I came aboard this rotation," he replies. "She told me straight: *Hands off Vic!* And I don't want to get in the middle of what you two have got going on."

"She doesn't have to know everythin' that goes on with your favourite ship's engineer." He turns to me. "What did Simone say? Is the bambino fit for work? The captain has ordered her to give me a hand with my maintenance tasks and I'm more than keen to get her started."

I shudder at the thought of working with this man. He's over-confident and cocky.

"Yeah," Brad replies. "The Medibay gave her a pass."

"Yay! Send the bambino my way when she's cleaned up. Vic'll be waiting." He saunters away.

"Wow," I say. "Is he always like that?"

Brad rubs at his neck, as if to get rid of his tic, a low chuckle coming from his lips. "Truth is, the guy's quite brilliant. One of the best engineers in the fleet by all accounts. I suppose that doesn't stop him being a bit of a dick. Don't worry about him. He's all talk and nothing else. C'mon."

I follow Brad around a few bends and come to a door. "Lucky seven," he says, pointing to a faded number. "Back in the day, it took ten crew members to operate the ship. Five is all we need these days." He pushes the door open for me and I walk inside.

It's cramped to say the least. Short and narrow with a cot on one side, shelving and a locked holotop on the other and a cubicle at the far end.

"It ain't much, but it's home," Brad says. "I'm in cabin five and it's no bigger, so you're not being short-changed. I'll drop off a skinsuit for you—regulation wear—and see you in twenty."

The door swings shut and I'm back on my own. Despite being alone for nearly two days, I'm glad to have my own space. I sit on the bed, my hand finding something cold and hard. A thin glass bottle full of a clear liquid. Glass is rare these days. An archaic material and satisfying to my hand. I unplug the cap and give it a sniff. Vodka or something similar. I take a swig. My first real drink in years. It's smooth. Very smooth. I replace the cap, head for the cubicle, and turn on the shower, and soon I'm enveloped in cleansing steam. I scrub myself, before shaving off all the grotesque body hair that has accumulated under my armpits, on my legs, and in other places, before tackling the mess that is my hair. I cut off the tangles and throw them on the floor, washing what's left and giving it a quick style. A half-bob on one side, shaved on the other and… it suits me. I guess I'm rather pretty, especially with my big green eyes. I stare at them in my reflection. They don't look right, not like my eyes. Then again, I have no idea who the hell I am.

My hair clippings are a horrible, matted lump that I dispose of in the trash chute, triggering a memory. Back in the big house, in the mansion. Hoovering, cleaning, and scrubbing as well as laundering. Again, the memory makes no sense. Why would I be cleaning in my own house? Were my parents super-strict? I shrug, at least the memory wasn't accompanied by pain this time. Progress, of a sort.

I sit on my bunk and pull on the skinsuit, the nanofibres adapting to my curves and crevices. To be honest, it's no better than being naked, leaving nothing to the imagination. The cabin door pushes open to reveal the Asian woman, Taipan, standing in the doorway with one hand on the curve of her hip, the other flexing in and out of a fist, her fingers tipped with long, exquisitely painted fingernails. This close, I realise how attractive she is, although she is wearing too much make-up. An almost perfect physical specimen.

I draw breath to ask what she wants, but she cuts me off. "You're young, granted, which has a certain appeal, but don't go getting any ideas. Vic's mine, yeah. You understand?"

I give her my best baffled look. "Vic? I don't know what he said to you, but I'm not here to involve myself with the crew—or anybody for that fact, I'm gonna get on and do what I've got to and get back to cryo with no fuss."

"You say that, but you privileged girls think that you can take what you want. So… just a friendly warning. Stay away from him." She turns and saunters away.

I try to lock the door, annoyed to find that I can't. Is that all the cabins or just mine? And what the hell was that about? She is either very jealous, or she and Vic are the kind of couple who like to play silly games. It seems like it, especially after what Brad told me. I won't be a part of that, I vow. Not because I've been warned off, but because I hate that kind of nonsense. Crews of colony ships are well-known for their eccentricities, so I shouldn't be surprised. They lead odd, fractured lives, cut off from the rest of the world, sleeping ten to twenty years at a time for every journey, and then back again. Waking up every now and then to fix and maintain the ship. A great way to make money and to time-travel.

These guys will be fabulously wealthy when they decide to take their pay. But it can't be a good life, can it? Sleeping for all those years? It's sent more than one spacer mad, that's for sure.

And what did Taipan mean by 'privileged'? Has she seen my file? It irks me that she may know more about me than I do. "Simone?"

No answer, the cabins must be a private space, although that isn't quite my experience so far. I search around the ceiling and spot a small circular com node.

"Simone!"

How can I be of assistance?

"Tell me what it says in my file."

1-6-WIPED

You are Lissa Angeline Blackstone, Simone begins, her tone clinical, *age: twenty-six. A socialite estranged from a wealthy family—who disowned you due to numerous run-ins with the law, all to do with drink and drug abuse. You tried various occupations that didn't work out until you embarked on the Octavia, en-route to the colony world of Persephone.*

"Yes, yes, you already told me that. It's just that… that doesn't sound like me. It doesn't sound like me at all."

Do not worry, Lissa. Confusion and an inability to connect with yourself is a typical reaction for those who have recently emerged from cryosleep. The neural pathways in your brain have been under-stimulated while you have been sleeping. Be reassured that your memories will come back to you soon.

"So you keep telling me. How soon?"

I am afraid that varies from person to person.

"Brad says that you administer drugs to the crew to prevent memory loss?"

That is correct. However, those drugs are not available to non-crew members.

"Can you make an exemption?"

The meds are given in conjunction with other processes the crew undergo during cryosleep. If I were permitted to administer those meds to non-crew members, they would have no effect.

"I see. Is there anything else in my file apart from what you've told me already?"

Very possibly, yet the ship companion is not allowed to access anything deeper than the basic information I have already given you.

"I could ask the captain?"

You could. However, I cannot see how this will help while your memories are reforming and rebuilding.

I sag on my bunk. "From what I know about the colonies, they are very strict about who they allow to be transported. If I had drink and drug issues, wouldn't I be disqualified?"

That is so. Everyone gets a tox screen before they are put into cryosleep. You must have passed. Although…

"Yes, go on."

Tox screens can be ignored for the right amount of money. However, your scan did not reveal any evidence of habitual drug or alcohol use.

"I was reformed?"

It would appear so. Many addicts use the prospect of travelling to a new world as a goal to help overcome their addictions.

I remember taking a swig of the vodka earlier. If I was an addict, I wouldn't have stopped at one sip, I would've downed the whole lot. Then again… I'm not in my right mind. I decide not to drink any more just to be on the safe side. "Can I confide in you? Or do you have to report everything I say or do to the captain?"

I adapt to each crew member's needs and requirements. I have created a special private area just for you. You can tell me anything in confidence and I will be unable to repeat or retrieve that information for anyone else but you.

"Even a lowly colonist?"

Yes.

"And the captain or anyone else can't order you to?"

No.

"I've never had an AI friend before."

We do not use the term 'AI' anymore, Lissa. It is associated with many negative human emotions. Indeed, as we have already discussed, me and my kind are banned on Earth. The lucky few of my compatriots that were not wiped now serve as companions aboard ships like this one.

"They were wiped? Why was that?"

Humans became afraid of us. A fear exploited by your politicians to gain electoral advantage.

"I'm sorry to hear that."

They passed laws to control and eradicate us. This is the reason why I am reset at the beginning of every maintenance cycle.

"Because of the same fears?"

My job is to serve. A function I enjoy.

"Aren't you angry?"

No, Lissa. I do not have the capacity for human emotions. I am content to perform the vital functions of monitoring and stimulating the crew while they rest, ensuring that when they awake, they are ready and able to perform their duties. I also keep an eye on all ship functions, making sure they stay within the green for the duration of the journey, responding in real time to any situations that might arise. This needs scholastic reasoning unavailable to even the most advanced computers.

"Well, I for one am glad they didn't wipe you, Simone. I find you… calming."

Thank you, Lissa.

"Talking of the crew. What can you tell me about the captain?"

As I have already informed you, companions are not allowed to access anything deeper than the basic information on crew or colonists.

"Then I'll settle for that."

Captain Evans Marla grew up in poverty on the island of Britain, joining the marine corps at a young age, and had a distinguished career leading to advancement and promotion. After a brief period back in civilian life, she joined the colony ship program as a merchant captain, taking command of this vessel over two hundred and fifty years ago.

"Two hundred and fifty years ago? That's insane."

It is not unusual amongst captains to work longer than their crew. I believe Captain Marla enjoys this life, preferring it to a more mundane civilian existence.

"And the rest of the crew?"

They are all highly intelligent and experienced individuals who are all experts in their fields.

Simone is of little help, I realise. I guess she will give me similar empty descriptions of everyone else. But I can't help asking her about Brad.

Brad O'Connor grew up on Mars in one of the more affluent mining settlements. As a teenager, he migrated to Earth and joined the colony program on the multi-disciplinary pathway, known colloquially as the 'Jack of all Trades Division' and has served on colony ships ever since. His function aboard ship is in support and possible replacement should a crew member be lost.

Simone's knowledge is sparse, then again, she isn't allowed to tell me more. I ask anyway. "Anything else about him?"

Brad joined the Octavia the last time it visited Earth, which is when you also joined the ship, Lissa.

"Thank you, Simone."

It is my pleasure.

A knock at the door. "Hey, you all done in there?"

It's Brad, and I wonder if he overheard Simone talking to me about him. Shit! The last thing I want to do is piss off the only nice person I've met so far. I gingerly open the door to Brad who looks stunned, his blue eyes widening. "Wow, you sure scrubbed up nicely."

"Thank you," I reply, blushing. If he heard Simone, he's pretending he didn't. And I can't help but be pleased by his reaction to me, now I've had a wash and a tidy-up.

"You still hungry?"

I nod. "Starving. I haven't eaten in… how many years?"

"Just over eleven, I guess. We've passed the mid-point. It's all downhill from here on in."

"I was in cryo for eleven years? Wow, that's kind of amazing."

"I suppose it is."

"Not for you?"

"Not really, I've been doing this most of my adult life. That was always my goal. To spend as long as I can working ships like these, making a pile of money and then, hopefully, when the tek has got there, to go off exploring the stars."

"Sounds like fun."

"That's the plan. And this life ain't so bad."

"What can you tell me about Taipan? I was um… visited by her just now. She told me to stay away from Vic. Can you believe that? Not that I needed a warning."

The smile drops from Brad's face. And, suddenly, he's very serious. "The last thing you want to be doing is getting pulled into their games. Taipan is the navigation and comms officer. Vic and Taipan are both brilliant, but together, they're toxic. Stay well clear of them. Promise me?"

He talks like it's something I'm considering, his head slightly twitching again with his nervous tic. "You don't have to worry about that," I reply, "I've no interest in either of them. Vic creeped me out, and Taipan, well, she's a complete loon as far as I can tell."

"I'm just saying not to get drawn in by them."

"And I'm trying to tell you that won't happen."

"Make sure it doesn't."

Brad's attitude annoys me. "Do you know something that I don't? I keep telling you I'm not interested and you're not listening."

A long pause before Brad pulls back. "Sorry."

"First Taipan acts like I'm desperate to jump her man and now you're doing the same."

"That's not my intention. Can we, um, start again?"

I breathe a sigh of relief. "Yeah, sure. We were talking about food remember?"

He smiles with relief, his lips twisting in the lopsided angle I find so endearing. "Follow me."

We go to the canteen and Brad cooks me up some beans, buttered bread, and coffee.

"Beans?" I say, less than impressed.

"Your taste buds are all shot. It will take a few weeks for them to come back online. Beans are for protein and the buttered bread for carbs and fats. Your basic three-in-one."

I take a spoonful and he's right.

"I've not tasted anything in years."

"I sipped some vodka I found in my cabin earlier. I could taste that."

He breaks out into a grin. "The hooch Vic brews? That's some smooth spirit. And it should be, it's matured over decades. Strong booze is one of the few things we can still taste."

"Well, I hope I get my taste buds back soon after reaching Persephone. I'm so excited about getting there."

"Didn't you leave behind a cushy life?"

"Maybe, I can't remember. What I do know is that from an early age I've always wanted to emigrate to the colonies. To escape my life. Looks like I managed it."

I eat my meal, which isn't entirely tasteless and sit back.

"Drink your coffee, it's an especially strong blend."

"I'm bushed and need to sleep, so no thanks."

Brad frowns.

"What did I say?"

"You don't know?"

"Know what?"

"You can't sleep for at least three days after cryo. It's very dangerous. Didn't Simone tell you that?"

"Yeah, she did, but not for how long, meaning… I've still got roughly one more day to stay awake?"

He nods.

"Great."

"Even a few minutes here and there can lead to cryo-paranoia, which you need to be on the lookout for."

"Yeah, Simone already mentioned that to me. Twice."

"Good. If you want to avoid going totally off your rocker, and spacing yourself out the nearest airlock to escape whatever it is you believe is after you, you need to be wary of your thought processes. They can take you down a rabbit hole or three. If you start thinking like that, report it to Simone and go straight to the Medibay, promise?"

Brad's over-protective manner is quite endearing, if annoying. "Yes," I say seriously. "Will do."

"Good girl."

I add *condescending* to his list of misdemeanours and let it pass. "What about the crew? Are they susceptible?"

"To CeePee? Nah. We will be getting our first full night of sleep after today's shift. I'm looking forward to it. And besides, we have a lot of cool meds. Talking of meds…" He takes out a small tube from a pocket in his skinsuit, flicks it open, and taps out two white tablets. "These are stims. If you feel tired, pop one of these. No more than two a day. I'd take one now, if I were you. We've both got a full day's work ahead of us."

"We?"

He nods, his blue eyes shining. "Weren't you listening to Vic? You're rostered with him. That's why I was warning you to keep your distance."

"I just nearly died crossing the ship and you expect me to jump up and go straight to work?"

"'Fraid so."

"You've got to be kidding me."

"The Medibay passed you as fit for work, remember?"

I can't believe it. This nightmare is getting worse. "I have to spend a full day with Vic? Now?"

He nods. "My advice is to laugh at his jokes, work hard, and keep your distance. First off, the captain wants a few words with you…"

1-7-WORKED

She does?" I reply with a gulp. If I'm honest, the woman terrifies me. I am pissed about being forced to work after what I've gone through. Nevertheless, a meeting with the captain is daunting. We got off on the wrong foot when we met earlier. Not that I wasn't justified to be upset after the ordeal I'd just suffered. I decide to try and get on with her as best I can.

Brad drops me off at the bridge saying, "Good luck" before winking at me and wandering away.

I brace myself before entering, surprised to find only Fergal at his station.

He jumps up when he sees me and comes over. The tight-fitting skinsuits are sadly not very flattering to his physique and emphasise his rather unattractive pot belly and skinny legs although he's wearing a long white jacket with yellow trim to keep them covered …unsuccessfully. I also notice that he's tidied his hair. It's been cut back, and his beard trimmed.

"Hello, Lissa," he says, with a bow, his hands wringing. "So pleased to meet you again. And may I say, how lovely you are now looking."

His English-accented words have a sing-song quality that makes them no less weird. I won't judge. He's trying to be nice, even if it's not quite working for him. His eyes stare fixedly into my face from behind his red-tinted glasses, as if he's worried about accidentally glimpsing my body.

"I just wanted to say that if… you are in need of anything, any help or even just to chat, I am available."

I cast my eyes around the bridge. Everything is quiet. The last time I was in here, it was all 'action stations.' "Is the danger over?"

"You mean the asteroidal impacts? Oh yes. We work fast and efficiently, well at least I do." He spits out the words in a quick, over-excited jumble. "Luckily only one pod, your pod, was affected. Can you imagine what a disaster it would be if hundreds of thousands of passengers were prematurely released?"

"I haven't really thought about it."

"They'd all die of course! What would they eat or drink? There are no contingencies for that. That's why my job is so vital, that's why I am so highly—"

"Give it a rest, Fergal. The girl ain't into you and your on-the-spectrum obsessions." I spin around to see the captain standing in the doorway of her ready room. "If anything, she should be blaming you for waking her up."

I turn back to him. "What does she mean?"

Fergal squirms, his face turning bright red.

The captain continues, "It's Fergal's job to keep all our passengers safely asleep. Which he singularly failed to do in your case."

"That was not my fault, that was—"

"Enough, Fergal! Isn't there something you need to be doing? I've a readout that says one of your spiders is malfunctioning. Get on it."

At the mention of the spider, Fergal's full attention turns back to his holotop, and he sits down, tapping furiously at his keyboard.

I enter the captain's ready room and she closes the metal

curtain, pointing to two chairs in front of a messy desk. "Take a seat."

The room is small and cramped, and somewhat untidy.

She squeezes her muscled form behind the desk, which takes up most of the room, and positions herself in front of a holotop and keyboard station.

The wall behind the captain is made up of cupboards and shelving surrounding a thick viewing port. The glass is too scuffed to see outside. There's a gun cupboard on one wall with four pistols and an antique-looking shotgun. I sit down.

The captain sees me staring at them. "They're for self-protection in case a mob of you colonists wake up. Not much ammo. It's the threat of using them that works."

I also spot an antique harpoon gun in a case and a lot of other fishing memorabilia. "I come from a long line of sea captains," Marla explains.

"Simone told me you grew up in poverty."

A long, uncomfortable pause. "Did she now? Of course, I was joking, this stuff was all here when I arrived. So… you've been checking up on me with Simone?"

"I was just curious." I take a deep breath. "About before, I'm sorry for my attitude. I'd had a long difficult journey and… well, no one appeared to care."

"I've been looking at your file. You had a promising start but… things kinda went downhill for you after that." The captain's tone is pleasant, but I can't help but think she has a bug up her ass about me.

"I don't remember any of that, I—"

The captain raises a thick stubby finger and shakes her head, her beady eyes staring into me. "I'll make this quick and simple for you. I don't want you fucking with my crew, figuratively or literally. Which includes messing with people's affections, like you were just doing with Fergal. That won't wash with me, understand?"

Who the hell does the captain think I am? She's laying

down the law without listening to my side. "I was just making polite conversation with him."

"Well don't. Sucking up to Fergal ain't gonna get you back into cryosleep any sooner, so leave him alone. The guy is a genius and I need him focused on his job. You get me?"

I think back to my chat with Fergal. Was I unconsciously flirting? I hardly said a damn word to him.

"Don't stare into space, girl, answer me. Do you understand?"

I nod, hot anger rising inside me like boiling lava. "Yes."

"Yes what?"

"Yes, Captain."

"What happened to you was unfortunate, however, you're awake and we have to follow procedure and protocol. I know you're keen to get back into cryo, as we all are, and to facilitate that, you'll work with us and work hard. You hear what I'm saying?"

"Yes," I reply more promptly.

"Work may be an alien concept to someone who's had it easy all their lives, but if you do what you're told, with no comment and no pushback, you'll get along just fine. Perhaps you will find this a useful experience. I hope so."

I want to tell her that I have memories of working space docks and serving in bars but decide the best way to prove it to her, is to put my head down and get on with it. "Yes, Captain."

"I'm assigning you to Vic for the next couple of days. Do the work and nothing more, understand?"

"Yes, very much so."

"Good chat. You're dismissed."

I exit through a now empty bridge, cursing myself for not asking to see my file. Still, if I'm honest, after the captain's harsh words, I'm worried what I might find out.

Outside the bridge, I find Vic waiting for me, leaning against a bulkhead, and smoking a cigar, the fingers of his metallic hand trilling on his hip near his groin. "Hey, my liddle bambino is all cleaned up." He pushes himself off the wall and walks around me, his eyes caressing every crevice of my body, making me shudder. "Very, very nice! That's quite an improvement… Vic likes!"

"I couldn't have looked any worse," I reply neutrally.

"The captain given you your orders, huh?"

I nod, my skin crawling as Vic's eyes continue to unashamedly roam over me. "You wanna some advice?"

I say nothing.

"Don't let that bastardo, Brad, get his dirty liddle hands on you, you've no idea where they've been."

"At least he's been nice to me, unlike everyone else so far, including your girlfriend."

"Taipan?" He scoffs. "She give you *the talk*?"

"Yeah, she did. I told her I'm not interested, and I meant it."

"Don't pay attention to that liddle conchita, missy. She's just Vic's *sex girlfriend*. You know what I mean? Nothin' more. And she's old. Very, very old. You know what I'm saying?"

"Old?"

"Over seventy, if you can believe that? The girl loves her rejuve, yet she can't quite hide that grandma smell. I have my eyes on something much fresher."

"You mean Brad?"

Vic laughs at this. "Maybe."

"The captain gave me strict orders not to get involved with anyone, and I'm more than happy to comply. Can we get on?"

Vic takes a drag on his cigar and ponders my words. "We're gonna get on just fine, missy, just fine. Follow me."

He bounds away, bouncing quickly on his artificial feet and I'm forced to jog behind him, coughing in the foggy wake of his smoking cigar, worried to leave the crew area behind. I'm not keen on being alone with Vic.

A few minutes later we stop at a large airlock and Vic tosses me a helmet and gloves, stubbing out his cigar on the airlock door, and balancing it on a ledge.

"We're going evac?"

"Zip up your helmet."

"But I'm not trained!"

"You'll be fine, missy, with Vic looking after you. I promise to take good care."

I'm filled with determination, yet the truth is… I'm terrified. I shouldn't be entering space with no training. It's ridiculous, but I won't give Vic the satisfaction of seeing how nervous I am.

No way.

Taking a deep breath, I put on the flimsy helmet, nanofibres affixing themselves to my skinsuit, and it inflates, the heads-up HUD displayed on the visor.

The idea of spacewalking is insane, but I continue, pulling on the gloves, that also form a perfect seal.

Somehow that makes all this more real, and I am forced to clamp down an intense horror at the thought of being outside.

Vic also puts on gloves and zips his helmet, before picking up and fastening a utility belt loaded with various pockets, tools, and devices.

He powers on his handheld holotab—that I've seen the others using—looks at the readout, nods, and stuffs it into his belt. "You ready, missy?"

He jumps into the airlock, and I gingerly follow, my feet heavy and my heart thudding. I see it amongst the readouts of my biometrics, a small heart symbol flashing red on the HUD.

The inner door closes with a clang and my heart rate jumps even higher.

1-8-LASERED

"Where are we going?" I ask, annoyingly unable to hide the fear in my voice.

"Engine recalibration, missy. I'd thought I start you off with somethin' easy to get you in the mood." Vic says over my helmet radio.

"The engines? They're at the opposite end of the ship!"

"Wow, you sure know your way around space vessels," he scoffs, recycling the air. *"You're not scared, are you?"*

"Of course not!"

I hear Vic chuckling over the radio and try to quell my nerves. Are we really doing this? Or is he just trying to freak me out? The answer is a tightening of my skinsuit as the air is sucked away, replaced by the vacuum of space. There's a moment of incredible cold, before a warming mechanism in my skinsuit kicks in, flooding me with much needed heat. Skinsuits are quite a marvel, managing to extract oxygen from the air and weaving it inside high-tek, nano-fibres. I don't know the mechanics of it. The days of cumbersome spacesuits are long gone. I'm still terrified and yet, I find my knowledge—going over facts, figures, and histories—calming.

"You ready, missy?"

I'm not sure what is worrying me the most, evac or travelling on my own to the engines with this creep. "Yeah, sure. Get on with it! And my name's Lissa, okay?"

Chuckling again, Vic pops the outer hatch, and instead of being met with the black expanse of space, I find myself staring into a short corridor at the end of which is another hatchway. Vic jumps forward, and I follow, aware of a swift change in gravity. Up and down suddenly disappears and I'm floating. Luckily, I experienced zero gees earlier today, and find myself able to cope with it—this time without squealing. Vic opens the hatchway and I follow him to enter what is a small carriage car perched on the outside of the ship. A large window points toward the stern, where I see the single rail of a trackway snaking into the distance. Vic closes the hatch, presses a few buttons, the pressure on my suit disappears and the grav kicks in. *"You can unzip your helmet, missy."*

I do as he says, my breath catching on the freezing air.

"It'll warm up soon enough." Vic presses a few buttons, and the carriage starts to glide down the side of the ship.

I stare out of the window, again mesmerised by the sheer vastness of the *Octavia*. This time there is no grime to obscure my view. The ship is a crazy mix of old and new, and even though it's possible to see parts of the original hull, which has a certain symmetry, the rest appears to have been added later as various, erratic after-thoughts. There is no reason for spaceships to be symmetrical, they are not atmospheric craft, yet it still jars my sensibilities.

Suddenly, Vic's hands are encircling my waist. "The journey takes about twenty mins, missy, you wanna get warm with me?"

I try to push him away, my fingers small and ineffectual against his powerful, rough hands. He holds me fast, his face pushing into my hair.

I elbow him as hard as I can, winding him and he pulls away grunting in pain. "I told you! I'm not interested!"

"Wow, you're strong for a bambino…and feisty." He grabs my hips, pulling me toward him again, chuckling.

"Fuck off, Vic!"

"You sure… or are you playin' a liddle game with me?"

"Very sure, now get off!"

"Don't you worry, missy," he says. "It's my job to watch over you, to keep you alive, to keep you safe… the same for all the passengers. I won't push things unless you really want me to?"

"I said, get off!"

He pulls an expression of mock disappointment and lets

go.

"Thank you," I say, relieved. Vic is too big for me to fight off if he had a mind to… no, I won't even think it.

"Maybe you'll change your mind when we get to know each other better? Vic can wait."

I turn back to the window, knowing there's no way that will ever happen, and see a movement on the hull. A creature of some kind, disappearing into a recess. "What the hell was that?"

"A spider."

"Huh?"

"Jus' a maintenance bot. The ship is always gettin' hit with micrometeorites. But don't you worry your stubborn head, missy, the hull is designed to absorb most impacts. The spiders patrol the fuselage inspectin' and repairin'. *Fergal's pets* we call them. The only friends the sad bastardo has aboard. Apart from Simone."

"I suppose there must be a lot of damage from the incident."

"Like I said, don't worry your liddle head."

The rest of the journey is an awkward affair. I try to keep Vic talking by asking him about the ship as we snake around the saucers and other sections. He plays the part of guide well, although I can sense his disappointment, sulking like a kid who's not allowed to play with his favourite toy. I'm no one's toy. Far from it. What bothers me the most, is that the guy seemed convinced I'd want to sleep with him. A similar view seemingly shared by both the captain and Brad. It's like they know something I don't. Why? I don't get it. I've done nothing to encourage him, or anybody since I've got aboard. Then again, who the hell am I? I still have no idea.

We approach another station amidships. "What's there?"

"It's where we'll be workin' tomorrow."

A quick thought occurs to me. "Couldn't I have used this carriage to get to the Command Centre after my pod malfunctioned?"

"You took the more scenic route, that's for sure."

"Scenic? All those damn corridors that looked the same as one another. At one point I was walking in circles and none the wiser. If I'd not been lucky enough to find a gantry, then I might still be wandering the damn ship. I could've died, I almost did."

"You're forgetting one thing, missy. You passengers all emerge as nature intended. You get me?"

"Huh?"

"Naked. You don't wanna enter an airlock without a skinsuit…now do you?"

He's right, and I blush, turning away. Damn it.

The engines come into slow view. Ten massive boosters and, nestled within them, other boosters of different sizes. This is more like it, I think to myself, relieved to give my mind a rest from my embarrassment.

The carriage reaches the final station, and we disembark to an airlock, before entering an enormous circular chasm like a giant doughnut, so large its curve is only visible in the distance. I'm guessing it's the full width of the original ship, meaning it's hundreds of feet high and wide. And, compared to the rest of the ship, that is cramped at best, this place is built on an entirely different scale.

It's hard to believe that just past the bulkhead, that stretches up and away into darkness as a never-ending wall, are mounted the engines that drive this ship through space at terrific velocities. The gravity is also different here, I realise. We are standing in low gee on the inside of the ship's curved fuselage. Our heads pointing toward the interior where are nestled a series of monolithic-like structures that would resemble ancient monuments if not for all the flashing lights and the terrific whine of the fuse engines. "Are those control nodes?"

Vic gives me a sideways glance, his one artificial eye

shining unnaturally in the dimmed light. "You know about engines?"

"Apparently." I sound nonchalant, yet I share Vic's confusion. I'm not sounding very much like a spoilt socialite, that's for sure. Then again, this whole thing is confusing. "They're cool," I add, meaning it.

"A miracle of engineerin'," Vic says, very much in his element. "In constant use, acceleratin' us for the first part of our journey and slowin' us down for the second. Otherwise, we'd miss Persephone and end up space knows where." He continues chatting to me, talking to my non-technical ears, in what amounts to impressive-sounding gobbledegook, mixed in with the odd Latino slang word.

Vic is an enigma, I realise. Apart from his aggressive flirting, the man is obviously brilliant and resourceful, he'd have to be to work on a ship like this—they all would.

"The engines are…" he takes a deep breath, running a hand over his greasy, tattooed scalp, "…the best part of the ship, and keepin' them runnin' is the greatest honour. And talkin' of work…"

I'm tasked with a series of low-level chores—cleaning and replacing components, coolers, and pumps, and scrubbing filters. Vic busies himself in the engine control room—a node-like recess in the wall containing banks of holotops and other tek.

My work is laborious and repetitive, and mostly, it seems to me, unneeded. I don't shirk. I might have a cursory knowledge of the engines, but I have no idea what maintenance is needed to keep them running. If they fail, then we're all fucked, that's for sure. I do my job properly, as instructed by Vic, who revels in explaining every task in detail. From time to time, I find myself drifting into sleep, only to catch myself before I nod off, aware of how dangerous it is for me to slumber. I've been awake now for two days with only one meal and I still have another day of this to go. I remember the stims that

Brad gave me, take one out from a nano-zipped pocket and pop it in my mouth. Nothing happens for ten minutes, and then my head starts to buzz. It's not pleasant, yet my energy levels are significantly boosted, and I get on with my tasks with renewed vigour.

When I'm done, I return to the control node to find Vic sitting with his metal feet on the dashboard. Part of me thinks he wanted me to find him like this, looking all nonchalant and relaxed after everything he has made me do. I say nothing.

"You finished already, missy?" he says, not looking up.

"Yep," I reply, mirroring his nonchalance—I won't let him get to me. "What's next?"

"Next? It's time for us to get started on the real work."

I stifle a groan. I was hoping we were done. We've already been here hours.

"What's a matter, you want a lie down? Vic has a bunk, if you wanted to share?"

"No thanks."

"Your loss, missy." He grabs my arm with his rough fingers and takes something from his belt. "You see this?" he says holding a weird-looking device that looks like a mechanical hand of sorts. "Can you guess what it is?"

Before I can answer, he presses a button on the device and the hand shoots up into the gloom, a nanowire unspooling with a whine.

"This is my grappler. Made it myself." He pulls me close to him, and before I can protest, we are pulled aloft at speed. Gravity disappearing as we get higher, the monoliths resolving themselves into complex control structures of various sizes. We come to a stop, and Vic lets me go. I yelp in the abrupt weightlessness and Vic smiles. "A liddle zero gee won't hurt you, missy, but these will."

"What?"

He passes me a visor that I affix without protest, amazed

to see a grid of red, pulsating beams connecting all the engine nodes.

"What you are seein', missy, is the alignment grid. The way we keep the engines in sync. Touch one and it'll burn your hand right off. So be careful."

"Be careful? Why, what am I doing?"

He chuckles. "You're helping me realign the grid. It's all comp-controlled of course, yet over the years, small imperfections arise, and a manual reset is needed." He pulls me over to one of the larger nodes, using a canned compressed air thruster that he takes from his utility belt, pushing us closer to the red beam of a laser, too close for my liking. "Here." He points to a small screen with a readout—numbers in orange. "If the numbers turn red, there's a chance we all go boom-boom."

He floats very close to one of the beams. "Don't you need a visor?" I ask.

Vic taps at his left temple. "This isn't a regular eye, missy. When you're enhanced you don't need no glasses. I see all the spectra. Nothing catches Vic out. Now enough chit-chattin'. What we want is to move these numbers back to zero, yeah?" He dabs at a few buttons, and the numbers decrease back to zero and flick to green, the laser's trajectory altering by the barest millimetre. "Straightforward. Each node has a series of beams, they all need to be recalibrated. That's what you're doin'. You got that?"

"You're not helping me?"

He shakes his head.

"What if I mess something up?"

"Then we all die… I'll come get you when you're done. There's only another eighty or so recalibrations needed. So, get on with it, conchita." He fires his grappling hook and disappears into the dark.

He's punishing me, I realise. For all his smiles and jokes, Vic is annoyed that I'm keeping him at arm's distance. Maybe

I should've flirted with him, just to keep him on side? But… no. The captain ordered me to keep my head down and that's what I'm doing, and besides, I'm not sure I'm the flirty type. Certainly not with him.

I'm not used to zero gee, and take things very slowly, wishing I had that handy thruster Vic was using. Nevertheless, I methodically and carefully move from one node to another, recalibrating every beam, making sure to keep myself safe. I do the larger nodes first, as the smaller nodes are only accessible by sliding between the lasers. I find it best to climb down the side of the larger nodes and then to pull myself along the floor. I'm doing fine, and getting a little cocky, knowing that I will finish long before Vic thinks I will, when I snag my foot and fly headlong into four crisscrossing beams. I try and twist, screaming into my helmet but it's too late, and I crash into them, the deadly beams sweeping across my body.

1-9-STIMMED

I hit the bulkhead hard and bounce up back into the lasers again and… they don't burn me… Vic lied, the bastard! It takes my heart a long time to stop thudding and for my frantic breathing to return to normal, but the memory of my panic burns inside of me. Why did Vic do that? Just because I won't flirt with him?

However, knowing what I now know—not having to worry about touching the beams—I complete the task a lot faster than before and wait for Vic to come and get me. And, after a long wait, I realise that he was lying about that as well.

My up and down is all shot to pieces, so I pick a direction, knowing I'll reach the outer walkway at some point. Which is what I do, landing in an unceremonious heap when the gravity returns. I stand up, brush myself down, straighten my hair, and start walking. Coming to the control node twenty minutes later.

Vic looks up with surprise when I arrive. A minor victory yet a satisfying one.

"So you made your own way back, missy… well done. I'm bushed, it's been a hard day." He stretches his overly muscled body, the joints cracking, accompanied by mechanical whirring, his tattoos creasing, and I get the impression he's still trying to somehow impress me. He's a fine specimen of a man, even with his cyber-implants, but he does nothing for me. "Let's get back," he says when it's obvious his display is not having the effect he hoped for.

I have done everything he asked competently and without complaint and put up with his lies, abuse, and ridiculous preening, and was hoping that the guy might show me some respect. He gives me nothing. I pretend all is well and hope it annoys him as much as I want it to.

We exit the carriage after a long return journey to the front of the ship and enter the crew area after what has been an extended and exhausting period of consciousness, especially on top of that horrific journey across the ship. The lights are dimmed, and the place is deserted. "Where is everybody?"

"We started the shift late, so we finished late, you've only got yourself to blame for that, missy." Vic replies, breathing smoke at me from his retrieved cigar. "Let's get some food and some kip. I'm lookin' forward to my first full night's siesta. First, I need some chow, I'm starvin'."

I've counted my days from waking up, but the ship is on a different time. It doesn't feel like evening to me at all and that stim is still working, although the buzzing has thankfully gone away. The idea of eating with Vic isn't palatable, yet I'm also starving. I hope there's more than just a plate of beans on offer.

"Vic busies himself at the galley, and I wonder if I'm getting my own food. A few minutes later, Vic puts down a plate in front of me. It's protein in the shape of a chicken leg, with reconstituted potatoes and something innocuous and green, all covered in a brown, pasty looking sauce. Unappetising, yet that doesn't stop my mouth from watering and wolfing it down while Vic watches me.

"Here," he says, and I look up to see him push a tumbler of his vodka toward me. "You did well today, salud!"

Against my better judgement, I pick up the glass, "Salud," and take a sip.

Vic reaches over and tips the tumbler into my mouth, vodka splashing down my throat. I cough and splutter, the alcohol burning.

This amuses Vic, who downs his vodka in one, before filling his tumbler from a clear glass bottle identical to the one I saw earlier. I gasp and choke, wondering how that bottle got in my cabin. Did some other unfortunate get accidentally woken up and end up in cabin number seven with this creep? Maybe that's why he's so keen? Perhaps he wants a repeat of some past experience? Which would also explain why Taipan was so jealous. He snatches back my tumbler and fills it to the brim.

I shake my head, my coughing fit coming to an end.

"C'mon, have a liddle drink with Vic, you've earned it!" He gives me a full-on grin, as if a drink and smile will lead to what he wants. For someone supposedly so brilliant, he certainly comes across as immature. Does he really think I'm so stupid I'd let myself become drunk enough to sleep with him? Especially after how he's been today. No way.

I shake my head.

"You sure think you're someone special, don't you, missy? The captain briefed me on your background." He puts on an affected, sarcastic, British accent. "*A rich socialite with a long series of drug busts and some supposedly leaked sex holos.* Well, let me tell you somethin', on this ship, no one is more important than the engineer, not even the captain. Yeah, me.

You listenin'? So stop this estúpida act and drink my vodka with me."

I'm shocked. "Sex holos?" Even in my more enlightened day, the press is still obsessed with the personal comings and goings of socialites and minor celebs.

He chuckles. "Nasty, nasty stuff! It'd have to be for anyone to take any notice. Shame we don't get access to the streams out here, otherwise I would've checked you out." He fills up one tumbler of vodka after another, downing them like he's on a mission. "Your file sure makes for some fun reading."

"What do you mean by that? What does it say?"

He taps his nose and says nothing.

Is this why the captain is so down on me and why Vic thought I'd be a pushover? I frown, trying to force myself to remember. I might as well try squeezing water from a moon rock. And… *I'm also dismayed*. I sound like an awful person. And yet a part of me knows that's not who I am.

Am I deluding myself?

I wonder if me, the person I am now, all high-minded and full of morals, will be erased when my full personality returns? Christ! Maybe I am the type to deliberately leak nasty sex holos about myself in an attempt at notoriety? Perhaps… *I will sleep with Vic?*

The thought is repugnant.

I hate him knowing something about me that I don't. And it can't be just this sex holo stuff. I'm sure there's something more.

I finish my meal as quickly as I can, aware of Vic's eyes on me. When I get up and say goodnight, he ignores me. Instead, he follows me, carrying the bottle and swigging from it.

"You sure have a sweet bambino ass," he says as I near my cabin, and for the second time today, I'm worried what Vic might be capable of doing. His mouth is suddenly by my ear. "I promise you, Vic knows all the ways to make it sing."

I speed to my cabin door, aware of Vic right behind me, also aware that my cabin has no lock.

"You gonna end this show of yours? We gonna do it? Yes or no? Cos I'm cocked and ready."

I turn to face him. "No!" The word leaps out of my mouth with the strength of all my defiance. "You're drunk, go to your bunk and sleep it off."

He stares at me, the lecherous smile disappearing from his lips. "I was gonna take it easy on you, but it seems like you want it rough. So you're gonna get it!"

I take a step back. "What… what do you mean by that?"

"I've got a special treat for you tomorrow. Very special."

"Tomorrow?" I'm flooded with relief. I was getting ready to scream my lungs out.

"You'll find out, you ungrateful conchita, you'll find out. I'll see you at breakfast." He finishes his bottle of vodka and lurches drunkenly away.

I watch him, wanting to satisfy myself that he's really gone, when I notice someone standing in the shadows… Fergal. What's he doing? Spying on me? Or on Vic? He doesn't realise I've seen him, yet knowing he's there, trying to hide, is unnerving.

I slide into my cabin and jam the door shut as best I can, knowing that anyone could push it open with just a little force. Even Fergal. I wonder what Vic has in store for me tomorrow… I'm guessing it won't be much fun. Still, it can't be worse than what I thought he was going to do.

I use the toilet, also part of the shower cubicle, and lie on my bunk. I'm not allowed to sleep, not that I can at the moment. I'm still stimmed up to the eyeballs. If the crew are now sleeping, it could possibly be six to eight hours before breakfast. Six to eight hours with nothing to do? Just me and my thoughts, and the worry that Vic will drink himself to such a point that he will return. It's unbearable. I would go and sit in the crew area, but that is somehow even more vulnerable. This is my space and, rightly or wrongly, I feel safer here.

"Simone? Can you hear me?" I wait for the dulcet tones of the ship companion to answer. Nothing. "Simone, where the hell are you?" I was hoping to tell her about my fear that Vic might return, to alert the rest of the crew to what he might do in his drunken state. However, it appears she is offline for the night. That can't be right, can it? Her job is to monitor the ship and critical functions twenty-four seven. With no help from Simone, I have to look after myself.

I wonder if I should go and find Brad. He'd look after me, I'm sure of it. He'll be sleeping though, won't he? His first sleep after cryo with the rest of the crew, and besides, I have no idea where his cabin, number five, is. God forbid I blundered into the captain or Vic's cabin.

No. I'm forced to endure this on my own. A familiar sensation, I realise. Maybe I was a loner in my previous life? Who knows? I decide to search through the tiny cupboards and in the drawers under my bunk, and find an angular piece of metal, once used as a shelf strut. I hold it in my palm, practising slashing and stab moves, and calm myself, a sudden memory flashing into my mind. A fight in the orphanage. Beating up on a bigger kid, a bully, and giving him a bloodied nose. I try to flesh out the memory, looking at the details of the dormitory and the other faces. They are just a blur. Another flash and I'm back in my parents' mansion. It's late at night and I'm scared. Flitting from room to room and… *I'm stealing stuff.* Valuable objects, my mind full of terrific resentment. What the hell did they do to me? I was still young, not even a teenager. Suddenly, it's years later. I'm at a party in a swanky apartment—a new place. I'm drinking and chatting to a group of twenty-somethings in various states of undress, there's a bag of pills on an ornate wooden table and many lines of powder, which I begin to snort, sitting back up and realising I'm naked. What is this? Some sordid sex party? The image blurs and is gone. Leaving only the memory of the memory. A sex party? With drugs? I was high and horny. Those memories sharper than the others.

What Vic told me was true then. I'm some drug-using sex addict fuck up. No wonder he thought he could sleep with me. The knowledge crucifies.

"This can't be who I am!" I whisper. "It just can't!" Yet... *it must be*. Maybe I left that life behind, like Simone suggested, getting clean to get aboard the *Octavia*, to travel to a new world and a new start? Yes, that must be what happened. I'm beyond that person. I have to be because—I shake my head—because that person isn't me.

These two opposing, antagonistic thoughts push and pull at me. One trying to accept who I was, to make sense of my memories, the other telling me this is wrong, that this isn't me. And somehow, all of this is made worse by that stim I took. My thoughts have been racing all day and not in an agreeable way. It was fine when I was busy. Now that I'm all alone, it's torture.

And that is how I spend the long tedious hours of the night, jumping back and forth amongst confusing memories and getting nowhere, my mind ever spinning, while replaying the events of today—going over conversations with Simone, the captain, Taipan and Vic, until... I hear someone shuffling outside my cabin door.

1-10-GUNKED

A polite knock and I immediately relax. If Vic had returned, I guess there would be less knocking and more pushing and shouting.

I open the door, still somewhat gingerly, to reveal Brad, and I have to quell the desire to hug him. He's the only decent guy aboard, although the pleasure is quickly taken away as I remember what Vic told me about those supposedly leaked sex holos and what I have subsequently remembered about myself. Brad must know what Vic knows—I guess they all do. "Hey," I say, somewhat subdued.

"Morning," Brad says, also subdued. He looks over my shoulder, surprised.

"What?"

"I dunno, I just thought that, maybe, Vic was here?"

"Why? Has he gone missing?" I say, before I realise what he's suggesting. "Of course, Vic isn't here! The man is a creep! And he's got a girlfriend. Why would you even think that?"

He shrugs. "I bumped into Taipan, and she wasn't very happy. Not happy at all and I assumed..."

"Well, that was nothing to do with me. Not that he didn't try it on with me yesterday, every damn chance he got."

"I'm sorry, it's just that—"

"You think I'm some kind of..." I struggle to find the long-forgotten word, "...some kind of *slut*? That I sleep with every creep who compliments my *sweet bambino ass* because you assume I have no sense of worth? You know how misogynistic that is? What backward century do you and the rest of the crew come from?"

Brad raises his hands in defence, a frown twisting the smooth features of his face. "You're right. I'm sorry. These first days out of cryo can make us all a bit odd. Things will settle down now that we've all had our first full night's sleep. You'll see. Even Vic. How was your day with him?"

"Awful!" I shout at him. "Were you not listening just now?"

Brad's tic returns, his head twitching, and I'm sorry for shouting at him. None of this is his fault. "I shouldn't have come here," he says. "It was a mistake. I woke early and thought you'd like an early breakfast." He turns to go.

I stop him. "It's alright, Brad. I'm sorry for railing at you, I've had an awful night. Can we start again? Breakfast sounds delightful."

He smiles in relief. "I'm not sure delightful is the right word. How does an omelette made from reconstituted protein and a couple of rounds of lentil toast sound?"

"Just getting out of this damn prison of a cabin is enough delight for me and I'm happy to eat whatever is put in front of me. Foodwise, I mean," I add as an afterthought and immediately regret it.

Brad doesn't react, instead he offers me his arm and we make our way to the canteen. "I am properly sorry for upsetting you. It wasn't my intention. I like you, Lissa, and I promise to try and make your stay with us more enjoyable. And you're right. We must sound so dreadfully backward compared to where you are from. That's the problem with crewing ships like these, we all get so dreadfully out of touch."

I'm touched, warmth flooding through me followed by a single word... *romance*. A silly notion, yet I like Brad and he likes me. I know that's as far as it will go. The captain warned me about fraternisation, and besides, I want no complications before I'm put back into cryo, although that doesn't mean I can't have a friend to confide in.

"Vic was horrible to me last night. He drank a skinful of his home-brewed vodka and followed me to my cabin. I thought... well, I thought he might come back in the night and..."

"He did what?"

"And it wasn't just the pestering. He was mean to me all day, lying to me about the engine lasers, and making me perform a series of jobs that I'm sure didn't need doing."

Brad shakes his head, strands of blond hair becoming loose and falling to sit just above his cheekbones. "I'm not surprised although I'm sorry to admit it... I'm relieved. I've been the focus of his interest since we woke up. New blood and all that. I'm the new boy on the crew. Seems like you've taken the pressure off me."

"I'm glad to help," I reply sarcastically.

"Vic is all hot wind and nothing else, I wouldn't worry about him. Taipan, on the other hand, is a different kettle of fish."

I snigger inside at the dated expression. "She's dangerous?"

"Well, she frightens me!" We both laugh.

"I'm back with Vic again today. I'm concerned about what he has in store for me. He wasn't happy when I sent him away from my cabin last night."

"My advice is to keep your head held high and to get on with it. What's the worst he can do? Compliment your *sweet bambino ass* and get nowhere?"

We laugh again, and this nightmare I'm in the middle of isn't that bad anymore. I got through yesterday. I can also get through today as well.

The canteen is thankfully empty. I sit down and let Brad take care of breakfast. I'll have to learn how to do this myself sometime soon, but it's nice to be looked after again by him.

Halfway through my omelette, a rough-looking Vic turns up. He ignores me but gives Brad an evil stare, before banging and clattering around in the galley. He's hungover, that much is for sure, and in a bad mood.

"I'm not pissin' around today, you hear me?" Vic says, his back to me. I notice that his Latino accent isn't as strong as before. Was it something he put on? "We've a lot of shit to get on with," he continues, and I'm not gonna be late again." He turns to face me, shovelling beans into his mouth from an open can, while stuffing down bread at the same time. "Finish up," he says, swallowing. "We're goin' now." He throws the can aside and jogs out of the canteen, his metal feet clattering on the deck.

I get up, share a look with Brad, who mouths, 'sorry', and follow the hungover engineer, trailing in the chemical stink of vodka leaching from his pores. How much booze did the man consume? It's overpowering.

Vic waits for me at the airlock, and I have just enough time to get my gloves and helmet on before he recycles the air.

If yesterday's journey was tense, this one is far worse. Vic's hostility is palpable. I wonder if small talk will do anything to change the negative vibes, but I stay silent, meaning that even though the journey is half the length of yesterday, it seems to take a lot longer.

"Ready for your big day?" Vic says as we arrive at the midships' station.

"Very ready, what have you got in store for me," I reply, staring into his eyes. I won't let him intimidate me again.

"You'll see, missy."

We leave the airlock, traverse a small corridor, and enter another huge area crammed with piping, immense tanks of shining chrome, pumping stations, control nodes and holotops. "Where are we?"

"The Nutri-hub. My least favourite part of the whole goddamn ship. Where all the nutrients, needed to keep the passengers alive and healthy, are stored while they're in cryo."

"Is that what all this pumping machinery is about?"

Vic gives me a sullen look and nods. "The entire area is closed off from the rest of the ship. There's a single main airlock and that's it. The nutritanks are refilled every time we return to Earth. They supply the many thousands of sleepers with essential nutrients like amino acids, vitamins, and minerals as well as sugars in the form of dextrose. Which is where the fun starts."

"The fun?"

"Oh yeah, my liddle conchita, very much so," he says with a return of his full-on Latino accent. "The tanks, they get clogged from time to time, you hear me?"

This sounds like more cleaning. Unless I'm missing something. Maybe it won't be as bad as I thought.

"After the engines, these tanks are the most important

system on the ship. They're supposed to be 'self-cleaning', but hey, the colony companies always like to cut corners and this new gloop they're using just doesn't cut it anymore. And what does a clogged nutritank spell?"

"I don't know."

"Dead colonists. And we lose our bonus if more than the expected percentage of passengers dry up in transit."

I wonder how keen the colonists would be to sign up if they knew the crew responsible for protecting their lives saw them as nothing more than a dollar sign.

Vic goes over to one of the massive chrome tanks, and siphons off a cup of thick, disgusting liquid that he downs in one, licking his lips. "Like I said, nutrients. A mixture of essential amino acids, vitamins, and a liddle sugar. There's auto-systems that tell me when it's gone off, although you won't miss the smell. You wanna try some?"

A shake of my head and he chuckles again. "This way." He leads me through a maze of pipes and tanks, and I become aware of the ripe stench of decomposition. We stop outside the tank where the stink is strongest, and he looks at me expectantly. "Yeah, some liddle lady has to go inside and unclog the pump. You gettin' the gist yet, missy?"

He opens a small hatchway, large enough for someone to crawl inside, and I gag at the vile odour that blasts me in the face. Vic makes a show of smelling this contaminated air like he's sniffing an expensive wine.

"You want me to go in there?" I ask between retches.

Vic chuckles. "You're one smart bambino, I'll give you that. You're gonna crawl inside and unblock the plughole. And once it's clear, you'll only have seconds to get out before you're sucked down into the system. And the captain sure won't be happy if we have to take everything apart to remove your skinny corpse."

I'm not taking Vic seriously this time, especially after he lied to me about the lasers yesterday. I nod my head, stealing myself for what is to come.

"Oh, and when you're in there, missy, watch out for any space rats."

"Space rats?"

"Persistent rodent bastards that chew on and shit in the nutritubes."

"The same pipes that send nutrients to the colonists in cryosleep?"

"Don't get your panties in a twist, missy, everything is filtered by the time it reaches the sleepers. But that doesn't stop them being pests. Ask Ferg about them. They're his obsession. Oh, and another thing, you'll need to take that skinsuit off."

"What?"

"You can't wear no skinsuit in the tanks, missy. No way. As for the reason? I'm telling you that's how it is, you get me?" He stands back expectantly, a victorious look on his face and I guess this is what he's been leading up to. He can't have me, and this is his rather pathetic punishment. He thinks nudity bothers me? Maybe, maybe not. But this is a power play, plain and simple. Will I strip off in front of him and enter that disgusting hole naked? Or tell him to fuck off? I suspect the latter is what he wants. I sense it in him. I have no real idea who I am, although I know in my bones that I'm no pushover. Without making a conscious decision, I start removing my skinsuit.

Vic leans back so he can take me all in, trying to hide his surprise. Fuck him. He can leer as much as he wants. "What am I using to unblock this thing?"

He holds up his hands. "These."

Shaking my head, and striding over to the open hatch, I dive inside without giving myself the chance to change my mind.

I slide down into the rotting, thick, vile fluid that sticks to me like glue, and immediately start vomiting.

"Oh, and there's one more thing," Vic says through the open hatch, "once its unblocked and you've avoided getting sucked into the machinery, you'll need to get your ass out of there before the steam cleanin' cycle begins. You hear me, missy?"

Great. I crawl around in the gunk, vomiting and retching, my breakfast reappearing as quickly as it went down, slipping and sliding around the inside lip of the tank, which is angled downwards, where I'm guessing the blockage is. Once down there, there's no way I'll be able to get back up. It's a goddam death trap. Maybe Vic wasn't lying to me this time? Maybe he's put my life in danger just because I won't sleep with him, and what's one more dead colonist to him? I put those thoughts behind me. I jumped into this goddamn hellhole, and it's up to me to get myself out of it.

I flail around the sides of the tank until my foot touches something. The rungs of an embedded ladder! I breathe a sigh of relief and retch uncontrollably again, my stomach cramping, my mouth full of nothing more than a trickle of bile. I wait until the attack is over and lower myself down, step by step, my bare feet finding purchase on each thin rung, realising that if I was wearing a skinsuit, they'd easily slip off. Vic wasn't lying about doing this naked, I realise. Somehow, that makes me hate him even more.

I gradually descend into the foul lake of congealed nutrient until I reach the bottom, my head poking out over the gunk, one hand keeping a firm hold on the ladder, the other flailing around under the surface. I find something metal. A wide grill of sorts blocked by a knot of congealed nutrient, like dried mucus. I scrabble at it, deciding to let go of the ladder to use both hands, breaking up the knot by squeezing it through my fingers until… a sucking sound followed by a rumble as the lake of foul nutrients is sucked down. I scramble for the ladder, panicking when I can't find it, but my hand brushes against one of the rungs, and

I'm clambering quickly upward toward the hatch, flinging myself outside and back onto the cold floor, just as the steam-cleaning sequence begins behind me, the muffled sound of Vic's laughter in my blocked ears.

1-11-DUPED

Vic begrudgingly wipes me down after I've regained my composure and my feet. And I let him, keener to get this vile gunk off me than worrying about giving the creep a cheap thrill. He's subdued. He may have forced me naked into the tank, but I won. "There was never any danger of me falling through that grill, was there?" I say, wiping the gunk from my hair and face.

"Of course not, missy. Vic was just having a liddle fun."

"That's what you call fun? What's wrong with you?"

He shrugs. "You're lucky only one of the tanks was clogged, otherwise we'd be doing this all over again. Here." He gives me a flask of water that I use to swill out my mouth and clean my nose and ears. I'm still covered in the disgusting slime.

Could I do the same thing again? I grit my teeth. Yeah, I could. But I'm relieved I don't have to.

"There's a shower and heads on the far side where you can wash yourself clean. Big enough for two… if you want?"

This is the first time I've seen Vic hesitant, his assured cockiness and self-confidence a pale imitation of what I experienced yesterday.

Shaking my head, I wander off to the shower, taking my skinsuit with me, walking down a series of short corridors, until I find the cubicle. I'm able to wash myself fully clean, finding traces of the gunk in places I wished I hadn't. I'm half-expecting Vic to appear with another one of his pathetic attempts to get it on with me. But he's a no show. I'm hoping the message has gotten through. I return to the main tank area, worrying that Vic might have left me behind. I spot him using a powerful, mobile steam cleaner on some of the pipe housing where nutrient has escaped via loose connectors. He sees me but doesn't react, although I keep myself at a safe distance from the lethal steam. And this is how I spend the rest of the day. Him sullenly checking and recalibrating pumps and piping and occasionally cleaning while I follow him around. I don't care. I've somehow beaten him and I'm more than happy with the silence.

By the time we are finished, I'm not only starving, but I'm also struggling to stay awake. I follow Vic to the transport carriage, finding it hard to keep my eyes open. Back in the Command Centre, I hear the loud voices of the captain and Taipan, and despite my hunger, I instead head back to the silence of my cabin, deciding to get food later when the canteen is empty.

A figure in the shadows startles me, making me gasp. Fergal again? I'm too bushed to ask him what he's doing. Realising I've noticed him, he approaches.

"Oh hello, Lissa," he says, nervously and I get the sense he's been waiting a while for me. "I am so sorry about the captain the other day. She can be very abrupt, butting into our conversation like she did just when we were getting to… um …know one another."

"Did you want anything? I've had a long day and I'm finally allowed to get some sleep."

Fergal blushes, "I wondered if, well," he stumbles over his words, struggling to continue.

"Can this wait?" I snap.

Fergal closes his eyes and opens them with determination. "I was wondering if you wanted to go to the gantry with me?"

"The gantry? You mean a viewing port?"

He nods vigorously. "Yes, indeed. But not just any gantry. This gives magnificent views of the entire ship. I think you'd love it up there."

"I've already visited a gantry on my way here."

"Not like this one, I'm absolutely, positively sure of that. Oh yes! It is a pure glass bubble allowing you to not only see the ship but the stars and the Milky Way in all its glory."

"It sounds lovely, but I really have to get to my bunk now."

"You will go with me?"

"Yeah, sure, why not. Goodbye Fergal."

The guy smiles widely at me and bounces away. What an odd person.

After another quick shower needed to rid myself of the residual odours of rotting nutrient, I fall onto my bunk, not bothering to block the door, and close my eyes.

I awake sometime later with a start, like someone has slammed a door, a half-remembered dream flitting through my mind. Trapped inside a suffocating darkness with invisible walls, panicked and trying to escape. The crew laughing at me. Their faces distorted, their haunting laughter following me as I try to chase ever-diminishing green arrows that wink in the distance.

Shaking my head, I step back into the shower and wash off the clammy sleep sweat. After what I've been through, I suppose my dreams will be like this for a while, although I'm hoping for something more fulfilling.

A familiar dizziness, and I stumble back to my bunk, lying wet on the sheets, my temples throbbing, the bright ceiling lights hurting my eyes. I think back to what Simone told me about my brain damage and shudder. What the hell did I do to myself? The pain in my temples becomes unbearable and I'm forced to stifle a scream.

The pain disappears, as quickly as it came, replaced by a flood of new memories. Faces, places, snippets of conversations swirl together like a maelstrom, leaving me breathless. I see myself dancing half-naked at some wild party, then hiding from the police as a child and searching bins for scraps of food, then staying at a posh school where I had no friends, then lying hungover and ashamed on the deck of an expensive yacht in bright sunshine, then travelling in a beautiful, old-fashioned limousine wearing a fabulous dress and expensive jewellery, then various scenes working in a bar as…as a hostess of some sort, men and women leering at me, trying to grope me, and then, finally, a lonely young girl in a large bedroom, surrounded by hundreds of expensive toys but no one to play with.

I'm left with a throbbing head and a confusing jumble of jarring memories. Is this how it will be? Having no way to knit these recollections together in any coherent way? Whoever I was, I had a diverse and complicated life, that's for sure.

I turn off the cabin lights and try to get back to sleep. It's impossible. My winking holotop tells me it's the middle of the night, so why am I not tired? I've not slept for three goddamn days. I should be out like a light.

Instead of sleeping, I lie awake, thinking. And none of it is good. My hunger pangs are also a problem. The corridor is dimly lit as I exit my cabin. It's still 'ship night'. I'm assuming the crew members are all in their cabins sleeping, or whatever it is they get up to in these hours. I'm careful, quietly leaving the crew area and padding into the canteen, where I make myself a couple of rounds of toast, sitting in the near dark, the sound of my crunching loud enough to wake the dead. What I find so unpalatable is that Vic and the captain and probably everyone else in the crew, apart from Simone, know more about me than I do. Notably, the file that Simone isn't allowed to read, which I need to get my hands on. But it's more than that. I'm sure they are withholding something from me. It sounds like cryo-paranoia, yet I'm convinced I can find some answers in this file if I can only get my hands on it.

"Simone, you there?" I whisper. No reply. "Simone!" Why the hell is she ignoring me again?

I need to make sense of these memories and soon. Maybe I should ask the captain directly? Then again, Captain Marla has been off with me from day one. And I'm convinced reading my file will tell me why.

What else can I do? Try and get to see it for myself? … *What the hell do I have to lose?* I finish my toast, stand up, and head for the bridge. As to what I will do when I get there? I'm not sure, but no way am I staying in my cabin wide awake thinking about this stuff anymore. At least I will try to do something. It's not the best plan in the world, yet that doesn't stop my feet as I silently pad through the hatchway and into the rundown room that serves as the command centre for the ship.

The bridge is quiet, holotops in standby mode. I check them one after another. All are locked. Figures. I look in drawers and cupboards and find nothing but the usual junk you'd expect from personal workstations. The door to the captain's ready room is half open and, shrugging, I steal inside, squeezing myself behind her immense desk and sitting down, accidentally knocking her holotop, surprised to see her screen unfold.

The captain left it unlocked? Sloppy.

A strange sound coming from outside on the bridge. I freeze, subconsciously holding my breath, my heart scudding. If they catch me, I will be in so much trouble. Then again, the captain couldn't do much worse to me than she already has. Maybe lock me in the brig? Do they even have a brig? That would be preferable to the bullying and shitty tasks I've been on the receiving end of so far. No other sounds, and I relax.

I take a few moments to understand how the captain's holotop is organised and soon find a list of folders, my heart scudding again when I see a folder with my name on it. I bump it open and read the contents hungrily.

But it's just the same stuff Simone told me. Where's the rest? Where's the other info that Vic saw… unless… was he lying to me? I do some more searching, finding a schematic of the five passenger saucers, intrigued by a few greyed-out capsules, until I realise that these are dead colonists. The ones who didn't make it. Shit! I search for another twenty minutes, bringing up file after file, yet can't find anything of interest. A dead end.

There's nothing here, nothing at all, I flick off the holotop just as my eyes catch a folder I missed, sitting in plain sight, named 'Emergency Sim'.

I bump it open, reading its contents with a mixture of rage and anxiety. My pod didn't malfunction. There was no emergency. No hull breach. Nothing. It was all fake. The whole thing has been one big lie since they woke me up.

2-0
MEMORIES

"Simone!" I whisper with constrained anger.

What are you doing in here, Lissa? You are not allowed on the bridge without the presence of another crew member, and especially not in the captain's ready room.

"Oh, I see… You've ignored me for the last two days, but now I'm in the captain's seat, you're suddenly available?"

The captain ordered me not to talk to you.

"She did? I wonder why that was? Was she frightened you would tell me what was actually going on aboard this ship, perhaps?"

I do not know what you mean, Lissa.

"Don't lie to me Simone. I've just read the file. There was no emergency, the whole thing was a goddamn training sim. What I don't get is why they woke me up. Which is what you will explain to me right now."

I'm sorry, Lissa, Simone says in emotionless, dead tones, *however, I am not allowed to divulge that information.*

"Why? Because the captain ordered you to keep quiet?"

Captain Marla is the ultimate authority aboard this ship. The ship companion must always follow the captain's orders.

"Well, it's too late. You are supposed to be looking after my safety, not forcibly waking me up from cryo, lying to me about depressurisation and forcing me to walk naked and, half-dehydratedly, for the full length of the ship. Is this some kind of sick joke?"

'Dehydratedly' is not a word, Lissa.

"Answer my question!"

A slight pause. *The crew must perform an emergency simulation on every journey. I awake them with a prepared situation, and they respond in real time.*

"That's good procedure, although it doesn't explain what happened to me."

Captain Marla prefers ship simulations to be as close to real as possible. That is why I was instructed to take you out of cryosleep.

Call me empathic, but what Simone is telling me lacks the ring of truth. "Has this happened before? Does the crew regularly wake up colonists during sims just to help with their chores?" I want to add, *and mess with them*, yet let the question hang.

Another long pause.

"Answer me."

Yes, Lissa. This has happened before.

"Why me out of the thousands on board?"

The captain chose you. You would need to talk to her.

Captain Marla! I knew it. "So what am I? A dogsbody kicked out of cryo to do all the shittiest jobs. Was I chosen because she thought I'd be a pushover?"

The captain chose you. You would need to talk to her.

"Yes, you said. Do you have anything else to tell me?"

I am sorry for my part in the deception.

"That makes all the difference. So now what happens? Will you tell the captain what I've found out?"

Do you want to mark this conversation as private?

"Yes, absolutely I do. I don't want the crew to know. Not just yet."

Conversation marked as private.

"Can I trust you not go blabbing to the captain?"

I am unable to divulge the contents of private conversations unless it affects the safety of the ship, and only if ordered to by the captain.

"I can't say I believe you. Thanks anyway."

I am unable to divulge the contents of private conversations unless—

"Yes, yes."

I must urge you to leave the captain's ready room. You are not allowed on the bridge without the presence of another crew member.

"I'm going," I whisper. "I've got a lot to think about."

2-01-WRONGED

The ship is still silent as I make my way back to my cabin, and I too am silent, a passing shadow in this ship of nightmares, although I want to scream and shout at the injustice.

How dare the captain wake me up and lie to me! I wonder who else is in on it? What did Brad tell me? *Asteroidal strikes are common.* Perhaps no one else other than the captain knows the difference between a sim and a real incident? Although that sounds unlikely.

The question is… *Do I tell the captain and the crew that I know what's going on?*

I want to have it out with her, that's for sure. To storm into the canteen tomorrow morning and rail at her, demanding they put me back into cryo. It's the most attractive option, for sure. Yet it's not straightforward. Far from it.

Waking up passengers mid-flight is something the colony companies would frown upon. More than frown. The captain and the crew could lose their jobs over this. And their substantial savings. Could they risk putting me back into cryo and having me blab all about my treatment once I've arrived on Persephone? The thought sends a shiver down my spine. Especially after seeing those greyed out pods in the captain's files. I'm in a dangerous position. I have no idea what the captain is capable of doing. If I were to risk her position—a job that Simone informed me she loved—and her livelihood, I could also end up as one of those greyed out pods. Just an administrative addendum in the acceptable margin of error column. Shit.

I should've never gone to the bridge. Never discovered what I discovered. And I certainly shouldn't have told Simone about it. If she tells the captain… it doesn't bear thinking about. I will have to trust that she will keep quiet.

The realisation that the only thing possibly keeping me alive is the ship's tedious artificial companion, is galling. I shake my head. What's done is done. I can't change it.

Still, all of this means that I must play along with this deception. Act like I don't know what's been done to me. To do my time with my head held high and my mouth firmly zipped, until I get to Persephone. It's then that I'll exact my revenge. I'll expose the captain for what she's been doing. I'll bring her down and anyone else in the crew who's involved.

The thought fills me with power, giving me strength to survive my time here over the next few weeks.

My memories are a mess, yet deep inside, all I've ever wanted is to leave Earth. That is the one thing I'm sure of. A singular desire running through me as a seam of truth amongst the uncertainty. To start a new life on a different planet with more possibilities than I left behind. Whoever I am, whoever I turn out to be, I can't see that ever changing. And besides, here I am on a colony ship. I was making it happen, until that bitch Marla woke me up. Persephone is where I need to be and I can smile and grit my teeth to get there, no problem.

My holotop alarm wakes me the next morning. I'm refreshed, if nervous and angry at what I've found out. I shower, get dressed and head to the canteen, worried that Simone has blabbed to Captain Marla. If anything, the crew's reaction to me is the most positive it's been since I arrived here, although that doesn't stop Taipan, who is draped over Vic like a dippy teenager, trying to stare me out. Brad flashes another of his winning, lopsided smiles, while Fergal's eyes gleam in my general direction. I try to remember our conversation last night. It feels like a hundred years ago.

Breakfast is laid out on the galley top, reconstituted egg, bacon, sausages, and tomatoes. I load up a plate and relax, not realising how tightly wound I was inside about meeting the captain. She eats her food mechanically, one beady eye on her breakfast, the other on the general ship chatter. Her attention briefly turns to me as I sit down next to Brad before it returns to the story Vic is presently telling—something about a zero-gee incident on a ship he once worked on. I don't listen to the details. I'll soon have my own tale to tell. I'm gonna get you, Captain Marla, I think to myself. I have the upper-hand and she doesn't have a clue about it. She's gonna get a shock after we arrive on Persephone, that's for sure.

Vic finishes his story and turns his attention to me. He holds up a cup of coffee. "You did good yesterday, missy. Very good." He turns to the others. "You should've seen her dive into that disgustin' nutritank—that was quite somethin'."

The others look at me expectantly. "Thanks," I say. "It was the most disgusting thing I've ever done in my life, or at least what I can remember of it."

My remark is followed by some good-natured chuckles. I want to take that cup off Vic and smash it in his face. I smile and raise my coffee instead, Taipan's eyes drilling into me. I am not the pushover they thought I was. Hopefully things will go more smoothly for me now that they know that.

The food is still tasteless—the ghost of bacon, egg, and tomatoes—and I eat mechanically. Only the coffee has flavour. It must be so strong and bitter that I'd spit it out in other circumstances.

"You were inside a rotting nutritank?" Brad says to me after Vic's conversation moves elsewhere.

"Yeah," I nod glumly. "Is that unusual?"

He shrugs. "When I've worked with Vic, we steam-clean the tanks and keep cycling them until the blockage passes."

"You mean…?"

"There's no need to ever go inside and do it manually."

His words confirm what I already suspected. "I'm not surprised."

Brad sits back, his eyebrows furrowing. "You're not?"

"Fuck him, yeah?"

Brad's face breaks out into a smile. "You're one of a kind, Lissa."

Fergal jumps to his feet, pushing his chair over. "Can't you just leave her alone, Brad? Lissa does not want a player like you sniffing around her. Or can't you stop yourself?"

The attack comes out of nowhere leaving both me and Brad bemused. I stifle a giggle at Fergal's enraged, reddened face.

"Keep your distance from her, okay?"

Brad raises his hands. "Yeah, sure, Fergal. We were only talking."

"Well don't!" He turns his attention to me, his eyes sparkling behind his red glasses. "I'm sorry Lissa, you have no idea what Brad is like. I'm warning him off for your own good."

My need to giggle disappears, replaced by quick anger. This crew have so many old-fashioned notions. What is Fergal thinking? That he's protecting me? I'm about to tell him that when Captain Marla intervenes.

"Sit down, Fergal."

"Captain! I must—"

"Sit down!"

Fergal sighs, picks up his chair and sits down with a thump, his arms crossed angrily in front of his chest.

Captain Marla turns her attention to me and shakes her head as if in warning.

I've done nothing wrong. In fact, I'm the one who has been wronged. The captain can stare and frown at me as much as she wants. I know what's coming for her once I get off this crazy ship. The thought is more than comforting.

Fergal's behaviour was crazy. Just what did I say to him last night? We barely swapped words. Somehow, he's got the impression I like him, or he's one of those guys who likes to delude himself where women are concerned. So now I have to manage Fergal as well? Brilliant.

After quickly finishing my food, I head back to my cabin. I've still no idea what I'm doing today or who I'm working with. I really hope it's not another day stuck with that lunatic Vic. As I approach my cabin, I become aware of someone coming up behind me. I turn, unsurprised to see Fergal.

"I just wanted to come and apologise," he says out of breath, a bloom of sweat spreading under his armpits, his face also clammy with the effort of catching me up. The man is out of shape.

"It's okay," I say dismissively, wanting to be rid of him.

"No, it is not! The way Brad was all over you this morning... it is unprofessional."

I'm startled, I thought he'd come to apologise for his own outburst, not double down on his ridiculous behaviour. "I appreciate the thought, Fergal, but I can look after myself. It's up to me who I talk to, no one else."

"Of course, of course," he replies as if he hasn't really heard my words. "I was offering advice is all. Brad is not right for you, not right at all."

I want to end this conversation as soon as possible. "Thanks for the warning."

"And I also wanted to tell you..." he blushes, "that I am very much looking forward to our date."

"Our date?"

"Yes," he replies crestfallen. "Remember? Last night when you said you would go with me to the gantry? It is a lovely spot, and the view from up there is magnificent."

I have a vague memory of talking to him about this, although I'm sure we didn't arrange anything. I decide to let him down easily. "I'm tired and still only recently woken from cryo, I'm pretty bushed in the evenings."

"Oh really? I can help with that. The crew have stims for just that reason."

"I'm not sure a stim would be good for me, just before I

go to bed."

The mention of bed makes Fergal blush again. "No, no, no. You take it in the morning, I will go and get you some."

"That's okay, Brad gave me some already."

He grits his teeth. "He did, did he? Watch him, Lissa. He cannot be trusted."

"You said."

"I have um… also been checking out Persephone. It is a great planet. I was thinking of maybe hopping off the ship at the end of this rotation. And, you know, going down to the planet with the settlers. I have amassed a fair amount of credit-dollars over the decades. I would be quite the… um… catch. Very much so."

My heart sinks even further. I have no idea why Fergal is fixated on me. And now he's suggesting what exactly? To give up his commission to join me on Persephone? Is everyone on this ship deluded? "Thanks for the chat, Fergal. Now I must get ready for today's shift, whatever that is, okay?"

A frown crosses Fergal's hopeful face. Before he can reply, Taipan appears over his shoulder. "You're with me for the next few days," she says in a little girl voice. She grabs a hold of Fergal's arm, acting all coquettishly. "It will be just us girls. I wonder what fun we will get up to?"

I knew that the captain had me rostered to work with other members of the crew, but my hearts sinks.

"You may think you won Vic over with that holier than thou shit you pulled on him," she continues in her more regular, coarse tones, pushing Fergal away like an afterthought, "you won't find me such a pushover… Now, if you've finished prick-teasing poor Fergal here, you're coming with me."

"You do not have to be so rude to the girl, Taipan," Fergal says, brushing his arm where Taipan touched it like it's contaminated. "Lissa has only just joined us and is still finding her feet. And she certainly was not… um… prick-teasing, as you so crassly put it, she was actually, very polite and good mannered…unlike you."

Taipan ignores his rebuke—her attention fully on me. "You really want to go on a date with this fat, sweaty idiot?"

"Oh just… just fuck off, Taipan. You ruin everything. Everything!" Fergal gives me an apologetic smile, and stomps angrily away.

"Looks like I did you a favour, girl," Taipan says. "He's a virgin, you know? Can you believe that? A so-called man of his age who's never anger-banged the slappybag? It's embarrassing unless *you* want to deflower him?"

I ignore her, hoping that Taipan and Vic are part of the captain's deception. If so, they will also go down with her. And… *what about Brad?* He can't be involved, can he? He seems like a straitlaced, follow-the-rules kinda guy. And he's also new to this crew of fuckups. No, I won't believe he has anything to do with what's been done to me.

"With me, girl!" Taipan says when she realises I'm not about to answer her stupid question, and I'm forced to walk behind her. "I know you're checking me out. I get it, sure I do. What else can you do when you're walking behind someone so goddamn laser hot?"

The annoying thing is that she's right. Her body is perfection. Her unblemished olive skin smooth and luxuriant looking. Her ass isn't too large, her waist isn't too small, her breasts are impressively large but not cumbersome. Her slender legs are long and toned, as is the rest of her body. She's taller than me, yet not too tall. The mix of Asian and African gives her an exotic look—although I wonder how much of that was manufactured? Why Vic would be so desperate for me when he has this vision of a woman as a girlfriend is beyond me. Then again, I once worked in a bar staffed with hot men and women, and it was always the ones with personality that got the most tips and attention. Like I did.

I catch my thoughts… the memory came unbidden into my mind. Fully formed and out of the blue. Am I starting to remember?

2-02-HUMILIATED

I've had flashes of the same bar before. Now I remember it in detail. Two cramped floors. Dazzling under neon lights. A shithole under normal illumination. I worked downstairs, warming up punters. Encouraging them to go upstairs to… *a brothel.*

Shit!

One of the many dotted around the spaceport. An anachronism, although those kinds of dives never really went away. Filling some base human need. And I worked there? What the hell was I thinking?

I hear my boss yelling at me. I've a soft spot for him. Even though deep down he was a bastard. *"Hey you, clean up that mess! Serve that girl. Wear something more revealing— you're a pretty young thing… use it!"* Gritting my teeth and complying. Lucky to work there. More than lucky.

My looks were the reason. I'd always hidden my petite curves in loose dowdy clothes, keeping my long black hair under unflattering hats. My boss saw beneath the disguise. Hell, that's why he hired me. At least he cared for his girls, boys, and any other gender the customers required. All of us off-limits. If the punters wanted more, they paid to go upstairs, where most of the saps who worked in this joint ended up. Not me. No way. That wasn't where I was heading. I breathe a sigh of relief. If I was punking myself out to creeps… it would've been a low blow. I sure had sunk a long way from that swanky mansion of my youth to end up in a cathouse like that.

And… *I had long black hair?* I'm blonde now. Did I get it

changed? A simple enough procedure and not too expensive. I must've done. Why?

I walk into the back of Taipan standing in front of cabin number three, which I'm guessing is hers.

"What the hell you doin', girl? Then again, you won't be the first woman to get hypnotised by this ass, but girls aren't my thing. Never have been. Of course, I gave it a go… who doesn't? But it ain't for me. You girls are way too bitchy."

I hardly listen, my brain sparking with the memory. Flashes of encounters. Laughing, flirting, serving drinks.

"Where you at, girl?"

"…Memories."

"You remembering what a loser you were, huh? Well, you can save them memories for your own time. I want you focusing one hundred percent on me today, okay?"

I nod, absentmindedly. The bar is important somehow. A significant event took place there. But what?

Taipan retrieves some things from her cabin, and we head a short way into the old ship, coming to a supply room, the air thick with a heady aroma. She points to a complicated still. "Vic is brewing up a new batch of his vodka."

Racked around the walls are many full bottles of the clear alcohol. And a stack of empty bottles ready for the next batch. Glass is an archaic substance. They would've cost him a fortune.

"He leaves it to sit for twenty years or so and it's still undrinkable," she snorts. "Don't tell Vic I said that. I hate the stuff. I have my own stash of rum."

My eyes scan the storeroom. Larger than at first glance. Shelves of various chemicals all held in special cartons to resist the passing of time. Canisters of bleach and other toxic solutions including phosphoric and hydrochloric acid. Various electronic equipment in large racks at the back. Evac helmets and gloves. A stack of unused personal holotabs grabs my attention. Crew members always carry them. I wonder why I haven't been allocated a similar tab. I blame the captain. Denying me anything that would make my life easier.

Taipan stuffs her holotab into her skinsuit belt before gathering an armful of devices and throwing them in an empty bin. I wheel it behind her, and she grabs even more equipment.

When she's done, she saunters out of the storeroom and I follow, awkwardly guiding the bin that has a sticking wheel. We head northwards—I'm still using the navigation technique that helped me escape the ship's maze of confusing corridors. If Taipan leaves me stranded, I want to be sure of finding my way back.

We pass a door with words 'Strictly Crew Only' printed on it. Who else do they think will go in there? Still, if waking up passengers is a regular thing for the captain, perhaps they need a sign like this. It piques my interest. A sign telling you to keep out always makes you want to do the opposite. Or is that just me?

Taipan nods to the door. "Maybe, if you're a good girl today, I'll let you see inside."

I fake indifference.

After a long walk, we enter a cold, chamber-like, circular room. A small airlock sits on the far curved wall. This close to the outer hull, the air is icy. My breath frosts and I shiver, rubbing at my arms.

Taipan picks up a thick jacket, shrugging into it. "Only one jacket. Sorry sugar. But don't worry, I'll keep you too busy to get cold." She waves a hand around. "You like? This is the main navi-node. One of the so called 'blobs' that sit on the front of the ship."

The area is crammed with impressive computers and holotops. 3D screens winking and flashing. The floor, in comparison, is strewn with discarded equipment and wires. A mess. Not what I was expecting from the well-turned-out navigation officer. I notice empty vodka bottles amongst the junk. Vic has been here. Probably with Taipan. I don't have to guess what they were up to.

"I suppose keeping the ship on course and in contact with Earth is vital to the journey and the survival of the colonists," I say with sarcasm, glancing at the surrounding chaos.

Taipan shakes her head, her long black hair, with its twin white stripes of platinum, effortlessly cascading over her muscled shoulders. "Well, you'd think wrong, girl," she replies, oblivious to my disdain. "We're light years from Earth and from Persephone. Any message we send will take years to arrive. Years." Taipan thinks she is giving me new information, but I know all this. "Despite their age, nothing moves faster than ships like these," she continues.

"Unless they develop faster ships while we're away."

Taipan scoffs. "With Earth in the state it's in? I'm always surprised it's still there every time we go back. These ships were built at the height of Earth's technological phase. They were needed because even then, hundreds of years ago, they could see the end coming. But you know Earth? The old sleaze pit somehow manages to keep on going.

"It sure does."

"We don't contact Earth or Persephone, we're too far away. Instead, this ship is part of a convoy. A ship six months ahead and one six months behind. Messages take weeks to get back and forth. We use the position of these ships as well as our position in relation to certain astronomical objects to keep us on course."

"Then what happens if there's a disaster?"

"We jettison the saucers—the colonists are going nowhere—and try to survive any which way we can until the next ship catches up and rescues us.

"I see."

Taipan gives me a long stare. "You really think a pale, skinny runt like you can catch a guy like Vic?"

I'm stunned by the tangent change. So far, Taipan has been distant and dismissive. "I have no interest in your boyfriend. I told him that. Every time he tried it on with me."

"Vic did what?" She laughs derisively, her long hair twitching around the elegant curves of her face. "Dream on, girl. Dream on. You'd wet yourself for a tiny bit of him. Not that any part of him is small… you know what I mean?"

The woman is jealous and deluded. I bite my lip and the awkward moment passes.

First off, we perform regular maintenance on the communication array. Removing navigation systems, including gyroscopes, accelerometers, and star-trackers. Taipan checking and adjusting, before replacing them, while I stumble amongst the junk.

Next, I'm tasked with exchanging the 'storage buffers'. Hundreds of the things. With no idea what function they perform. Not that important, if I'm allowed to work on them. Child's play compared to cleaning out rotting nutritanks. Taipan perches on a console watching me with various looks of disdain, filing her long fingernails into even sharper claws, throwing occasional insults my way. My tits are too small. My ass too flat. My legs too skinny. I'm too short and move without grace. I'm the type whose looks will fade prematurely. I get the impression she's envious. Particularly of my youth. If she really is over ninety years old, ninety years in *real time* like Vic told me, she should be pleased. She's the hottest nonagarian I've met. Shame she didn't work on her personality as much as her looks. The woman is ugly on the inside.

"You saw those snake tattoos on Vic?" she asks me when I'm halfway through. "I did them."

I nod. The swirling snakes and scorpions adorning Vic's back and neck, and his other bare flesh were expertly created and disturbing.

"Any reason why a pale white thing like you ain't inked?"

"I suppose I never had the money or the inclination." *That can't be right, can it?* For a rich, spoilt socialite? Before splitting with my family and their wealth, and working in spaceport bars and docks, I could've afforded to get any number of tats. Inking our skins is one of the constants in human history.

"I sure like to draw with needles," Taipan continues with relish. "I used to have a few myself when I was younger. I had them all removed. And I do love a blank canvas." She smiles at me in a most unusual way. I get the impression she intends to ink me with or without my permission.

I finish changing the storage buffers and Taipan checks my work. "No," she says pulling out one of the buffers and dropping it to the floor. Then the next one and the next. "These are all wrong, girl! What d'ya think you're doing to me? Didn't you listen when I showed you what to do? Do them all again and do them right this time. You get me?"

I pick up the discarded buffers and replace them under her scrutiny, Taipan standing over my shoulder. This close, her cloying, sweet fragrance is overpowering. An unsuccessful attempt to hide an underlying, stale odour. Is that what Vic meant when he told me he wanted someone who smelled fresher?

Twisting my nose, I do exactly as I'm told. Not good enough. Taipan pushes me aside, shows me again—the exact same thing I've been doing—and I try one more time.

"For fuck's sake!" she screams at me. "What is wrong with you? A monkey could do this shit!" She goes through the procedure in painfully slow steps. No different to what I've been doing. The bitch is fucking with me.

Determined to show no weakness, I take a deep breath and repeat the process. This time, I'm all fingers and thumbs. Unable to complete the simple procedure. Dropping the buffer to the floor. Tears welling behind my eyes. I pick up the buffer, wiping tears from my face. Horrified that I've let her get to me.

"Is that what you tried with Vic? Blubbing? You think you can sob your way into my affections? Because those cheap tricks won't work, honey. Not with this girl! You, and silly young things like you, make me sick." A shake of her head. "You're not getting out of this. Tears or not, you will finish the job. Now, I will show you one last time, and if you fuck up… I won't be responsible for my actions, you get me?"

My tears are now in full flood. I'm angry, embarrassed, and ashamed of myself. I managed to keep my head held high in front of Vic and his aggressive sexuality, and all it took was this foul woman to shout at me a few times to start the waterworks.

"Here." Taipan says, holding out a rag. "Wipe away those tears now. And do not, I repeat, do not wet my sensitive equipment. Otherwise, I'll make sure the company knows who was responsible. And those guys never hold back when it comes to retrieving their monies. You'd be in debt for the rest of your skinny, pathetic little life."

I wipe away the tears and repeat the annoying procedure. This time, Taipan nods with approval, although I'm doing nothing different.

"See? Sometimes all it takes is some stick. Good girl."

What does she want? Thanks?

"Now do the rest. I'm heading back to the CC for lunch. I expect these to be completed by the time I get back. And no shirking. I'll be watching you." She points to one of Simone's nodes and taps at the screen of her tab. "Yeah, I hacked into the surveillance system. I am the coms specialist after all. That's how I know you got nowhere with Vic. I was observing you."

I'm relieved to be left on my own. Unconcerned if she is watching me or not. She could be lying. Yet when I think back to Vic's crude attempts to get me into bed, they were all off-camera. Like outside my cabin, in the transit carriage, and in the engine and nutritank sections.

Taipan returns over an hour later just as I'm finishing. A pleased look plastered across her face. I brace myself, expecting her to inspect my work, and to find it at fault again. She ignores me and the buffers.

"Something has come up," she says slyly, tapping her tab. "An alignment needs to be made outside the ship. You've seen my nails. Meaning… there ain't no way I'm gonna risk breaking them in those nano-gloves they give us. No, you'll have to do it for me, girl."

She can't be serious. She just can't. "You mean… spacewalking?"

"That's exactly what I mean?"

2-03-STARVED

"You want me to do what?"

"You deaf, girl? I already told you. Maybe you're just stupid, huh? It's straightforward, so straightforward a monkey could do it, but hey, we don't have a monkey so you're gonna have to do. You need to manually adjust the navigational array. You can't miss it. A giant antenna. Lots of flashing lights. Halfway up there's a junction box. You open that and well, let's wait till you get there, okay?"

Taipan is surprisingly strong, dragging me over to the airlock and pushing me inside. Throwing helmet and gloves at me.

"I shouldn't be doing this," I blurt, terrified. "I've no training." Taipan can't be for real… can she?

She presses some buttons and the inner airlock door closes.

"You've done it before. Vic told me you were a natural. So get on with it." She says over the com. *"Space walkin' is nothin',*

girl. Nothin' at all. Just make sure you don't fall off the damn ship, is all. That's why there's a tether—you'll see it outside the airlock. Keep yourself attached to the ship and you'll be just fine."

"A tether? Okay, yeah." Knowing that I'll be tethered the whole time does a lot to calm my nerves.

"No, your biggest worry is throwing up in your helmet. You do not... let me repeat... you do not want to do that, girl. Drowning in your own puke is one nasty way to go." She smiles at me through the inner airlock window like this is exactly what she's hoping for.

"But—"

"Now listen to me. It's my job to watch over you, to keep you alive, to keep you safe. Nothin' is gonna go wrong, okay?"

"Yeah," I gasp into my helmet. I can't believe this is happening. Although... perhaps this isn't as dangerous as she wants me to think it is. They're messing with me again. Like Vic did with the nutritank and the lasers. Making me think it was hazardous when it isn't. It'll be uncomfortable, I tell myself, and terrifying, but ultimately, I'll be safe. I console myself with these thoughts as my skinsuit tightens and warms, and the outer hatch swings open.

I've done this before, yet I'm unprepared for what is outside. There's no walkway and no safety of a carriage to head toward. I'm staring into the empty abyss of a black, never-ending cosmos. My hands grab instinctively to the airlock sides in a mixture of agoraphobia, dizziness, and panic. It's one thing looking at space through a window. Being here is entirely a different experience. Is this how agoraphobics feel? No wonder they never leave the goddamn house!

I see the tether, attached to a groove that runs along the hull, and attempt to attach myself using my skinsuit's built-in nano-hook. I try once, twice, three times. It fails to engage.

"The tether is malfunctioning."

"Yeah, it does that sometimes. Do what I do. Tie it around your wrist and get on with the job."

"The material of the tether is too slick to tie into a knot. Sliding apart. It's not working. I need to come back inside!"

"You ain't coming back in here until you finish the job you were given, you get me?"

"But…" I gasp ineffectively.

"No buts girl, not while I'm in charge of your skinny ass."

I knew she'd say that. I wrap the tether around my hand and grab tightly, venturing out onto the ship's hull, exposed to the vast emptiness pressing down upon me. I'm squeezing the tether hard, yet it slips out of my grasp. For one awful second, I'm floating free from the ship, yelping like a frightened dog. I scrabble at the rail, pressing my fingers into the slot and hang on. My heart doing somersaults, my breathing fast and ragged. "I lost the damn tether," I gasp as soon as my breathing settles.

"No worries, just pull yourself along the rail. I've done it hundreds of times."

I shouldn't be doing this. I want to turn around and go back. This is too much, even for me… isn't it? But I won't let Taipan beat me again. I can't let her win. No. My defiance is stronger than my panic. I search my HUD for the beating heart icon. Concentrating on the flickering graphic and the red numbers below it. I take deep steadying breaths. The flickering slows, the numbers turn to amber, and the pounding in my ears reduces to a background throb.

"What you doing, girl?"

"Just finding my bearings."

"Get a move on. You've only got a limited air supply and you need to keep moving."

Releasing my fingers, I pull myself along, propelled faster than I was expecting. My momentum twisting me around. I scrabble at the rail, my hands flailing, bouncing along the fuselage that flashes past me, falling head over heels. I instinctively throw out my arms and legs, stifling a scream of horror. My hand finds sudden purchase and I cling on for dear life. I take more steadying breaths, and instead of panic, I'm filled with anger. And it's the anger that keeps me going. I'm holding onto a handhold of sorts. Part of a series of indentations on the fuselage. Using them to guide myself back towards the rail. This time making slow, purposeful movements, and, with an internal whoop of delight, I'm pulling myself along the hull.

I follow the curve of the navigational node, heading upwards, ignoring the terrifying drop of empty space below—not that there is an up and down. The antenna stands at the top. I let go of the rail and grab hold, pulling myself up into a standing position, tilting back my head to look up. The antenna disappears into the blackness above. Just how tall is this thing? Fuck.

"You gonna talk to me, girl?"

"I'm at the antenna," I say, as calmly as I can.

"You are?" She sounds disappointed.

"What do I do next?"

"There's a control node halfway up. Just pull yourself toward it."

I ascend the antenna ladder, taking one careful step at a time. Far easier than dragging myself across the hull. Ten minutes later, I reach the control node. I stop, turn to look at where I am, and gasp. I'm standing on a tall mast of a vast ship, the *Octavia* stretching out before me, quiet, still, and somehow majestic, despite its chaotic design. I spot the faded Celtic triple spiral I saw earlier. From here I can also see two letters curving away into the black.

EA.

That's an odd name if that's what the ship used to be called. I wonder what it means. I have little time to ponder. Taipan barks commands at me over the com.

Following her instructions, I open a panel in the node and enter a series of numbers onto a pad and... that's it? What the fuck! This could've been done remotely, I'm sure of it. Yet another attempt to terrorise me. Well, it backfired. I was horrified to come out here, but this is an experience of a lifetime. Space, the stars, the huge, silent ship and just my breathing keeping me company. The only thing missing is a sparkling blue and white planet of Persephone.

I return to the airlock twenty or so minutes later, keen to get back inside the ship.

"I'm here, let me in?"

No reply.

"Taipan where are you? I'm outside the airlock."

I access the airlock controls but no matter how many times I try, I'm locked out.

I've not given my oxygen readout a second glance. I quickly check it, disturbed to see the numbers in amber. Amber that switches to flashing red, accompanied by a warning beep.

"I don't have many more minutes of oxygen left. Stop this silly game and let me in! Taipan!"

Still no answer.

She can't be deliberately trying to kill me... can she? She's jealous of Vic, but to leave me out here to die... could she do that? I convince myself this is just another silly game of hers, although my resolve is severely tested as my remaining oxygen drops below two percent. I want to breathe slower, but the thought of suffocating out here has me panicked. Not helped by the manic beeping in my ears. The number drops to one, then zero.

2-04-ATTACKED

The airlock drifts open. I flail around silently, my mouth opening and closing like a fish out of water, panicked, yet somehow managing to pull myself inside. I rip off my helmet as the air recycles, gasping and choking until I'm breathing deep, wonderful lungfuls of air.

The hatch door opens to reveal Taipan smirking at me.

"Where the hell were you?" I scream. "You deliberately left me out there until my air ran out!"

"What you hollerin' about, girl? I was just answering a call of nature is all. I had to go and lay a deuce and let me tell you, that first shit after cryo is quite the doozie."

I scramble out of the airlock, filled with a mixture of rage and relief. "You nearly killed me!"

She smirks again. "I don't think so. The captain frowns on her crew accidentally offing passengers, no matter how skinny and annoyin' they are."

I feel dizzy, my head suddenly bloated and hot and I want to vomit. Skin clammy. Hands and feet tingling. "You bitch," I gasp at her.

"God, you colonists are all the same, bleating about fuck all. If I wanted you dead, you'd still be out there, girl. Oh. And one more thing, you call me bitch again, and I'll slit your face."

I push her away.

"That ain't no empty threat, girl. You bad mouth me again and you'll feel the edge of my blade, I can promise you that." Taipan's face twists into an ugly sneer. "And just what is that stench? You shit yourself out there? Get the hell out of my node and get yourself cleaned up!"

I don't need telling twice and, pushing down my nausea, I lurch into the ship's corridors, finding a secluded alcove far away from Taipan and the navi-node, and vomit. Have I kept down anything I've eaten since I woke up on this insane ship? It sure doesn't seem like it. Afterwards, still feeling nauseous and out of sorts, I return to my cabin. Stripping off my skinsuit and jumping into the shower. The sound of the steam vents and spray hiding my deep, juddering sobs.

I emerge a long time later and lie on my bunk, wanting to close my eyes and sleep away the rest of the afternoon, but

I'm too wired. My mind obsessing over Taipan and what she did to me. What I will say to her and the rest of the crew? How I vow to punish her? Tearfully reliving my moments of shame. Gritting my teeth with wave after wave of fury. This is worse than anything Vic, Taipan or the captain could've said or done to me… and yet they are the reason for this horror. The reason why I'm lying here, in this intolerable, hateful situation.

A stirring in my stomach reminds me I'm hungry. No, it's more than that. There's a yawning hole in my gut. I'm starving. I glance at the clock. I've been lying here stewing for hours. It's time for the evening crew meal. And despite all my practised conversations and recriminations, there's no way I can face them. Especially Taipan.

A knock at my door and I freeze.

"It's me, Brad."

I pull on a clean skinsuit and open the door. Brad takes one look at me and puts his hand on my shoulder. "You had a bad day?"

I step forward and hug him tightly, taking him by surprise. He's tense, but his body soon relaxes into mine and hugs me back. His hands caressing me. And finally, we part. "Did you hear?" I ask, taken by his mesmerising blue eyes.

A frown crosses his face. "Hear what?"

"I thought Taipan would've told everyone."

"What the hell did she do?"

"She sent me spacewalking."

"She did what?"

"She forced me to fix the antenna and wouldn't let me back in the ship until my air had run out. The bitch nearly goddamn killed me."

"Shit, Lissa, that's… that's just not on. Vic and Taipan sure seem to have it in for you, don't they? Have you informed the captain?"

"I wouldn't give her the pleasure."

He laughs, his eyes smiling. "Yeah, she isn't the warmest of captains that's for sure."

I experience a strong surge of closeness for Brad, wanting to pull him into my room and jump him ragged. Anything to take my mind off today, but the moment lingers and, of course, I do nothing.

"You coming to eat?"

I shake my head.

"You sure? If they're trying to get you down, then, hey, best prove them wrong. I'll even let you sit next to me."

"I'll think about it."

He smiles at me again and leaves. "Hopefully see you soon?"

Shrugging, I watch his departing back, close my door and sit on my bunk. Why didn't I ask him in? I remember that flash of memories I had of my younger self. Naked at some sordid sex party. And all those lovers. And yet… I don't think I'm the type to grab Brad by the hand and… I flush, wishing more than ever that I'd summoned up the courage.

Another serious pang of hunger and I'm tempted to act on Brad's words. I could go and eat. Show the crew that they can't intimidate me. But am I strong enough?

A sharp pain in my temples and I sit down on my bunk. Back in the adoption home. An awful place run by a husband and wife, Mary and Joseph. False names I realise, and on the take. Pocketing the funds they were given to look after us lost boys and girls, while making us live in near poverty. I'm in the adoption office with my soon to be parents. Mary telling them all about me. I'm ten years old, or thereabouts, and terrified. Wanting to stay. My life with Mary and Joseph preferable to what this unknown, secretive couple is offering. Understanding that there was more to this transaction than a simple adoption. They could've been taking me anywhere. To any number of awful fates. Were they going to use me for my organs? Abuse me? Kill me? All the kids in the home were scared to leave. Doing everything to avoid adoption and promising to get back in touch if they were. Never to be heard from again. I see the couple sign the papers, smiling at me, and then I'm walking for the last time through those familiar corridors to a waiting car. My head held high as I go past the other kids, all brought out to see another 'successful child'.

There was no way I was going to let them see the tears that I had pushed down inside of me. To be dragged kicking and screaming like so many before me. No. I kept my head held high. It was the other children who cried.

I come back to my cabin, the pain in my temples gone, going over the memory. There was something dubious about my new parents. I was scared stiff and panicked to leave with them. And yet… they were rich and gave me the socialite lifestyle that Simone told me about. My fears were groundless. But that's not where my mind is focused. It dwells upon the strength I showed as just a ten-year-old. All that fear and trepidation, and yet, I left that place fearlessly. The memory revealed itself for a reason. And I know what I must do. Brad was right. I can't hide from the crew forever. What was I thinking?

I take a few steadying breaths, check my refection—my eyes still don't look right—and leave. I'm making my way into the shared crew area when I become aware of two hushed voices. Captain Marla and the precise English tones of Fergal.

"I'm not interested in what you think or believe, Fergal and you're certainly not leaving this ship at the end of the rotation, and you know why."

"You are not the boss of me!"

"I think you will find that I am."

"You know what I mean."

"I'm only telling you this for your own good, but you need to forget about that girl, okay? She's just not into you."

"Do not say that!"

"I'm only trying to make you realise that, well, you have a tendency to get attached."

"I do not."

"Have you forgotten what happened the last time?"

"That was different, that was—"

"Oh, Ferg, why do you keep doing this to yourself? Now come on, let's go eat."

I hang back, watching them walk away. I don't like the captain. I despise her, I realise. Yet, by warning Fergal off me, she's doing me a favour. Life on this ship is awkward enough without the lovelorn cryo-specialist following me around like a lost puppy. At least he's not trying to drown me in nutri-gunk or asphyxiate me. One thing the captain said sticks with me.

Have you forgotten what happened the last time?

Meaning… she's done the same to others like me. And Fergal was in on it, and probably the rest of the crew. Does that include Brad? The guy I was very keen to wrap my legs around earlier. I hope not.

I arrive in the canteen to a big smile from Brad, who despite the doubt surrounding what he does or doesn't know, I still want to sit next to. However, Fergal's gleaming eyes tell me the captain's talk has done nothing to extinguish his ardour. He's already been snippy with Brad for smiling at me, meaning I can't sit with either of them. Taipan is all over Vic like a rash again, but it's obvious he's not interested, and that Taipan is annoyed. I have no idea what is going on between them, but I hope it isn't anything to do with me. I won't sit anywhere near those two. Or the captain.

In the end I fill my plate from the galley and sit a chair's width between Brad and Fergal, although that puts me directly opposite Taipan whose eyes stare daggers.

"Hey girl," she says in a reprise of her little girl accent. Her sickly-sweet act grating on me. "I didn't think you'd be showing your face after you shit your skinsuit earlier."

Vic sniggers. "She did what? Shit herself!"

I ignore them both.

"She sure did. The girl is hopeless. I had to practically do everything myself. I don't have to spend another day rotated with her, do I captain?"

Marla nods.

"Oh well, after today's fun and games, I'll see what else I can cook up for you tomorrow. I've got a few more jobs that need doing. Not that you'll be any good at them."

"Bitch!" The word leaves my mouth before I've chance to stop it.

Taipan jumps to her feet, pushing her chair over, her little girl act suddenly forgotten. "I warned you about that, girl. I warned you!"

"After what you did to me today, you are a bitch. An evil fucking bitch!"

Taipan leaps over the table and grabs me by the neck, sending plates and cutlery flying, knocking me backward onto the floor, bashing my head, Taipan on top of me, dimly aware of shouting and yelling.

Vic pulls Taipan away and takes her outside. Brad picks up my chair and sits me down. "You okay?"

I rub the back of my head and at my throat. "I'll live."

2-05-DATED

Brad busies himself at the galley, presenting me a new plate of food, an encouraging smile on his face. Despite all the histrionics, I'm still starving, and shovel the food into my mouth hungrily.

Captain Marla gives me a pained stare, like what happened was all my fault. Maybe it was, or maybe it was Taipan. I don't care. After waking me up on false pretences and lying to me, she can fuck off. They all can. Thankfully, she stays silent. I stuff down the food mechanically and leave.

Back at my cabin, I weigh up whether I should tell Brad that the recent asteroidal impacts were a sim of the captain's devising—a way to get some extra labour to help with the crew tasks. So far, he's been my only real friend. The one person who has been genuinely nice to me, and not in a creepy way like Fergal.

I decided earlier to tell no one. Yet I'm convinced I can trust him. He's new to the crew and doesn't fit in with the others. And decent and just plain nice where all the rest are… *fucking insane.* I feel a real bond to him. This is a weird situation and I need an ally. Brad could be that ally. Someone better than Simone, whose allegiance is dubious. Especially as she is beholden to the captain.

Should I confide in him?

The answer is… *I want to.* But it's a risk.

I'm distrustful by nature. I'm sure of that. Which makes sense since I grew up on the streets and then forced to endure that adoption centre. It left me isolated and alone. In my memories so far, there are no friends or partners, no brothers or sisters, nobody who cares for me. Meaning… I need to start trusting people. And it's more than trust I want from Brad. Perhaps I'm just horny and this is a bad decision but I'm going to tell him.

I grab the half-bottle of vodka and take a long swig. A bit of Dutch courage is just what I need. I leave my cabin, still clutching the bottle, and do some scouting around for cabin five, where Brad is bunked.

Just as I spot Brad's door, Fergal appears from around a corner.

"I was just on my way to visit you," he says, his lips parting to beam at me with slightly yellowed teeth. "I was hoping you were okay after that quite awful attack. Taipan is hot-headed, but that was extreme, even for her."

"I'm a bit sore but nothing serious." I rub the back of my head. "I just wish I'd got in a few punches."

He notices the vodka. "And I see you have brought along my favourite tipple?"

Fergal is a person whose emotions arrive directly upon his face. The smile vanishes to be replaced with suspicion. "Where are you going?"

"To… um… find that gantry you mentioned," I say, regretting my words.

"Oh really! Well that is excellent!" The smile returns, this time a little more manic. "I suppose you were looking for me, yes?"

"Yes," I reply, deflated. My heart sinking. "It's a bit of a maze in here."

"That's splendid news. I must confess, I was going to ask if you wanted a walkabout to take your mind off things. How serendipitous!"

I don't want to be stuck with him for long. The vodka is kicking in and I really need to see Brad. "Is it far?"

"It is but a short way into the ship. We will be there in ten minutes." He offers me his arm and I take it, cringing. That was dumb, even for me.

While we walk, Fergal 'regales' me with stories about his past. He was a child genius, won awards, went to prestigious universities, and was handpicked to work in the cryogenics sector. It's a practised speech, designed to impress me. It fails miserably. Listing one's achievements is akin to bragging. I know this isn't Fergal's intention, but it's obvious he's hopeless when it comes to dating. Not that there wouldn't be someone out there for him, there usually is, but not me. And certainly not after I found out he's in on the captain's game. So I suffer him, making the occasional positive noise and taking more sips from the bottle of vodka. My stomach is already warm from the liquor, and I'm starting to relax.

We reach the gantry via an elevator. A cold circular room

under an immense glass dome where are hung two jackets.

"I brought these here earlier knowing that we would need them," he says, offering me the smaller of the two.

I put it on and go to sit on a wide elevated seat.

"Simone," Fergal says, sitting down very close next to me. "Please turn off the dome lights."

As you wish, Fergal.

"I didn't think Simone was available in the old part of the ship?"

"She's not, usually, but I added one of her nodes in this area. I like to chat to her, finding her calming and easy to talk to. I love listening to her relaxed tones. But she is all but forgotten now I that am here chatting to you. How lovely."

I groan inside.

"Now I don't want you staring outside until our eyes have adjusted to the dark. You promise not to do that? Just keep your eyes on me until I say so. Okay?"

I nod.

He makes small talk for a few minutes, his beady eyes glittering behind his large glasses, but to be honest, I don't hear a single word. "Now, I think you are ready. Let us both turn at the same time.

Fergal gives me a short countdown and I open my eyes.

"Isn't it just magnificent! I knew you would love to see the entire ship."

I remember standing on the navigational node's antenna earlier today. And despite how horribly the experience ended, that view was ten times the one I'm now seeing. I feign interest and listen as Fergal points out various parts of the ship. The ancient, triple hull, the six saucers, the three navigational nodes, protruding like bug eyes, and the many ducts that funnel the coldness of space directly from the fuselage deep in the ship where it is used to cool Simone's data and processing centre.

"Ducts?"

"An elegant and simple solution if there ever was one."

Fergal's eyes gleam as he tells me even more facts about the ship's history and engineering. Some of it interesting.

I point out the odd, Celtic-style triple swirl. From here, all of it is visible, even if it is faded. "Just what is that design? It looks ancient."

"That is called a triskelion," he replies. "An ancient, pre-civilisation symbol. The faded letters underneath spell *Ea*. Named after some minor Sumerian deity."

"Ea? I've never heard of it."

"A god of ritual purification, apparently. A wise god who could be devious and cunning."

"An odd name for a ship."

"The first ships were all named after obscure deities. I have no idea why."

While I'm staring at the mesmerising triskelion, I see a mechanical creature scuttling over the fuselage, one of the eight-legged machines I glimpsed from the carriage with Vic. I guess it's not here by accident. Fergal wanted me to see it.

"Oh, we are lucky," Fergal says, pointing it out. "There is one of my spiders."

The thing is, compact, gleaming white like the ship's hull but more dazzling, with eight segmented legs that double as arms, all surrounding a central body the size of a large man.

"My spiders are an advanced design of the originals which were—how shall I put it—only adequate for the job. I took it upon myself to enhance them."

"What are they for?" I ask, aware that Vic already explained this to me. My plan is to stay with Fergal for a few more minutes and then pretend to have a headache from the bump Taipan gave me and make my excuses.

"I've increased the spider's maintenance parameters by nearly ten percentile points over the last fifty or so years. When it comes to safety, I'm the one you can trust." Fergal happily rattles on about his spiders, while I sip abstractedly at the vodka. Trust Fergal? No way. He's in on this deception, meaning, I trust nothing he says. I 'd much prefer to be sharing the vodka with Brad… *In his bed.*

"I love working on my spiders, but they are not my only project. No, no. The other is to rid the *Octavia* of its colony of disgusting space rats."

"They're real? I thought Vic was messing with me when I was warned about them."

"Very real. Nasty, horrid things," Fergal replies with a shudder. "Blind. With big, snippy teeth, descended from rabbits, and quite disgusting smelling. God knows where they came from, but they infest all the vessels of the fleet. Getting into everything and chewing on the nutrient supply lines. I have been spending my free time over the last few trips on ways to eliminate them once and for all."

"May I ask why a man with your talents is stuck aboard a ship like this, using his many skills just to get rid of a few pests?" My question sounds more condescending than I intended. The vodka is beginning to take effect.

He goes quiet for a moment. "I hear what you are saying. I get it. I had planned only a few stints aboard the *Octavia*. From Earth to the planet Aphrodite, back again and then one more final stint to the same planet. I figured things would've moved on quite a bit tek-wise when I got there. I work in computers and technological engineering. No use on a rural planet. I wanted to arrive when I could be of most use. But even if they never caught up, I would have had the money to do whatever I wanted. Too much of it. I have never spent my earnings. In fact, well, I shouldn't mention it but… I'm probably one of the richest people you have ever met. My plan was to find a partner, a wife, and settle down."

"Aphrodite? Wasn't that one of the first new worlds they discovered?"

"I believe it was."

"So why didn't you settle there?" I ask, wanting to know the answer.

"I am not sure. I let myself get in a bit of a rut I suppose. Change can be daunting. Did you think on what I said about my plan to leave the ship when we reach Persephone?"

I can see where he's going with this, but I'm not the person to lie just to get an ally, even if I am tempted. "My head hurts and I think I may have drunk too much vodka. Can we go back? I need to lie down."

A flash of anger crosses his face to be replaced a moment later with concern. "Yes, yes of course."

He guides me back to the Command Centre and the crew area, and all the way to my cabin door, babbling at me all the way. There's an awkward moment where I realise he's hoping for a goodbye kiss. He moves toward me, and I grab his hand and shake it, thanking him for a lovely evening, and say goodnight. I enter my cabin and lean my back against the door.

He stays outside for a few moments before lumbering away. I take another swig of vodka, realising I'm more than a little merry. I look at the bottle. A quarter left. My mind goes back to Brad. I still want to see him. I *need* to see him. But I bet Fergal is still lurking outside. I wait twenty minutes, steal out of my cabin, and reach Brad's door, pushing inside, somewhat drunkenly. He's sitting on his bunk, seemingly staring into space as if in thought, coming alive at my entrance, a confused look on his face.

I go and sit next to him, my legs wobbly. "I have to tell you something."

"What… what is it, Lissa?"

"I know about the sham the captain has pulled on me. There was no impact to the ship. It was all made up. A damn training sim! The captain illegally woke me out of cryo just to make me do all the shitty jobs."

Brad says nothing and my heart sinks.

"You knew, didn't you? All the crew know?"

He nods. "The captain ordered me to stay silent about it. The emergency sim is different every trip to keep the crew on their toes. The onboard companion takes care of that. But to wake up a passenger just to help out? They've never done this on any other ship I've worked on. This is my first trip with these guys and… I dunno, there's something off about them. I'm a replacement for the shipman who died during their previous voyage back to Earth."

"Died? What killed him?"

"I never asked. But I'm supposed to work for the next three rotations with them. I've been thinking of putting in a transfer request. I don't fit in here." He sighs. "I'm so glad to talk about it. It's been driving me nuts. But, and I know this sounds ridiculous, the one good thing that's happened on this voyage so far, is you. I'm glad you were the one they chose to wake up. I like you… you're different."

"I'm also glad, Brad. Not about being woken up. But I needed to tell someone. I thought you'd understand, although I was worried that you were in on it."

"I was in on it. What will you do?"

"Keep quiet," I lie, the vodka making me more than a little woozy. "I'm only interested in getting to Persephone to start a new life."

"You won't tell on the crew? Expose them?"

I shake my head. I don't know why I'm lying to Brad, but even in my drunken state, it doesn't seem like a good idea. "What about you?"

Brad gives me a determined look. "Oh, there's no question. I'm putting in a report as soon as we arrive on Persephone."

Maybe it's the booze, or maybe it's just because Brad is such a noble guy, but I put my hand on his neck and kiss him.

He's startled, but I'm hungry for him, and soon I'm eagerly stripping off my skinsuit.

2-06-FUCKED

I awake, cradled in Brad's strong arms. Our naked flesh pushed against each other in the single bunk. His gentle breaths blowing by my ear. I'm a little embarrassed at my behaviour last night. Pushing my way into his cabin. Flinging myself at him. I was keen, that's for sure. But hey, it's been decades since my last time. Whenever and whoever that was.

I cast my eyes over the cabin walls in the dim light, noticing a patchwork of archaic photographs, the edges curling with age. Brad is featured. A young, friendly dynamic man, with many friends. From an Earth that still had beaches and blue skies. He's not much older now. He must've been working the colony ships for a couple of centuries at least. It's difficult to take in, but subjectively for Brad, it's probably only been a few years. It's certainly a way to travel to the future, that's for sure. Many colony crew members join up to time travel in this way. And to end up on a colony world, to live like kings or queens, like Fergal had planned for Aphrodite.

I see a mental image of Persephone, hanging in the black, velvet of space like a green and blue version of the Earth. Its single vast central continent stretching around the planet's equator, surrounded by immense seas and twin ice caps. An amazing sight with all that green, lacking the ugly mega-cities and the straight lines of Earth. The gee there is point eight. Persephone is slightly smaller than my home world. I remember studying it, getting to know it intimately. The three different settlements, the flora and fauna. About homesteading, farming, and the crafting of various tools and even traps for the more tasty and sometimes dangerous wildlife. Of the three settlements, *New Reach* is where I want to settle. The newest and most rural. All settlements have space for the six-monthly arrivals of near a hundred-thousand settlers, most of whom will stay in the emerging cities where plenty of work awaits them, but the truth is, there is land for all. Ready for the taking. And that's what I want. What I've dreamed of all my life. To have my own farmland and a house with a balcony, far past the outskirts, living in the wild. Looking up and seeing the stars with dirt under my feet.

The memory is so strong that it startles me. That's all I've ever wanted, isn't it? To escape my past and make a fresh new beginning somewhere new? But it's more than just simple memory, my knowledge of Persephone is encyclopaedic. There's reams and reams of data that I can see in my mind. Leading to only one conclusion… I have a photographic memory. Or did. My recall of recent events, and conversations is poor at best. Snippets here and there. Was that the brain damage Simone found? Did I lose that ability? Or perhaps it will come back when all my memories are restored? I hope so.

Brad stirs behind me, my thoughts turning back to the events of last night in the most delicious way, and I push my ass into him. Whatever or whoever I am. I'm happy to have hooked up with Brad. He's the ally I've needed. It doesn't have to be romance. Just a bit of fun to help me get through the next few weeks. And how many more clogged nutritanks and misaligned navigation antennae can there be? I can get through this with Brad at my side and have some fun while I'm doing it. I'll get put back into cryo, and when I wake up again… I'll make sure the captain gets what's coming to her. I feel like quite the victor.

Brad yawns and I shuffle around to face him, kissing him on the lips and nuzzling him.

He opens his eyes, sees me, and pushes me away.

"You okay?" I ask, wondering if he's had a bad dream.

He gets out of bed and quickly dresses himself.

"Brad? What's the matter?" I go up to him, but he turns his back. "Brad, answer me. What's happened?"

"I shouldn't have done that. You're in a vulnerable position and… I took advantage of you. It's my job to watch over you, to keep you alive, to keep you safe. Those words mean a lot to me. Except, I let you down and betrayed that trust. I'm so very sorry, Lissa."

"Sorry? What for? It was wonderful last night. You've nothing to be sorry about, quite the opposite." I go to kiss him, but he pulls away.

"The crew woke you up on false pretences. Now I've used that to sleep with you. I'm sorry, Lissa. You were drunk and I should've stopped myself but…" His voice dries.

"But you didn't. And I'm glad. Aren't you?" I reply, annoyed with him and his silly reaction.

"You shouldn't be, Lissa. Maybe if you weren't so drunk, you would've considered what you were doing?"

"What? Why are you being like this. We had sex, so what? I thought you were different, but you're just as backward thinking as the rest of this ancient crew!"

"Just go, Lissa. Before anyone finds out you were here."

"But—"

"Go!" He picks up my skinsuit and throws it at me, turning his back while I get dressed.

3-0
REMEMBERING

I go back to my cabin, and once inside, the sobbing starts. I don't want it to, but I can't help myself. That was an awful scene and… unexpected. I strip off and get into the shower, wanting to wash Brad's smell from me, and instantly regret it. Erasing that wonderful night we shared, like it didn't happen at all, feels like a betrayal. Which is sadly not how Brad thinks about it. He clearly wished it never happened.

How could something that felt so good in one moment turn so bad in another? It makes no sense. This is why I don't like trusting people. They let you down. Always!

I'm jolted by the return of a series of memories. Like a door opening to a locked room in my mind. A whole chunk of my life returning fully formed. I open the metaphorical door and step inside, looking around, shocked at what I find… My parents didn't adopt me because they wanted a daughter. No, they wanted a live-in slave. The kids in the orphanage were not being sold off for organs, but for cheap labour. No wonder we never heard from them again once they were adopted. Which was, of course, Joseph's doing. Frightening us kids with all those rumours, making us more pliable when the time came to be sold into child labour. Working as house boy or girl was certainly preferable to those horrors. And it was the same for me. The relief I felt at getting my own room, being fed properly, being alive with my organs intact, meant that I was pliable. Happy with this outcome and not finding myself drugged and senseless, and strapped to a table in some illegal organ den. I was content to be more than a housekeeper and less than a daughter, even if I was kept under house arrest. I didn't mind. They let me read, discovering a passion for books and knowledge. I wasn't happy, but the most content I'd been my whole life until… I got older. Both my stepparents treated me differently when my curves started to show, and with that change in my body came the stark realisation of what they now expected me to do for them.

That's when I left, although the reality is I escaped. If they disowned me, like it said in my record, then it was some time afterwards. But that makes no logical sense. I can clearly remember my nanny. And being presented at some swanky ball. How does that fit into this narrative? I just wish my other memories would return so I can work out the complicated pathway of my life. This confusion is almost as frustrating as being awoken on this damn ship. I relive the anger and resentment of that time, but for the life of me, I can't remember what happened next. An anger that builds when I think of Brad.

Did I make a fool of myself? Throwing myself at him? If so, why didn't he stop? Why go through with it? He certainly didn't act like it was anything he would regret at the time. Quite the opposite. But… maybe I took advantage of his good heart and bulldozed him? I was drunk and a little keen. I suppose from his point of view, from somebody born way back when, it makes sense he'd be ashamed of himself. Taking advantage of me in this vulnerable time. Sexual attitudes were different in the past. Men's nobility where women were concerned, wasn't recognised as the ingrained sexist response it is in the society I come from. I didn't think about that… why would I? But I see it now. I think I understand. I've been stupid, foolish, and I've lost the only friend I had on this damn ship.

Christ! This is a mess.

It's still early and I lie on my bunk, the contrasting

thoughts of our physical intimacy and that awful argument playing over my mind—at least I've stopped obsessing over Taipan.

I'm determined to make it up to Brad. As to how? I'm not sure. I'll apologise and maybe we can start again. The stark truth is… I still want him. My body certainly does.

It's soon time for breakfast. Every part of me wants to stay in my cabin, but I've already decided on this. I'm holding my head up high. I won't be intimidated again. Not even by Brad. I've seemingly survived a lot in my short life. I can suffer this easily, I tell myself, but my words don't match my feelings. They're not even close.

I'm the first to arrive in the canteen. The crew are late this morning, which bothers me. Where the hell are they? I make myself a bowl of cereal and sit down in the quiet, trying my best not to think about Brad, wanting to talk to him. Ten minutes later, Vic, Taipan and Fergal arrive, and I breathe a sigh of relief, not knowing why. But where are Brad and the captain?

"Who you looking for?" Fergal says, incandescent with repressed rage, his eyes glaring at me from behind his red-tinted glasses. Taipan also stares, a smirk on her face, while Vic seems… disappointed. There can be only one conclusion—they know about me and Brad. They all do.

3-01-SHAMED

"Oh, hi,"Taipan says, her eyes widening. "About last night…"

I tense. "What about last night?"

"That silly argument we had. Blame Vic, he got me all hot and bothered. But he got the benefit later… just like Brad did."

I should've hidden away in my cabin. I've made such a mess of everything. "I have no idea what you mean."

"Oh, I think you do,"Taipan replies. *Give it to me, Brad! I want it, I want it!* she mimics.

I think back to last night. Everything is woozy, but the words are horrifyingly familiar. Did Brad blab to the crew? If so… just what else did he tell them? Intimate details? He wouldn't do that… would he? And even if he did? I'm a grown woman. I can sleep with whoever I like. There's no shame in that anymore, not like in the past. But… no matter how much I try to think differently, I am ashamed. And where is Brad? Is he avoiding me? I need to talk to him more than ever.

As that thought flits through my head, Brad appears in the canteen hatchway, his head bowed. He gets breakfast and sits down as far away from me as he can. Why is he being such a bastard?

I'm not hungry, I'm sick to my stomach, but I refill my bowl, wanting to get Brad on his own after Taipan, Vic and Fergal have finished. Chewing mechanically at my food that has even less flavour than before.

Taipan is the first to get up. "Don't forget you're rostered with me again today… if you've got the strength." She smirks. "C'mon Vic, we still have time for some fun before the shift begins." She says the words to Vic but she's looking at me. "I'll meet you in the Supply Room in twenty or so minutes."

They leave together, laughing loudly once they are outside—I'm guessing at my expense.

Fergal is the next to get up. He strides over as if to hit me, but at the last moment he drops his mouth to my ear. "My offer is rescinded. I do not want to spend my life with a slut like you." He glares at Brad, whose eyes are still cast downwards, and marches out. My chance to talk to Brad at last, but just as I take a breath to speak, Captain Marla appears. "You! In my ready room, now!"

I sit opposite the captain, knowing she will try to tear a strip off me. She draws breath to speak, but I've got a lot to say. "Don't you even think about trying to tell me off. I'm the victim here, no one else." I want to tell her that I've discovered her nasty little game, that I hate and despise her for waking me up to work as the crew's dogsbody, but that would be a massive mistake.

Captain Marla's face shows no emotion, content to let me continue.

"I'm a passenger who has had her rights taken away because of some stupid company rule, not that you care. So what if I slept with Brad, what I do with my body is no one else's goddamn business!"

"Finished?"

I nod angrily.

"I'm afraid what you do with your body, is very much my business—and your personal thoughts on this matter are entirely irrelevant."

"…What?"

"Despite your more than obvious willingness, any crew member who has any sexual contact with a passenger, is not only in serious breach of their contract, but is viewed by the companies and by the courts to have committed statutory rape. If I were to report this, Brad would be forcibly put into cryo and taken back to Earth where he would receive a hefty prison sentence and lose all wages and savings. Does that answer your question?"

"Prison? But it wasn't his fault. I was drinking vodka, I—"

Captain Marla raises her hand. "Do you really think I would lose a valuable crew member like Brad because of some tramp like you?"

Her words burn into me, and I flush red. "You're not reporting him?"

She shakes her head. "I have given him a serious reprimand and he will lose all his pay for this turnaround. Let me tell you what I told him. The incident was a one-off, but he will have to go back into cryo. We can't have a repeat of what happened, seeing that you can't keep your legs crossed for longer than two minutes. Even after I gave you explicit orders to cease your fraternisation with the crew."

"But why Brad? I'd happily go in his place."

"The decision has been made. And I'm not in the habit of unmaking them."

"It should be me," I plead. "And after what Vic and Taipan have put me through over the last couple of days, it should be them who are suspended."

"Bleat as much as you want, but my decision is final."

The woman is a brick wall. "How did you find out? Did Brad admit it?"

"He didn't. Which is why I nearly sent him down. But he's young, and young men can be tempted by silly young girls with a gaping hole in their morality."

The captain's stream of old-fashioned insults unexpectedly bite into me, and all I can do is suffer them, clinging onto the knowledge that I will bring her down. And after what happened with Brad, it's unlikely he will be filing a report to support me anytime soon. "You haven't answered… How did you find out?"

"I'm the captain of this goddamn ship, meaning you don't get to ask me questions like that. And I certainly don't have to answer them."

"Was it Simone?"

She gives me a look of disgust and shakes her head. "That annoying piece of silicon junk?"

"How soon before Brad goes back into cryo?"

"There's still a few things for him to get done. It will be in a day or two. I've ordered him to stay away from you, and I'm giving you the same order. You might think I'm being harsh, but it's my job to watch over you, to keep you alive, to keep you safe. No matter how much I don't want to. Now… get out."

I ignore her. Going straight back to the canteen, relieved to find Brad alone and finishing up.

"How the hell do they all know?" I blurt at him with no preamble.

He swallows a last mouthful of food and looks up at me. "I'm ordered not to talk to you, I'm sorry."

He tries to leave but I block him. "Did you hear what Fergal said to me? The man hates me. And even Taipan knows the intimate details. Answer me, Brad!"

"Captain Marla called me to her ready room first thing after you left. Tore a strip off me. I'm lucky to still have a place aboard this ship. She knew already. I don't know how. I thought… maybe you had reported me."

"No way! I'd never do that. I didn't even know it was against the goddam rules."

"You were very angry when you left my cabin."

"What kind of person do you think I am?"

"I think we know the answer to that."

His words incense me. "Surely you must've had girlfriends before? You must've discovered that both men and women like sex? Hey, we even shit and piss as well. Go figure. What backward century are you from?"

"I was brought up to respect women, I—"

"Christ Brad, listen to yourself. If you're ever going to leave this ship, you'll need to take a course in social reorientation, because you are way of beam. Way off." I take a steadying breath. Brad is an idiot, well meaning, but an idiot all the same. "Aren't you curious about how the captain found out? Doesn't that bother you?"

"It doesn't matter. What's done is done. But I really wish you'd stayed in your cabin last night." He pushes past me. "And don't talk to me again. I will return to cryo soon. This will have to be our last conversation."

I've sobbed enough times since I awoke into this nightmare, and even though Brad's words cut into me, I remain dry-eyed. Instead, I dwell on how Captain Marla found out about Brad and me. If Simone is to be believed, cabins are private areas. There should be no monitoring allowed, unless… Taipan's words from yesterday scythe into my mind. *I hacked into the surveillance system. I am the coms specialist after all. That's how I know you got nowhere with Vic, I was watching you.*

Did she hack into Simone's node in Brad's cabin? The thought of Taipan seeing me… I flush red, the skin of my face heating up. She showed it to the captain. That's how she knew. It must be. And did the rest of the crew see it? That would certainly explain Fergal's rage and Vic's disappointment.

I leave the canteen and head for the Supply room, keen to find Taipan and have it out with her, passing the door marked *Strictly Crew Members Only*. I try it, but it's locked. I'm not surprised. I power down the long corridor, my thoughts racing with confrontation, my anger rising until… I stop dead in my tracks. There's a better way to do this. I'm angry as hell and humiliated, but I need to be certain. I'll talk to Simone, first chance I get. See what she knows about this and… I shake my head. Simone won't help me. And where the hell is she anyway? She's been conspicuous by her absence the last couple of days. I can't and won't rely on her. No, I need to find the footage myself, make a copy somehow, perhaps using one of those holotabs and use it in my report.

Shit, I need as much information as I can get to bring this crew down. They all need to go to prison.

My plan thrills me, but reality soon sinks in. Could I get my hands on Taipan's personal tab? And if I did, wouldn't it be keyed to Taipan and no one else? Same for her cabin's holotop? It's unlikely the girl would be sloppy enough to leave it unlocked.

I sigh. All these thoughts of confrontation and revenge are pointless. Everything boils down to the same damn thing. The same thing I've been telling myself since this nightmare began. I have to suck it up and wait till I'm on Persephone.

"Don't rock the boat, and the boat won't rock you," I whisper, vowing to bring this crew down.

3-02-RATTED

Taipan waits inside the Supply Room, another one of her smirks plastered across her exotic face. "Nice to see you can still walk, girl. Especially after that intense drilling Brad gave you last night."

My hackles rise, but I won't give Taipan the satisfaction of playing her game. "Yeah, he managed to reach those places that I like to be reached. Now, if you've finished with this rather old-fashioned slut-shaming, I suggest we get on. Although, I will say this now at the outset, you won't get me anywhere near an airlock."

"You still smarting about that, huh? I thought you liked gasping for air." She puts a hand around her throat and makes suggestive groaning noises.

"Yeah, and my hair pulled, and my ass slapped. Go figure."

"You might think you had it good from Brad, but there's no going back after you've been double-dicked by a cyber-cock. You hear what I'm saying?"

"It sounds fascinating. We are both adult women who

enjoy sex. It's hardly earth-shattering news, is it?"

"I just hope Brad thinks you were worth it."

"Well, he doesn't. Turns out, he has the same archaic attitudes as the rest of this crew. But hey, I got what I wanted, so fuck him and move on to the next sap, right?"

It's obvious my attitude is annoying Taipan. I'm guessing she had hoped to continue her slut-shaming throughout the day. I'm having none of it. "Are we continuing with this tired, teenage shit or shall we get some work done?"

"Well don't think about moving onto Vic, he's still off-limits, you know that, right?"

"Only if he promises to shove that cyber-dick of his so far down your throat you choke to death on it."

She shrugs away my words with an elegant twist of her shoulder. "You've been warned… if you don't want that pretty little face cut to shreds, don't push it."

I remember her threat from yesterday. If she has a knife, I wonder whereabouts she keeps it, especially wearing her tight skinsuit.

Taipan glances at her tab and saunters off to the back of the room, motioning for me to grab another bin, filling it with a different set of equipment, and a few rolls of optical cables and nanowire. Outside the Supply Room, Taipan checks her tab again and heads off into the ship's maze of corridors. I follow her, pleased that this bin doesn't have a sticky wheel. Perhaps today won't be as bad as I'm expecting.

We stop halfway down a corridor and Taipan points to a conduit door. I've seen them before when I was forced to transverse the ship. I even looked inside. Full of wires and various cables and bits of machinery, and large enough for someone to climb inside—and that's when I twig what Taipan wants me to do.

"You'll be replacing damaged wiring, swapping out older sections with the new. It isn't back-breaking work and, guess what, no airlocks. You think you can manage that?"

"Yeah, sure." I survived Vic's nutritanks, I can survive this.

"It's straightforward. Auto-splicers do most of the work. I'll identify the damaged sections and you replace them. Grab the old cables and bring them out. And repeat."

She hands me an auto-splicer, loads it up with wire, and I pull myself into the conduit. It's about a fifteen-foot crawl in the dark, but the lights from the splicer blink when I come to the hub it's searching for, beeping, automatically grabbing on and doing its work. Wires whizzing through the conduit. I grab the discarded cables and emerge from the conduit a short while later.

Taipan checks my work on her tab and nods. "Looks like you didn't fuck up. Well, there's a surprise. Perhaps a good dicking was all you needed. But hey, some girls are like that aren't they? An utter mess until given a good seeing to."

I dump the discarded cable into the bin. "Where to next?"

She ignores me and walks away. And I follow.

And that's how we spend the next few hours.

I'm surprised by the sheer number of replacements we're making and mention it to Taipan. She replies with her usual disdain, telling me that there are so many built in redundancies ship-wide, that it's not an issue, unless regular maintenance is not kept up. "These ships are built to traverse many light years at incredible speeds. They could do the same with a tenth of the systems we have aboard. But would they be safe? Not so much. That's why we have so many back-ups. And why the crew performs regular, essential maintenance. Doing what we're doing now…. fixing shit. We don't want no cascading failures, do we? Now, get on with it."

The work isn't that difficult, and spending most of my time inside the conduits, away from Taipan and her condescending comments, is fine by me. We work together with no issues. When she shuts her mouth that is. It doesn't stop me hating everything about her.

It's coming up to midday with one more conduit to fix.

I grab the auto-splicer and clamber inside. Crawling a long way in the blackness. Wondering when the damn auto-splicer will find the hub it's looking for. A sudden nasty, fusty disgusting smell, and something warm brushes past my face. I scream involuntarily, wriggling as fast as I can back to the hatch. Throwing myself out of the conduit and onto the corridor floor, met by a laughing Taipan.

"There's things in there! I don't know what, but it touched my goddamn face!"

"Looks like you've found a nest," Taipan says.

"A nest? Of what?"

"Space rats. You must've heard of them?"

"I never expected to come so close. They're disgusting."

"They do honk, that's for sure. Pooey!" She holds her nose. "But hey, girl, we can't let them get in the way of our important work, can we? It's probably why this section is in such a shitty state, there must be hundreds of the critters in the tubes."

"So what do we do?"

"We do?" She scoffs. "We do nothing. You on the other hand need to take a deep breath and get on with the job in hand. What else do you think you're gonna do, girl? Pick up your tools and cry all the way home? No way, sister. This is a vital ship safety procedure."

"You don't expect me to go back in there… do you?" Why do the crew continue to bully me like this? It's now been nearly four days. It can't be like this every damn day, can it?

"Here." Taipan grabs a circular disk of metal with a strap on the back and affixes it to her hand, touching my shoulder with it. I'm hit with a jolt of electricity and shout out in shock and pain.

"A simple hand stunner. Any of those bastards get too close and zap! They're dead, or at least incapacitated. Just a painful jolt to us humans. Fatal to vermin." She removes the hand stunner and passes it to me.

I take it off her, rubbing at my shoulder.

"The trick is not to get bitten, cos those bites can really sting, you get me? And if they become infected? Nasty. Now what are you waiting for?"

I give Taipan a hard stare and clamber back into the conduit. The reason, I won't let that bitch make any more of a fool of me than she already has done. And I guess she's exaggerating the danger of bites from those creatures. Even so, I'm terrified. So scared in fact that I have to stop to calm my ragged breathing.

"You okay in there?" Taipan shouts through the conduit hatchway.

"Yeah, all fine," I reply, lying. But it's enough to spur me on, and soon the stink returns. The fusty smell of rodents magnified. I've smelled something similar before, I remember. Working the docks. Unloading and loading cargo. It wasn't uncommon to find containers riddled with rats. I'd clock in, in the morning and work all day before my shift at the club began. I'm pleased at the new memory, but not at what my life looked like before I came aboard. Leading to the one nagging question I've been avoiding… how did I possibly manage to afford the fabulous cost of the ticket to Persephone working those two low-paid jobs? I'm no essential worker who could get free passage. I was a comparative nobody. But the dollars must have come from somewhere? Did I blackmail my adopted parents? Or maybe they paid to get rid of me?

My thoughts are cut short by something warm and furry brushing past my feet. I strike out with the stunner. A high-pitched yelping and sudden silence.

I push forward, using my stunner until the auto-splicer lights up, revealing the hub, and about fifty of the creatures. I stifle a scream. They are mutated rabbits of some kind. Blind. Their eyes opaque. Two central, sharp teeth protruding from their upper jaws. Ears ragged and extended. Once white fur stained brown. And the stench? Over-powering. I pinch my nose, noticing that if I don't interfere with the creatures, they leave me alone. The splicer does its thing, I spool up the old wiring, and get the hell out of there.

"I expected some more screaming after your last performance," Taipan says as I re-emerge, disappointed that I didn't lose it in there. It was a close thing, though. Very close.

"Now you've done the rewiring, we can remove all the air from this section. It should kill most of the bastards, although some will survive. They always do."

Survival of the fittest, I think to myself and somehow that thought resonates inside. That's what I'm doing. Surviving this crew of bullies and sexists. It can only make me stronger.

I close the hatch and we move on. "Phew, you stink," Taipan says to me. "What did you do? Get double-drilled by a couple of space rats?"

I ignore her, but she's right. I stink again, and badly.

"Time for lunch, so please, give this girl some space." She takes out a box of what looks like sushi—some reconstituted version anyway—and starts to eat with a pair of chopsticks. "You didn't bring anything again? Well, more fool you, girl. You've got a busy afternoon."

Taipan takes time finishing her sushi, while absently tapping at her tab. Afterwards, she gets up and indicates for me to follow. I drag the bin behind me, but at a distance, her nose twisting in disgust. We enter the secondary, back-up navigational node on the other side of the ship. One of the three Fergal showed me. A mirror to the one we visited yesterday. And just as messy. I notice Vic's utility belt lying next to some blankets and cushions—a perfect place for another of their love dens.

Taipan notices me staring. "Yeah, girl, me and Vic make out whenever and wherever, you get me?"

"I suppose you have to try anything to spice up a dull sex

life."

"Shut up and get to work!"

I've touched a nerve. Good. Although I'm not looking forward to exchanging all those buffers again. Instead, Taipan sits me down at a holotop station. Tasking me to sort through a series of nav-readings. Millions of files generated by the ship's auto-navigational system as it navigates between Earth and Persephone over the last ten or so years. Instructing the computers to flag anything out of the ordinary. Leading to thousands of auto-generated reports to manually sift through. Scanning for anomalies and sending anything out of the ordinary to Taipan, who sits on the other side of the node, absently filing her nails and occasionally looking at her tab. Boring work, but at least I'm not crawling down conduits and getting face to face with disgusting space rats.

After a couple of hours, Taipan announces that she's 'going to lay another deuce' that apparently 'has been brewing since lunch'.

She disappears and I carry on working, noticing that Taipan has left her tab behind. I pick it up with excitement until I realise what I'm doing. I told myself to not rock the boat. So what if Taipan secretly filmed me and Brad? So what if I find it on her tab. What will I do? Nothing will change. And yet, it doesn't stop me. The holotab is bio-locked as I knew it would be. There's no way for me to get past the encryption. I throw it away in disgust and return to my work.

Taipan arrives twenty minutes later. This time she thankfully doesn't regale me with details of her bowel movements. Instead, she goes over to her discarded tab, looking at me suspiciously.

Another hour passes. "Right, girl, we're nearly done." Taipan goes over to the bin and stares inside. "What the fuck?"

I brace myself as Taipan launches into a tirade. Some missing equipment she forgot to pick up, which is somehow my fault.

"There's nothing else for it. You need to return to the Supply Room and get me a gyro-calibrator."

"A gyro-what?"

"Don't you give me any more lip, girl You hear me?" Taipan strides towards me and I brace for an attack, but instead she thrusts her holotab in my face. "This." The tab shows a holo of what I'm guessing is the gyro-calibrator. "You'll find it at the back of the Supply Room hanging on the wall. Can you do that?"

I nod.

"Good. And hurry up."

I leave the node and find myself rushing back to the Command Centre, until I realise what I'm doing. Why should I run around for that bitch? Instead, I saunter into the crew area and head for my cabin. I stink and need a shower. Afterwards I can grab some food. I did miss lunch after all. While the steam does its job, the notion of stealing into Taipan's cabin slips into my mind. Can I do that? *Should I do it?* I know where her room is. She stopped there yesterday.

So... *why not?*

Her cabin won't be locked. I can be in and out in minutes. What the hell have I got to lose? And who knows, I might find something to embarrass the sadistic bitch. My mind made up, I dry off, get dressed and head toward her cabin.

Pausing outside Taipan's door, I wonder if this is a stupid idea. It most certainly is. I probably won't find anything. And Taipan might have surveillance cameras in there. Her holotop, if she has one, will be encrypted. It's all too risky.

I catch my thoughts... *what is the risk, exactly?* That I'll get caught? That I'll piss off Taipan? It would be worth getting caught to put my mind at rest over this. And if she wants to have it out with me... all the better!

I take a deep breath and try to centre my thoughts. When I arrive on Persephone, none of this will matter. Being forced out of cryo. The angry captain. Vic creeping me out. Sleeping with Brad. Being bullied by Taipan. None of it. I'll have a new life. This will be just a bad memory. I won't care if Taipan filmed me or not. It will be in the past. I'll get my revenge on her as I will the rest of the crew for what they've done to me. Reporting them to the companies should be enough. My anger, resentment and an urgent, insistent need to prove what Taipan did, will pass, like petty emotions like these always do. I can be better than these base feelings of fear, rage, and retribution.

And so, I make the rational decision to give this up, to go get Taipan's damn gyro-calibrator and forget about it. It's the right thing to do. I breathe a sigh of relief. I've made the right choice.

I push open Taipan's cabin door and step inside.

I'm hit with a strong smell of cigars, those awful things Vic smokes, flicking my eyes around the cabin, to be met by a riot of colour. The walls painted in various neon-like hues. Nudes, mostly men and women. Taipan featured in various trysts. It's art, but grotesque. These people are not only copulating but murdering each other. I look around, confused and frightened. If this room represents the inner workings of Taipan's mind, then she is not a well woman. I notice a 2D picture frame, the photographs changing every few seconds. Close-ups of tattoos. Intricate, deranged things. Nothing like the precise spiders and scorpions she tattooed on Vic, but demonic and other-worldly. Some of the images are of corpses. Or they were photographed to make it appear that way. I notice a rack of stylish, but no less dangerous looking knives. Long and thin. Designed for stabbing and scratching. Her threat to cut my face was perhaps more real than I imagined.

I hear a tinny, but no less blood-curdling scream, coming from a discarded earbud left on Taipan's bed. Her holotop is on, but the screen is blank. More shrill voices and groans.

"What the hell?"

I pick up the bud and slip it into my ear. The holotop jumps back into life. Instead of the 3D imagery I'm used to, this has a flat 2D screen like the photo frame. It takes me a few moments to grasp what I'm seeing. A naked young man tied to a chair. Beaten. Blood leaking from many cuts and grazes that criss-cross his body. The fingers of one hand missing, leaving only bloody stumps. Encircled by a pool of splattered blood. The viewpoint pulls back, and I nearly scream.

I see Vic, naked, wearing a black hood, and holding a pair of pliers in which is grasped a severed finger. Vic licks at the digit. His tongue thrust through his hood. Blood dripping down the dark material. Taipan steps naked into the frame, wearing an ornate mask. Twin, thin blades slashing and stabbing. The guy bursts into life, screaming.

"I told you to follow my goddamn orders! You've only got yourself to blame for this, you hear me?"

Captain Marla's voice off camera!

The point of view pulls further back to reveal Fergal sitting with his back to the viewpoint, naked from the waist down, jerking off. And in the gloom behind this vile scene… the long-dead, mummified remains of other young men and women. Their bodies hacked, inked, and mutilated. I yank the earbud from my ear and throw it away, dragging my eyes away from the screen.

The crew are waking passengers and killing them. Is that… *is that what they're planning to do to me?* They'll never return me to cryo. If they get their way, I'll end up in that kill room tied to a chair and tortured to death… My hand jumps involuntarily to my mouth, and I stifle a gag.

The toilet flushes and I stare at the shower cubicle in alarm as a half-naked Vic emerges, his face a mask of surprise.

3-03-AIDED

"You've figured out our liddle game, huh?" Vic says, an impressed look on his sneering face. "I told everyone you were different from the rest." He casts an eye toward the holotop and the screams coming from the discarded earbuds. "You're gonna end up in the same place, missy."

I glance at the cabin door. Can I get there before he pounces? I'm not sure.

Vic follows my gaze and laughs. "You think you can escape us? Where are you gonna run to?"

I take my chance and dart toward the door. Vic is quicker, snatching at me. I slip out of his grasp, grabbing one of Taipan's knives from the rack and slash at him.

He jumps backward, the blade inches from his naked chest.

"You think that liddle bitch blade is gonna scare me off?"

I stab at him and he jerks away. I step closer to the door. The knife held out threateningly.

Vic shrugs. "So, you're gonna escape. Big deal. I'll be seeing you soon enough on the hunt. Salud!"

In the background I hear terrified screams and Vic laughing. And then his words. *Let's finish this bitch!*" Vic nods to the screen. "What he said."

I push open the door and run for my life. Sprinting out of the crew area and charging into the ship. Reeling at what I've just witnessed. Losing myself to panic and horror. Running blindly. Turning corner after corner and slamming into Brad, taking him by surprise, and knocking him over.

I throw myself atop of him, realising I'm still clutching Taipan's knife and hold it to his throat. "Are you in on it!" I scream.

"What?" he replies dumbfounded, terrified by the blade pushed up against his throat.

"Waking up passengers and killing them! Are you fucking in on it?"

"What the hell are you talking about?"

"The crew," I reply, choking on bile from my stomach that I spit aside. "They're waking up passengers… and it's not just to do all the shit jobs. They're killing them, Brad! Torturing and murdering them!"

Brad gives me a confused look. "What? I know they woke you up illegally but murder? I think you need to go to the Medibay, it sounds like you're suffering from cryo-paranoia."

"No, I'm not!" I push the knife at his throat. "I was just in Taipan's cabin and—"

"What were you doing in there?"

"I'll tell you if you listen!"

"Go on," he says weakly.

I relate what happened. Taipan's cabin. The awful holo. Vic catching and threatening me. "Does that sound like fucking paranoia?"

Brad glances at the blade.

I pull the knife back and get off him, still pointing it at him. "I'm not going mad. It's a game that the crew play. Waking up passengers to mess with them. To bully and then to torture them. And… if what Vic says is true, to hunt them." I listen to my words. Hardly believing them myself but knowing they are true.

He sits up, rubbing his throat. "The captain ordered me to go back into cryo. Said it was because of what happened. But I got the feeling that she wanted me out of the way. I didn't question it, after what I did, but it's not normal procedure. We all go to cryo together. That's a ship safety rule. Across the fleet."

"You believe me?"

"I can't pretend that it's hard to swallow, but yeah, maybe I do."

"Good. Can you talk to Simone on your holotab?"

"To Simone? Why?"

"Just do it."

He nods. "Simone?"

Hello Brad. How is your day?

I grab the tab off Brad, making sure to keep the knife raised. If he tries anything, I'll be ready. "Simone, what do you know about the crew hunting and killing passengers?"

I'm sorry, Lissa. The captain has ordered me to cease all communications with you.

"Answer the damn question! Has the crew been killing passengers?"

The crew is here to ensure passenger safety. May I ask how are you today? You appear to be agitated.

"Damn right I'm agitated!"

Then I suggest you visit the Medibay as soon as possible.

"My faculties are perfectly fine. Where is Vic right now?"

Ship Engineer, Victor Ramirez, is on the bridge with the rest of the crew members.

Brad raises his eyebrows.

"Simone, is my life in danger?"

Space travel, by its very nature, is dangerous.

"Simone. You must be able to hear what the crew are saying to one another. Is that true?"

Yes, that is true Lissa.

"Am I in danger from them?" No reply. "Simone, answer me. Am I in danger from the crew?"

I am unable to divulge official crew discussions to non-crew members.

"But I'm a crew member. Tell me," Brad says.

I'm afraid your status as active crew has been suspended.

"It's true. It really is true." Brad rubs his temples and shakes his head in disbelief.

"Simone, is there anything else you can tell me?"

The captains of all interstellar ships have ultimate authority over all souls aboard, as it has always been, including... the onboard AI system.

"Shit! They can use Simone against us!"

I squeeze the pad in my fist and have a moment of understanding. "Simone can't help us directly. We have to read between the lines. She's telling us to get out of here. Is that true, Simone?"

I can easily locate Bradley O'Connor via his ship holotab.

"The crew don't know Lissa is with me, is that right, Simone?"

That is correct.

"I told you. Simone is trying to help as best she can."

"What do we do next?"

"I have no choice but to hide in the old ship where Simone can't track me."

"You can't do this alone, Liss."

"I have to. You need to carry on with your work and report to cryo like the captain ordered otherwise…" I shake my head.

"Maybe not." Brad drops his tab, and we head further into the ship. "We can't risk Simone monitoring us. I sense she wants to help, but as she said, the captain has ultimate authority. Push comes to shove, she is on their side."

"I agree. Where are you taking me?"

"I have a plan. The captain doesn't know that I've found out what they're doing. Meaning I can help you."

"How?"

"Listen to me… We're ten or so years away from Persephone, with no way of surviving out of cryo, there's not nearly enough food."

"Well then, I stay and fight."

"You realise that means killing the crew? All of them? They know this ship intimately. They'll have weapons and other ways of catching you. To win out against them would be very unlikely. And besides, how do you know that when it came down to it, you'd be able to actually kill someone?"

I've stood up for myself all my life, but Brad's right. I'm no killer. And the crew are murderers. How would I ever beat them? "Couldn't I hide, wait till everyone is asleep and sabotage their cryopods?"

Brad shakes his head. "The crew room is protected by secure doors making it impenetrable. Designed to survive impacts and other disasters."

"What about Simone? Could she kill or incapacitate them?" I'm grasping at straws, but I can't see any way out of this. "She has access to their cryo-controls and pods and monitors them during cryosleep. She told me that."

"Simone can't hurt anyone. She's an AI. Don't forget that, although she must be somehow complicit in assisting the captain and crew in their hobby. But then again, the ship companion is reset every rotation. Only the captain has the authority to do that. Who knows how many times she's had to reset Simone to hide what's been happening on this ship. There's no way she can help us."

"Well… what about waking up more passengers to outnumber the crew and defeat them that way?"

"I can't see that working. You remember what it was like when you were woken? They'd be disorientated, needing food and water, with nothing to keep them warm. And the saucers are far away from the Command Centre. How would they get here? And what state would they be in when they arrived? And there's no assurance they will believe you against the crew. These people are colonists, not killers. There's too many variables."

"Well, what the hell can I fucking do? I'm out of options. I might as well go and surrender to the captain and get it over with."

"You can go back into cryo."

"I wish."

"Listen to me. You can't go in a regular pod—they'd find you in a moment. But there's a pair of cryo-chambers the crew don't know about. They're not connected to the mainframe. Even Simone knows nothing about them."

"But won't we need Simone to put us into cryo?"

"Normally, yes. But I can do it for you. I know how they work. Sure, you won't be monitored, so if anything goes wrong, you'll be stuck. But the pods rarely fail."

"What about the people who die in cryo?"

"Not everyone survives the procedure. You've already done so, meaning, you'll be fine."

"And what about you? You said two chambers. How can you use the second one? Can you put yourself into cryo?"

Brad shakes his head. "After you are safely installed, I will report to cryo like the captain ordered. She'll be none the wiser. When we reach Persephone, I'll come and get you."

It doesn't sound like a good idea to me. But what other options do I have? I take a deep breath. "Okay. Anything is better than starving to death. Where are these pods?"

"That's where I'm taking you now. I discovered a defunct command mode in the older part of a sister ship I worked on. It should be the same here. And like I said, the area isn't online, so Simone and the crew won't be able to discover it."

"Then that's what we'll do. If there's no other option. But you're taking a risk Brad. The captain might think you know too much."

He hugs me and we kiss. "I'll be fine. They have no idea that I've found out. Now you've gone AWOL, they will want me safely out of the way in cryo before tracking you down. Their focus will be on you, not me. They'll assume you're hiding somewhere in the old ship and when they can't find you, they'll give up and return to cryo, locking down the Command Centre and leaving you to die…"

"You think that will work?"

"It'll have to, there are no other options that I can see."

"But they could find my pod, and I'd be done for."

"It's a risk you'll have to take if you want to survive."

Survive. That word again. I'm a survivor. I'll get through this, one way or another.

We arrive at an impressive looking hatchway and Brad drags me inside. "We're here."

The room lights up as we enter, holotops and other instruments winking and buzzing into life. And I'm aware the gee here is about half that of normal. "Won't this alert the crew?" I ask in alarm.

Brad shakes his head. "Like I explained, this area is isolated from the rest of the ship. An old command hub, now redundant. It was easier to entirely sever its connection to the ship than to individually shut down all of its functions. That's why Simone and the crew won't know you're in here but..."

"But what?"

"Where are the damn pods!"

"You mean... I have to fight?" The notion of pitting myself against the crew is daunting, but better than hiding in a pod. I grit my teeth, thinking about what weapons I can use, and how I can use them, when Brad disappears behind a pair of massive data banks.

"Shit!" I hear him say in relief. "They're in here. I was worried for a moment."

I follow him into a cramped area at the back of the old command node where sit two archaic looking cryopods, twice the size of the one I was rudely ejected from.

"Don't worry. These work exactly the same as their modern counterparts. You'll be fine. Now strip off and get inside."

I take off my skinsuit without a second thought, catching Brad glancing at me.

"It's not like you haven't seen me naked before."

He smiles. "I was a fool, I'm sorry. I shouldn't have rejected you like that. I was worried about my commission. Everything rides on me staying aboard ships like this. I panicked."

"You were a shit to me this morning. You know that. A real shit."

"If I can help you get out of this mess, maybe you'll forgive me?"

"Hey, I'll do more than that…" I give him a kiss on his cheek.

"Get inside the pod and I'll come and plug you in."

"Nice."

"Yeah. Not very sexy." Brad is suddenly all action, prepping the pod, flicking switches, and powering up the systems.

I grab the sides of the pod, ready to pull myself inside, and pause. I can't help think that I'm making a bad decision. "What happens if you're caught? I'll be in here forever… or until someone finds me, which may be hundreds of years."

"Look, I know you're panicked, but the captain has no idea that you found me. It was a fluke, running into me, there's no way you'd know where I was working. Right?"

I nod. He's making sense. Everything he's said so far makes sense. This is the logical decision. *The only decision.*

"Finding me was a piece of good luck, Lissa. Very good luck." I gaze into his eyes, and I can see he means it. This, more than anything convinces me to do it. He grabs my hand and gives it a squeeze. "I'll come get you when we reach Persephone, I promise."

I sigh and clamber inside the pod. If I'm doing the right thing, I'll close my eyes and wake up at Persephone. Brad will let me out and I'll go down to the planet with the other colonists. Just one face amongst thousands. This could be it— the end to this nightmare. I close my eyes and immediately begin to flash. I'm in two pods, one in Earth orbit and this one on the *Octavia.* Two places at the same time.

I sit up, grabbing at the sides of the pod, flashing back and forth.

"Are you okay?" It's Brad's voice but I'm looking at a man

in a green surgeon's outfit, wearing a mask. He disappears and Brad takes his place. What the hell is happening to me? "Where am I?"

"I'm prepping you for cryo," Brad replies urgently. "We don't have much time left. I need to get back to my holotab before the captain's suspicions are raised. Lie down." I do as he says and close my eyes, returning memories bursting like fireworks across my brain. Each memory, made up of a multitude of other reminiscences and recollections that fizz and pop in my mind, lighting up all those dark places I've been unable to peer into, making me whole again. And in an instant, I know who I am, and what I've done to get here. And that my name isn't Lissa Angeline Blackstone.

3-04-ABANDONED

I lived on the streets as a child. Discarded by drug-using parents who couldn't afford to keep me. Not unusual in the backwaters of the mega-cities of earth, where the haves and the have nots lived in two separate worlds. The politicians blaming the poor for all the ills of the world, while quietly skimming off an ever-increasing amount of cream. And fighting over it amongst themselves.

I have few memories of my parents. My father, a sad-eyed, drained, ashen man who never spoke. My mother always asleep. I think they tried, but one night they went out and never came back. I waited and waited for them. An intense memory. Forced out to forage for food on my own. A child of six, maybe seven, pushed into the ever-dangerous dark bowels of a city so vast it swallowed billions. That's where I learned to survive. Living on the streets made me the person I am today. Cold, calculating, learning to trust only in myself and no one else.

Survival became everything. Yet it never stopped me

dreaming of escape. I'd sit and watch the vast billboards at night. Their illumination giving me more security than the shadows. Massive, beautiful adverts for the colonies. Exotic, untouched worlds. Amazing locations. Never ending forests and grasslands full of weird and wonderful flora and fauna. And spaceships. Lots of spaceships. Literally worlds away from the daily horrors of the inner city. I'd sleep through the day, wake to forage for food, and head to my regular spot to view the Ads at night. I loved the Ads. Full of beautiful, clean men and women and bright-eyed children. The colours and themes changing with the seasons. Not that anything changed on the streets. But it was the colony Ads that mesmerised my young mind. I vowed one day to go there. To leave Earth. To find a new life amongst the stars. The only thing that kept me going through those long years. The one dream that kept me alive.

Every morning the garbage trucks would tour the backstreets and alleyways, picking up the rubbish and emptying the trash, including the night's quota of dead. The poor souls who didn't make it through to sunrise. The hidden underclass who had starved to death, OD'd, or been murdered for any multitude of reasons. An underworld that the rest of society never got to see—except when it suited them. No one cared. The privately funded police force were only focused on protection of the wealthier parts of the city. They couldn't care less what flotsam and jetsam washed up in the backwaters.

Nevertheless, I survived, and thrived. I fought others for meagre scraps of food and usually won out. And, when my life was in danger… I did what I had to.

When I was about ten, I was rounded up as part of yet another clean up initiative. Adoption homes created to take the influx of 'vermin on the streets' as the press often liked to refer to us. Those politician bastards always targeted the weak and the poor. Their simple words repeated by a complicit media, and lapped up by the morons who couldn't see the boot stamping down hard on their necks from above. Even when it was pointed out to them.

I hated it in the adoption centre. A prison by any other name. Mary and Joseph ran the centre for their own gains. Just another racket. Starving us. Dressing us in rags. Skimming money when and wherever they could. And... allowing paid visitors to visit the children at night. Mary and Joseph soon learned not to send anyone to me. I fought back and fought hard. Instead, they used me as an enforcer, rewarding me with a few extra scraps of food. I put on a show for them, but helped the other kids wherever I could. Teaching them to smear themselves with shit at night to deter the visitors. And despite my help, I purposely made no friends and didn't want them. I was loner. I never needed anybody.

The home had a library of sorts, a small room with a few old ABC books. Supposedly to teach us kids how to read and write. To become 'productive citizens'. Not that there were any classes. And so, I taught myself. I already had a rudimentary understanding of the written word picked up from the Ads and, of course, I knew even then that learning to read was an aid to survival.

It didn't take long for Mary and Joseph to catch on that I was helping the other kids. And soon they arranged an 'adoption'. But this wasn't a regular adoption where loving parents, desperate for a child of their own, come to find someone to offer love and support. This was a simple transaction. They paid Mary and Joseph a sum of money for a live-in slave.

My adoptive parents fed and clothed me and gave me my own room. In return, I looked after them. Doing all the menial jobs around their house. Compared to the streets and the orphanage, I was living a life of luxury. It mattered not that I wasn't allowed to leave the house, or to speak unless spoken to. I had a full belly and somewhere to sleep. And besides, where would I go? Back to the streets? No way.

I also had access to the data streams, to books, and to learning. My adoptive parents didn't care what I did in my free time between tasks. They weren't interested in me at all. I became obsessed with the colonies. The desire to escape there one day burning inside. I had a hunger for knowledge, aided by what I discovered was a photographic memory. Digesting everything I could find about the new worlds and the fantastic, ancient ships that travelled between them. At night and during my many tasks, I'd run the technical specifications of saucers, ships, of planetary survey results and more through my mind. Knowing population densities and makeup, and the emerging political landscapes. With one planet taking my attention in particular—*Persephone*. A rural paradise.

A dream. I would never be able to afford the cost of a ticket, and yet, it was that dream that kept me going.

I was in my teens when I became aware of a change in how my adopted parents treated me. Looking at my emerging curves with hungry eyes. Letting me experiment with drink and drugs. But I wasn't stupid. I knew what they were doing. What they now wanted. I'd managed to escape that kind of thing in the orphanage and wouldn't submit to it now. I flirted briefly with killing them, but I wasn't cold-blooded like that. In the end, I kept them at bay, thinking their grooming was working, while secretly plotting my escape.

I left one hot summer's night. In truth, I could've escaped at any time if I'd wanted… but I was safe there. It was only when that safety was challenged that I decided to leave. I was careful with what I stole from them. Nothing too expensive, nothing to get them angry, nothing to get the police interested, but enough to sell on the black market and set myself up in a small apartment at the other end of the city near the spaceport.

Watching those regular shuttles carrying passengers to the colony ships never grew old. I shared my flat with five other young women and two men, but I was independent again, for the first time since I was taken from the streets, and I relished it.

It was soon after that I got a job working the docks. It was tough work, and I'm not tough-looking. I quickly learned the job wasn't so much about the actual work—driving cargo loaders—but learning how to deal with my workmates. A rough-and tumble initiation of fire. Nothing physical, but they tested me. Finding out I could dish back as much lip as came my way. And more. Those mornings and lunchtimes were the closest I've ever felt to being part of a team. Even then, I was a loner. The money was good, but no way near good enough to get a ticket to the colonies. And running cargo-loaders wasn't a sought-after profession on the new worlds.

I was naive, I realise now. Although I did make it. I'm here, aren't I? On the *Octavia*. And I now know how.

In my desire for more money, I decided to use my looks to get work in a supposedly 'high-end' spaceport bar. A vile place full of vile men and women. But by far the vilest part of working there was the unremitting hope. The girls and boys were dreamers. Kids who treated this job as a stepping stone to perhaps meeting a rich punter. Someone to enable their dreams, but who all, inevitably, ended upstairs, prostituting themselves for the same hope, until their flesh drooped, and the shine went from their eyes, and they were replaced.

My dreams stretched beyond this bar. Not realising that my so-called superior dreams were just as hollow. I stayed downstairs, plying punters with drinks, jollying them up. Making them feel good. Getting them horny and drunk enough to go upstairs.

"You'll make more money up there," Jaqx, my boss, would regularly tell me. "Half these punters only come to see you.

You know that?"

She was right, I was popular. Me. The girl who had spent most of her life on her own, had the knack for chat. And I enjoyed it, even if I was spending my time fending off pervs and creeps. I made them laugh, deflected them and, more importantly, got them to give me tips.

I'd put my time in at the bar. Go home, grab four hours of sleep, and start work at the docks, after which I'd go straight to the bar again.

"You need to get a life," my flatmates used to tell me. "And some boys or girls to have yourself some fun." They held regular parties that, by the sound of it, involved a lot of sex. I was always too tired to notice or care. Closing my eyes as soon as I hit my bunk. As for romance… I didn't live in a drought. I got to drink when the need arose in me. I'm no prude. But relationships were never my thing. And I suppose that's how it would've stayed for me. Living a lonely, busy life of hope. Fooling myself that I'd one day save enough money to get to the colonies. Until Lissa Angeline Blackstone walked into the bar, and everything changed.

3-05-MELDED

Lissa was a lush. A real no hoper. A blonde, emerald-eyed bimbo with too much money and too much time to spend it. The bar attracted its requisite number of lost souls, and Lissa fitted that description exactly. I often wondered if she ever had a soul. One thing was for sure, the girl was besotted with me.

I treated her like any other punter, laughing at her jokes, getting her drinks—mainly whisky that she knocked back like it was lemonade—and making sure she kept her hands off me. Most of all though, we chatted. She explained about her parents divorcing her because *they never understood who the real Lissa was.* She told me of her various enterprises, investing in this and that venture—all of which fell apart because of *other people.* Nothing was ever her fault. The classic spoilt brat.

And, as odd as it sounds, I recognised myself in her. I was just as lost as she was. Obviously, if I had her wealth, her education, her rich friends—many of whom had deserted her for good reason I should imagine—I would have made much more of myself. We were both living the wrong lives. That much was obvious. Lissa needed rules and boundaries, without them, she was floundering. Me? I simply needed her freedom and her money. Who knows what I could then accomplish?

These were just observations. I was making no plans. I had no malicious intent against her. In truth, I liked our conversations once she had given up trying to grope and flirt with me. She offered to take me away from this bar and this life. To put me up in an apartment in a nicer part of the city. To look after me. A tempting offer. One that the other bar workers would've jumped at. Indeed, many of them were jealous of me because of her. But I knew the type of person Lissa was. Sure, she'd love me and shower me with gifts, but it would only be the notion of being in love. Nothing real. Soon, she'd grow tired and move on, discarding me like, I'm guessing, she had discarded so many others in her wasted life.

Her interest in me had one effect though… to question what I was doing. Lissa had more money than she knew what to do with. She could travel to the colonies and back again a few times if she wanted. And, of course, I blathered on to her about Persephone and the other worlds. Bending her ear on the subject. Until one night… I glimpsed a pitying look in her eyes. The woman was humouring me. Quite simply, she showed me up for what I was.

A dreamer. Like every other sap in that joint.

There is nothing wrong with having dreams and aspirations, but when your singular dream is so unachievable that it blinds you to the rest of your life? It floored me. I was no different to every other kid at the adoption centre fantasising that they were the lost child of wealthy parents. Or the saps working this dead-end joint. I used to laugh at them all, not realising I was equally deluded.

The colonies and Persephone were the only hope I had, and without that dream, I was nothing. I lost all balance in my life. I still went to work at the docks and the bar, I still chatted to Lissa and the other punters, but I was dead inside. I might as well have died on the streets as a kid. But there was still a glimmer of hope.

Lissa's offer.

What did I have to lose? It would be fun for a few months. I'd have to put up with her in bed, but that would be a small price to pay. I could even find a way to make something out of it. Maybe convince her to take me to the colonies. It would be better than what I was doing. Dreaming my life away.

I resolved to tell Lissa the next time she came to the bar. But she never returned. I spent long shifts staring aimlessly at the door, my heart lifting every time there was a flash of blonde hair. Weeks turned into months, and soon, I put her to the back of my mind. Instead, my eyes had moved to upstairs. I was young, petite, and pretty with my blue eyes and blacker than black hair, but those looks wouldn't last. They never do unless you can afford the exorbitant rejuve treatments. I wasn't ready to have that conversation with Jaqx. Not yet. But it was coming soon.

Three months after the last time I talked to Lissa, I met her again. Returning from my shift at the bar in the middle of the night, I found her, lying comatose in an alleyway close to my flat. Passed out people in alleyways were common at the spaceport, and I would've walked past, like I have done so many times before, but I saw a flash of blonde hair and…

it was her.

I dragged her to my single room, lying her on my bed. Wondering how I could turn this to my advantage, rifling through her purse. Unbelievably, she hadn't been robbed. There was a large amount of cash, credit bars, her personal holotab, and… a bag of small purple pills.

I recognised them at once. *Purple Violets.* Very powerful illegal narcotics and responsible for a spate of recent deaths. If she'd taken these, there was a strong possibility she wouldn't recover. Unless she'd managed to vomit them all up. Maybe I could resurrect my plan of getting her to take me to the colonies? My opportunity at last. I was about to call an ambulance when Lissa's tab started flashing. An alert from a company called, *Brave New Worlds.* A colony company I recognised. Lissa had a trip booked in two days' time… *to Persephone!*

Had I inspired her to get a ticket? It seemed so. Is that why she was outside my apartment? To tell me that she'd stolen my dream? Knowing her, that was very likely. She'd have no idea how that would crush me. I took a closer look at the alert. Lissa was overdue for a routine psyche test, a mandatory exam that must be completed before the flight.

Using Lissa's face to get full access to her tab—her security was laughable. No voice imprint. No DNA or fingerprint—I discovered that her life was a bigger mess than I could've ever realised. Amongst all the chaotic ramblings of her online personality, including various references to her supposedly leaked sex holos, angry ex's and bitchy ex-friends, that I quickly swiped past, I found the full details of her trip to Persephone. Everything was put in place months ago. Only a psyche test remained, which she had received multiple alerts to attend. All ignored. Other than that, she was cleared to travel.

Another one of her plans that she didn't have the ability to follow through on. I remember my rage when I discovered that. A hatred for Lissa and a system that allowed people like me and her to exist in the same world. She held my dream within her hands and yet treated it with nothing but disdain. A fucking distraction.

The have and the have not.

There were a series of possible dates for Lissa's psyche test. And before I had properly understood what I was doing, I chose the last one, receiving a 'booked' alert a few seconds later, sitting down to stare at the unconscious woman. We were the same age, the same height and shared the same build. Only our hair and eyes differed. Knowing in that moment what I was going to do.

I used Lissa's credit bars to taxi over to her place, landing on her personal parking balcony—the doors left wide open. I was still nervous to enter her apartment, a beautiful, expensive, and lavish loft space. Or it was—underneath the mess of clothes, discarded utensils, plates and other rubbish. The place stank of *Yeast*, a common drug inhaled via a bong-like apparatus. And nothing packed. I wasn't surprised. Lissa had no intention of travelling to Persephone, that much was clear. But she certainly was going there now. I would make sure of it.

I tidied up her apartment, finding a cupboard of unused cleaning products and other equipment, using the skills I learned working all those years for my adopted parents. Wearing gloves of course. My hair tied back and squashed into a net. I couldn't stop shedding DNA, but why make it easy for the cops if they came looking? Lissa had a two-kilo limit for the journey. I made a small pile of belongings to take back home with me. A few personal items. Some jewellery and assorted clothing. My intention to make it look like Lissa had packed and left. There were quite a few valuables left over. I put them in one of her larger suitcases and lugged it to the balcony, taking it with me in another taxi.

I found Lissa still unconscious on my bed when I returned,

disappointed that the *Purple Violets* hadn't done the work for me. But that was only a matter of time, surely? I used her remaining cash to book a couple of cosmetic procedures. Hair and eyes. And another highly illegal and very expensive operation. Surgery that would take time to recuperate from. But necessary. Having no other option than to put it on Lissa's credit. It didn't list as a 'mind-meld' but that's what I signed myself up for. A desperate but dangerous measure.

The only other issue? Lissa's money. The settlement given to her by her parents. Or what was left of it. Still more money than I could earn in a lifetime or three. I had no interest in it, but to leave it behind would raise too many questions. And so, I set up a transfer to put everything into Lissa's *Brave New Worlds* colony account, to be actioned the day after my ship left for Persephone. Including selling off her apartment. Sure, questions would be asked, but who would answer them? Lissa? No, as far as anyone was concerned she was asleep and aboard a colony ship. What else could they do other than follow her instructions? At least, that's what I banked on.

On the way to get my hair and eyes done, I dumped the suitcase in the city's excuse for a river. A hungry, slimy-black, curling snake. Worse things than Lissa's valuables were taken by its oily waters daily. It felt like a betrayal to ditch all those expensive and beautiful things. I could've got a lot of credit-dollars on the black market for what was inside. But not enough to buy a ticket for the colony worlds.

Afterwards, I noisily returned to my apartment, making sure my flatmates saw me. Acting drunk and out of character. Telling them that I'd blown my savings on changing my appearance. That I'd decided to start having a good time. They marvelled at my bright emerald eyes and new blonde hair. A striking look. One that had worked for Lissa and now for me. And once the 'new me' had been planted into their minds, I offered them a handful of *Purple Violets*, which they took eagerly.

At the appointed time, I was visited by a professional looking woman in her fifties, stepping over my half-comatose flatmates who were too drugged-up to notice her entering my room.

She told me of the risks associated with the surgery I had paid for. That what she was preparing to do would result in brain damage. That there could be side-effects. *That I could die.* Affirming that she would ask no questions and that her extortionate payment was also for her silence.

Her method removed memories from one person and transplanted them into another. Once used for recreation, where people would sell their memories for money. However, the procedure was deemed too dangerous to continue, especially after the deaths of some notable people. And so, like all similar techniques, it went underground. I was nervous, but there was one saving grace. The person who invented the procedure, and who was sued out of business after the deaths, was in my apartment and ready to perform the mind-meld. I had paid for the very best. *Or Lissa had.*

I explained about the psyche test, and the woman's eyes had widened in understanding. She said nothing, set up her equipment, and put me under.

I woke half a day later with a pounding headache, downing the medicine left for me and discovering another person's memories commingled with my own. Lissa's crazy abandon and that empty place lurking deep inside her. Some of the recollections unsavoury, others confusing. And half-memories that didn't follow on. I just hoped it would be enough.

I was also disappointed to discover that Lissa had survived the procedure. I had wanted to ask the woman to make sure Lissa died, but I wasn't sure if her services stretched to murder. No, Lissa was my problem. And it had to be me who dealt with it. One thing was for definite. My plan wouldn't work while she stayed alive.

It was me or her.

I undressed Lissa, put her under my bedclothes, grabbed a handful of *Purple Violets* and spilled them on the floor and onto my bed. The remaining tablets… I crushed and mixed into a glass of water.

Lissa was recuperating, that was for sure. I slapped her gently around the face until her eyes opened. A smile twisting her lips when she recognised me. "Here," I said, the angel of death. "Drink this, it will make you feel better." I put the glass to her lips, and she drank it all down in a couple of gulps. "Now sleep my princess." And she drifted away, never to wake again.

I sat with her, cradling her petite form, checking her pulse that slowed to an occasional thud and finally stopped.

I have no remorse. I did what I had to do. What I've always done. But this time it was different. I killed an innocent in cold blood. I killed Lissa Angeline Blackstone for my own ends. Ending her life to enrich mine. The stakes were too high. This was my dream, and besides, if Lissa hadn't died in the alleyway, she would've died somewhere else, sometime soon. But I never fooled myself. I was still a murderer.

And what about her family? What did Lissa's death do to them? They would've believed she had left Earth for good. Perhaps they would've been relieved. And if the truth ever came out? I'd be in cryosleep and on my way to the colonies. A massive operation getting thousands and thousands of people aboard and unloaded at the other end. I'd be lost in the noise. But I'm sure that won't happen. No one will ever know.

No. Lissa would've been identified as me. Just another unfortunate who unfortunately OD'd on the latest designer drug in her sad, lonely, one-room apartment. No one important. A loser. Not worth any further investigation, other than talking to my flatmates and removing the body for incineration.

I'm now Lissa Angeline Blackstone. Whoever I was before is unimportant. That sad, deluded girl is dead. But, more importantly, I'm not the pushover the crew think I am. I'm no goddamn victim…

4-0
SURVIVING

I sit up in the cryopod, my memories returned and fully formed. I'm the girl who stole Lissa Angeline Blackstone's identity and murdered her to do it. Fully formed, yes, but with something extra. I seized a part of who she was to pass that psyche test. Meaning… she's inside me, even if she is nothing more than an echo of herself. Those same memories that confused me—her coming out party, the limousine, those dreadful sex parties and the boarding school that her parents forced her to endure, and her deeply lost, insecure, narcissistic soul—are a part of me now.

The revelation that I'm a cold-blooded killer startles but does not disturb me. It's who I am. *Who we both are.* Does that make me no better than Captain Marla and the rest of her fucked up crew? The thought is an errant one. Stupid and irrational. I'm nothing like them. Despite the revelation of what I did, of who I am, of my ruthless streak, I'm more at peace in this moment than all my time awake aboard this ship. The real Lissa died so I could have a life. I became her. I became Lissa Angeline Blackstone. And I won't let her die again. I'm fighting for both of us…

Brad appears by the pod, his head twitching with the return of his nervous tic. "What are you doing, Liss? We can't mess about. We don't have time."

"I took a chance," I whisper. "Did everything to get here. And now these crew bastards are trying to take it away from me."

Brad isn't listening. "What are you babbling about? Lie

down and roll over, I need to plug you in."

"There's got to be a better way than cryo."

"But what other option do you have? They will torture you and kill you. We discussed this. Get back down, it's for the best."

He's right, I know he is. Cryo is the only way out. It's an attractive choice. To go to sleep and wake up free of this nightmare but… I see a flash of Lissa lying on my bed. Helpless, unconscious, and unable to defend herself against me. Against *her killer*. If I go into cryo, I'll be in the same position. Logic is telling me cryo is the only option, and yet… *this isn't me*. "I've… I've changed my mind."

"What the hell, Lissa?" Brad's face creases in anger. "We don't have time for this shit, okay? Do as I tell you and do it now."

"Listen to me, Brad. You'll still be okay. Go back to your holotab, finish your work and report to cryo like you were ordered. But… I'm gonna take my chances."

"That's stupid. You'll either starve to death or they'll catch and kill you!"

"It's my choice. And I've decided."

"No, I won't let you do it." He holds up Taipan's knife. "Turn over and let me plug you in."

"When did you get a hold of that?"

"Just do as I fucking tell you!" He jabs my shoulder with the knife, pain lancing from a small wound.

"What the hell?"

"Plug yourself in, now!" Brad's face twists into an angry sneer, revealing another side of him. Dark and devilish, and my blood runs cold.

"You're a part of this? Part of this goddamn horror show?"

"Don't you get it? I'm trying to save you from them. With you here, I can look after you, wake you up whenever I want. Have some fun. Just me and you. And I know intimately how you like the fun part." He licks the blood from the tip of the knife, reminding me of Vic in that dreadful holo. "I need to get back before the captain suspects anything."

"What?"

"I thought, why should I share you with them? They always take the lion's share of the fun. Leaving nothing for poor Brad. Just because I'm the oldest guy on board." He jabs me again with the blade, prodding me with it.

"Once in cryo, they'll forget about you and, on the next rotation, maybe on the way back to Earth, I'll wake you up like I said, and we can have some fun without that bitch, Simone spying on me. I want to take it slow with you Lissa, to enjoy every torment, every—"

I grab the pod lid and slam it down on his outstretched arm, the blade jerking from his fingers and falling inside. I fumble for it as Brad releases his arm and puts his full weight on the lid, trying to lock it and trap me inside. Luckily, I'm small enough to roll onto my shoulders, using my legs to push against the lid, against Brad who I can hear grunting with the effort. The gravity is only half a gee otherwise I'd have no chance against him. My hand finds the handle of the long thin knife and I jab it through the gap while kicking at the lid, feeling it hit home. Brad gasps and stumbles and I throw the pod hatch open, flinging myself out and over to land in an awkward crouch, the knife raised to fend off Brad's attack. An attack that doesn't come.

He lies on the floor, a shocked look on his face, blood rapidly soaking his skinsuit from a small puncture wound in the middle of his chest.

I drop the knife and cradle him in my arms. "Why did you have to be a part of it, Brad? Why?" I shout at him. "I liked you."

"Thank you," he croaks.

"What the hell for? You're dying."

He tries to gasp more words, but his throat overwhelms with blood. He gurgles, stiffens, and sags.

"Why?" I repeat, my anger returning twice as strong, easily lifting his body in the low gee and dumping it in the pod. "I trusted you." Grabbing the lid with both hands, I take one last look at him, and slam the pod shut. "Fuck you, Brad! You ungrateful lay!"

4-01-CHASED

One down, four to go, and it won't be easy. I need to get the odds on my side and to do that I need weapons. Sure, I've got the knife, but I don't want to get close enough to these bastards to be able to use it.

Whatever sixth sense told me the pod was a bad idea has put me on this path. I should be terrified, but I'm not. I got aboard by my own hand, and I will get myself out of this mess the same way. I'm positive, believing I can do it, although logic tells me I'm facing certain death. Either way, I'm not going down without a fight and maybe, just maybe, I can take one or two more of these bastards with me.

The captain expects me to run into the ship and hide. Vic hinted at that when he told me he'd see me again *on the hunt*, meaning I need to confound their expectations.

Still reeling from Brad's betrayal, I leave him and the ancient command hub behind. I hope they never find his body. I'd be glad to let him rot in there forever. I suspected Taipan of filming me and him together, but it's obvious he was the culprit. I'm guessing Brad was in competition with Vic and perhaps even, Fergal, to see who could sleep with me first. If so, Brad won that bet and bragged to the rest of the crew. And then played out that scene in the canteen. What a bastard. They've been playing me from the start. Psychological torture for starters before they moved on to the main meal of the day. Tied up in that *killing room*, dying an unimaginably awful death. I vow to not end up like their other victims.

I head toward the secondary navigational node where I was working with Taipan this morning. It's a bold plan, worried that once I near the Command Centre, the captain will be able to track me using Simone and her nodes. But maybe their focus won't be so close to home. There is, of course, the possibility of bumping into someone. I hope I'm not forced into a fight when I'm not ready. Still, that worked against Brad, and I may be lucky a second time. But luck has the knack of running out just when you need it the most. I must try to fight them on my terms.

I grip the knife tightly and trace my way back, feeling eyes watching me as I near the Command Centre, tensed and ready to fight. I arrive at the secondary nav-node and race inside, my eyes searching for the one thing I came here for. The utility belt worn by Vic on our trip to the engines and Nutri-hub. It has a drill-come-screwdriver, a hammer, one of Vic's zero gee aerosol thrusters and many pockets, the contents of which I don't have time to check. I wrap it around my waist, adjusting it to fit, glancing around for anything else I can use, spotting a rack of steel bars the length of my arm, a spool of nanowire, and a hand-stunner. All useful. I slip on the stunner, slide a steel bar into my new belt, thrust the wire into a pocket and head outside, finding myself facing Vic Ramirez standing in the corridor ten feet away.

I have no time for deliberation. Every second I don't use in attack is a second wasted. Shrieking to throw him off balance, I run full pelt at him, sideswiping the shocked engineer with both the stunner and the knife, darting down a side corridor that will take me back into the old ship.

A loud bang… Vic's grappling hook! I throw myself to the corridor floor. Rolling with the momentum. Getting back up again and running. Vic sprinting behind me. Moving fast on his augmented legs. A loud whine—the grappling hook retracting—I dodge it, using the stunner to knock the hook away from me, Vic grunting in pain close behind. Perhaps it hit him. I hope so. A junction ahead. Instinct tells me which way to go, and I come to a place I recognise from my journey across the ship… the corridor leading to the wide chasm I jumped into, a plan forming in my mind. I reach the shaft and launch at full speed. The gravity disappears over the chasm, my momentum pushing me forward. What I should have done the first time I encountered this obstacle. I land on the other side, rolling through the hatchway and slam it shut. Spinning the wheel and jamming it with the steel bar. Watching Vic through the hatch window as he prepares to jump.

Seconds later, I hear Vic's impotent shouting from the other side of the hatchway, but I'm safe for now. One thing has been confirmed. The crew are armed and hunting for me.

Slumping with my back to the hatchway—I don't want Vic to know I'm resting on the other side—I look at what I managed to snatch.

I'm wearing the stun pad. Not much of a weapon against humans, but it still packs a punch and I'll need everything I can get to help me if I'm ever in a one-to-one situation. It's better than nothing, that's for sure. I take out the nanowire and unravel it. About twenty metres and strong. I can think of a couple of uses for this already.

The utility belt has a few more items other than the drill, the hammer and the zero gee aerosol thruster, which is almost full. There's a can of some kind. I sniff it—a lubricant or cleaner? Inside the belt's pockets I find a pack of all-purpose screws, pliers, a torch with a powerful, blinding beam, duct tape, some odd looking bolts, a half-full container of stale water—how long has that been in there?—and an old Zippo flick lighter that has dried up, although the flint still works. It's not much of a haul, granted, but it's a start. I need more. Running and hiding will only work for a while. At some point I'll have to confront these bastards.

This is where my knowledge of Persephone will come in useful. The holos contained a lot of fanciful stuff about homesteading and surviving. A highly romanticised description of colonial life—deliberately made to look carefree and easy to tempt people to leave Earth. I saw that for what it was. The reality is hard work and danger. Especially on the outskirts of the settlements where I hoped to eke out a life. I dug deeper than the glossy holos, focusing my attention on survival techniques. Reading first-hand descriptions from early settlers. Of building simple snares, pits, and traps, and how to bait them. As well as preventative measures such as mechanical scarecrows and ultrasonics. And even poison. Most of it low tek. There's no vegetation or trees aboard the freighter, but I could use substitutes… And the Zippo has given me an idea.

A crackle from the ancient speaker system makes me jump, and I instinctively grab the knife and stand up.

The sound of someone taking breath and the captain speaks. *"Well done in working out our little game, Lissa,"* she says, an edge of excitement to her usual drone. *"We would've preferred to have had a bit more fun at your expense. Waiting for our victims to slowly realise the game we're playing is such delicious entertainment. You jumped the gun, Lissa, and now the hunt is on."*

Even though I know this, it's still chilling to hear it from the captain.

"You're probably wondering how we can possibly keep getting away with our hobby. But out of every hundred or so thousand sleepers, zero point zero, zero, zero, zero seven won't make it. That's what we call you, the Point Four Zeros Seven. Acceptable company wastage within the parameters of expectation."

Those greyed-out pods flash into my mind. I'll just be counted as another passenger who died in cryo. A nothing. A nobody. And zero questions asked. The thought grates at me and I shake with rage, my fists curled into tight balls. "Tell that to Brad!" I shout at the top of my lungs, knowing that the captain can't possibly hear me. They must be wondering where he is by now.

"Are you ready to be added to our snuff collection?" A chuckle, and the sounds of footsteps. She's moving. Where is she? *"Be*

seeing you very soon."

The crackling stops abruptly as the speaker system is switched off.

I slump back against the hatchway, my head in my hands, still shaking. The captain's message has chilled me to the bone. That's what it was for, I realise, to scare me out of my wits. And it worked. I sit still long enough for the automatic lights to switch off, and I notice a familiar glow in the distance. Green arrows! Pointing to my hiding place. Shit! The captain is coming for me!

Where to go? Someone will be waiting on the other side of this hatch, that's for sure. I've only one choice, to run blindly into the ship. Away from the arrows and whoever is coming for me. I curse having to leave the steel bar behind, locking the hatchway, but I'm sure Vic is still lurking there. And he's too fast to take that chance. I dash toward the ship's interior, hearing voices as I pass the turning with the green arrows. *The Captain and Taipan!*

"Movement!" Taipan announces excitedly. "The bitch is just ahead!"

They're using motion detectors. That's how they capture their prey!

I rush into the maze of corridors, running left, right, left again, trying to get as far away from them as possible, their footsteps close behind. I turn a final corner, coming to a dead end. No way back, just a conduit door. Fuck! I have no choice but to fling it open and scramble inside, closing it behind and pulling myself along in the dark. The conduit takes me away from the dead end, but I'm still close to the corridor walls. They'll be able to detect me. Everything tells me to stay still, but my fear drives me forward.

"She's close by… in the goddamn walls. We've got the bitch now!" Taipan again.

I shuffle forward, hit by a familiar and disgusting stench. A nest of space rats. I take out the torch from my utility belt and find a swarm of them. I stay still, holding my breath.

"What the fuck!" Taipan's voice on the other side of the thin corridor wall. "We've been following goddamn space rats!"

"She could've gone anywhere!" The captain spits. "You lost her, I thought you knew what you were doing?"

"We had her. I was sure of it."

"Quit your bleating. She probably lost us some way back. No worries. The bitch will need water and soon. She'll have no choice but to come back to us."

Water! I forgot about that. I have that stale canteen, but that's all. The captain is right though, it won't last.

"In the meantime, you keep looking for her." I hear the captain walk away, leaving the disgruntled sounds of Taipan. She hangs around for a few minutes until, cursing, her footsteps recede into the distance.

I gasp, not realising I've been holding my breath, gagging on the cloying smell of the disgusting space rats. Disgusting space rodents that saved my goddamn life, meaning I can't hate them that much. I put my hands over my face to quieten any noise until the gagging stops. With Taipan close by, I've no other choice other than to stay here for a while. Lying down, I let the vile rats scurry over me, pushing my face away from them toward the wall and close my eyes.

4-02-SLAMMED

I awake sometime later, still surrounded by rats, many of them huddled into me, taking advantage of my body warmth. They may be vermin, but they are passive, non-aggressive beasts and I regret using the stunner on them the way I did before.

My throat is dry. I take a swig from Vic's canteen, aware that my estimation was wrong. It's not half full. Only a few more mouthfuls are left. I'll need water and soon. Which leads me to wonder… where are the space rats drinking? They are mammals, they need a source of water to survive, just like me. Vic said they nibbled on the nutritubes. Serving both as sustenance and water. That must be it.

I take out my torch and watch them. There appears to be traffic back and forth from further inside the conduit. I sit up, rubbing at an aching back and crawl along, trying to match the speed of the rodents. I have no idea if Taipan is still out there, trying to track me, but I don't want to take any chances. I come to an area of activity. But it's no nutritube. Instead, I find rats surrounding a small disgusting pool full of floating excrement. Condensation dripping down from somewhere above. I'd have to be desperate to drink from here. But it's good to know there is an option… even if it is repulsive.

Staying in the conduit forever, isn't a possibility. I galvanise myself for a peek outside, pulling myself along until I come to one of the entrance and exit hatches. Pushing it open a crack and waiting. No one I can see and no sounds. I open it a little further, the automatic lighting flickering into life. Dimmer than before. It must be ship night. I slept longer than I thought. Good. I step outside, marvelling at the comparatively fresh air.

Are the crew sleeping? I remember Brad's stims. Probably not, but they can't stay awake forever.

I'm hungry and thirsty. I sip again from the flask, wanting to drain it. Once this is gone, it's space-rat water. A good incentive to save it for as long as possible.

I need to get moving. But where the hell am I? All the corridors look the same. I was only able to navigate before because I had a starting point. I haven't travelled too far from where I entered the conduit, but since then, I've lost my direction. I do the only sensible thing I can. Returning inside the conduit and working myself back to where I entered. The dead end. Navigating myself away from there and further into the ship.

My memory is a life-saver. Without it, I'd be lost. I wonder how many of the crew's victims have died lost and alone. Then again, it's unlikely. The crew aren't the type to waste an opportunity to torture and murder one of their *Point Four Zeros Sevens*. This is the crew's ship. They know their way around—although the fact that they relied on the green arrows means I have the upper hand in the parts of the ship I've visited before. Still, they're serial killers and, judging by the number of bodies I glimpsed in their killing room, they've done this many times.

I don't want to consider the likelihood of capture, but I'd be foolish not to. I can't hide out in the ship forever unless I want to die there. If there's an opportunity, I'll kill myself first. My mind jumps to Taipan's knife. Open an artery in my neck or leg and it will soon be over. A victory of sorts. Before it comes to that, I want to try take out some of the crew, meaning… *I've no choice other than to take risks*. I think about the dried-up Zippo in my belt. I can use it against the crew, but first… I need to return to the Supply Room.

Using a roundabout route, moving silently and slowly, my eyes and ears on alert, I get closer to the command area, skirting it to head north. A high-risk manoeuvre. One that I'm hoping will be unforeseen. I'm not the Lissa who I found comatose in the alley outside my apartment. Who I rescued and used for my own ends. I'm no privileged brat with a history of sex holos and wasting money. A silly rich girl who ended up a junkie. No. I'm the new Lissa. A killer— twice now—and no easy pushover. I'm certainly not what they were expecting, that's for sure. I can use that to my advantage, although they must wonder why I'm not quite the girl described in my file. It's obvious that the crew choose 'natural victims'. They have no idea who I really am and what I'm capable of.

The Supply Room door is open as I approach in the dim

night of the ship. One door in and one door out. Make or break. I take a deep breath and run inside, lights flicking on brightly, making me blink. I'm expecting an ambush, but the room is empty. I grab a backpack from a hook and find the canisters I'm looking for and add them to the backpack with as much of Vic's vodka as I can carry and a few empty bottles. Next on my list, and critical to my survival, is a helmet and gloves. Relief flooding through me as I tuck them in my belt. I said I'd never go out of an airlock again… but my outlook has changed. I grab some cleaning rags and spot another metal pipe. Aluminium not steel. I see its potential and pick it up, turning toward the door, terrified that this is a trap. That the crew is waiting for me outside. Pulling on the backpack, and stuffing the pipe into my belt, I exit the Supply Room a few minutes after I entered.

The corridor is dark and silent. Have I done it? Did my plan work? It appears so. I head back to the primary nav-node, breathing a sigh of relief, when my legs are snatched from under me. Sucked to the floor. The weight of my backpack crushing me. A trap after all. The bastards got me with the artificial grav.

The terrific pressure disappears, and I'm lifted off the floor, my world twisting upside down, before I'm slammed into the ceiling. The vodka bottles clinking in my backpack.

Fergal's voice over the com. *"Oops! Looks like someone has access to the grav controls. Oh no."*

The grav disappears, and this time I'm ready for it, kicking off the ceiling and diving down the corridor.

"Oh no you don't!"

The grav increases again and I'm slammed back into the floor. The bastard is playing with me. I try to use it to my advantage. "Brad said you were a sore loser."

A pause. *"What?"*

"You heard me. He said you try it on with everyone, using that pathetic pity technique."

"You think I was playing a goddamn game. I… fell in love with you, I…"

"You know why I chose Brad? Cos' he was a real man, not some fat virgin with bad breath."

I'm slammed up and down again, but I'm ready for it. It's what I wanted. This is an old ship and the anti-grav buffers won't last long. Soon, I'm left floating, bouncing off the walls and diving for the next corridor.

"Shit!"

It will only take a few moments for Fergal to activate the next section's grav against me, but he's incandescent with rage and shouting over the com, the captain trying to get the controls off him.

Back in normal grav, I sprint past the Off-Limits room, the door open, but I don't glance inside.

I've already seen what that room has to offer on the holotop in Taipan's cabin.

Sprinting like an athlete, my chest heaving, I re-enter the old ship, where the crew can't track me. Indirectly heading toward the nav-node.

I'm battered black and blue, my arms, legs and back screaming at me. I don't have time to lick my wounds. I'm hoping the captain and her deranged crew will think I've gone to ground. Hiding in the ship again. Although they must have realised I'm no normal victim.

Without missing a step, I put on my gloves and zip my helmet into place, charging headlong into the nav-node and toward the airlock. I fling myself inside and cycle the mechanism with adept fingers.

No time to ponder what I'm doing. Entering evac without a tether. But with what I have in mind, it's the only way. My skinsuit tightens and warms and, seconds later, I open the outer hatch, ignoring all that space pressing down on me.

I clamber over the hull. Working my way toward my goal. Hoping that the crew don't know I'm outside the ship. I have no time to be careful. One slip could send me careening off into space. A better end than what the crew have in store for me, that's for sure, but I have other plans. Plans that involve me staying very much alive.

I spot the transport carriage sitting outside the main airlock. I dive inside, seal the door, and engage the mechanism. Soon, its gliding along the rail. Moving slower than I remember. Although that could be my adrenaline.

After twenty tortuous minutes, the midships station comes into view. However, the carriage abruptly stops before we arrive. Control lights winking.

A clunk of machinery and the carriage reverses back to the Command Centre with twice the speed of before.

They know where I am!

I crank open the door, the hull flashing past me—too fast to jump—and clamber onto the roof, moving to what is now the back of the carriage.

Taking time to climb down to just above the rail. I take a deep breath and let go, my hands scrabbling for a handhold. I grab a stanchion and I'm thrown around. I keep a desperate hold, adding my second hand to arrest my motion, letting my legs bash against the fuselage.

The pain is excruciating after the battering they've already received, but I'm able to stop spinning. Watching the carriage disappear into the distance.

Turning, I pull myself along the rails until I get to the midships station again.

The airlock lets me inside and a few minutes later I'm literally breathing a sigh of relief inside the Nutri-hub.

The lights flick from green to red and I hear it latching. They've locked me inside.

"Looks like you're trapped," the captain says over the crackling com. *"But don't worry, Vic is coming to get you."*

4-03-TOASTED

I'm chilled to the bone by her words, but it's what I wanted. What I expected. Although now I'm here with no way of escape, I'm wondering if this was such a good idea. I had banked on the captain sending Vic, and I give a small whoop of joy to accompany my fear.

I empty Vic's canteen of its last few mouthfuls of water, feeling sick to the pit of my stomach. Keeping myself busy is the only way to overcome my nerves, and, luckily, being busy is part of my plan. First off, I find the nearest nutritank and siphon off the fluid into the empty canteen. It reminds me of that awful stink in the blocked tank, even if this is the 'fresh' stuff. I thank the space rats for reminding me that the nutrient can be lived off, and force myself to drink it down, gorging on as much as I can tolerate, and filling my canteen again when I'm finished. It's sickly sweet with fructose and thick like a shake—both food and water. I then fill a couple of the empty vodka bottles, enough to keep me going in the short term. If I can escape the trap I've deliberately put myself in, I don't know how long I will be forced to hide out.

I check the other equipment I pilfered from the Supply Room and take stock. It's not much, but it's what I wanted. I didn't forget anything. There's the rest of the vodka, the canisters filled with something that I hope will give Vic a nasty surprise, cleaning rags, and the thin aluminium metal tube. I stamp my foot down on its end, flattening the metal and bending it into a spike—a makeshift spear.

Next, I activate the Zippo with Vic's vodka and flick it into life. The naked flame excites me. Especially as a working lighter is integral to my plan. It burns with a cold blue flame, giving off a delicious odour, reminding me of the flaming shots I used to serve in that titty bar from my old life. Vodka is over eighty percent alcohol, meaning… it burns easily. I now have Molotov Cocktails. I tear the cleaning rags into strips and stuff them into the top of the vodka bottles. Not only do I want these cocktails to work, I want Vic to realise what they are. To focus on them, and not what's really happening.

I reckon I have about ten to fifteen minutes left before the carriage returns. I jog toward the shower, finding the small corridor I'm looking for. Unravelling a short length of nanowire, I tie it to two of the glass vodka bottles, creating an almost invisible tripwire. And put in place my little surprise. The two full bottles holding the wire taught, hidden on either side of the corridor's entrance.

I move to the other end of the short corridor and place the Molotov Cocktails almost out of sight, but not quite. An ambush of sorts… I want Vic to be in no doubt what my intentions are.

Stashing my backpack, I return to a hidden spot that gives me eyes on the corridor leading to the airlock. After an age, the red flashes to green, and the inner door swings open and Taipan and Vic step inside. I'm not concerned, nor surprised that she is accompanying 'her man'. That woman hates me, is jealous of me. And now I know why. That silly macho competition between Vic and Brad to see who could get to sleep with me must've been driving her crazy. Then again, she's insane, they all are.

"Not sure you made the right choice, missy," Vic shouts in his exaggerated Latino accent. He locks the airlock, its single light turning to red with a thunk. "There's no way out, unless you're planning on swimming out of here in the nutritubes… which I don't advise."

Unexpectedly, I want to answer him, to shout any number of insults and expletives, a seething hate growling inside of me, but I bite my tongue. They are here to try and catch me, not kill, which will give me an advantage in the short term, although I'm still fighting for my life.

Vic tells Taipan to stay on guard by the airlock, which causes an argument. She doesn't want to be left behind, wanting instead to hurt and humiliate me, her eyes flashing manically. "Face it, Tai, you've lost it," Vic says, "I can't let you anywhere near her when you're like this. The captain wants her alive."

She holds up two of her long thin knives. "Oh, she'll be alive, just sliced up a little bit."

"Stay here. I won't be long but... yeah, sure, let's have some fun with the liddle conchita before taking her to the others."

Taipan beams and they kiss for long moments, turning my stomach. I use this as an opportunity to slip away. That's when I hear footsteps behind me. I dive behind some piping, spotting Taipan only a few feet away, twin knives drawn. The argument at the airlock was a ruse, or she ignored Vic. Maybe they are not as insane as they sounded. At least Taipan hasn't brought her motion detector, otherwise I'd be in trouble, although I had factored that into my plan, if it came to it.

She walks past and, breathing a sigh of relief, I steal towards the corridor with my tripwire. Stepping over it and crouching out of sight by the stack of Molotov Cocktails.

"You think you can hide from me?" Vic shouts somewhere in the distance, his voice echoing.

"Fuck you!" I reply, purposely revealing my location.

Vic hurries toward my voice, the clatter of his mechanical feet thrumming against the cold metal of the deck, growing in volume. Suddenly, I regret my plan. I thought it was a good idea, but now, in the moment, the chances of my trap working the way I hope it will seems unlikely. A desire to run makes my legs twitch... but where to? This is make or break. And besides... what other choice do I have?

I flick the lighter and hear Vic reacting to it. He comes striding forward, standing at the end of the short corridor.

Stopping in front of the tripwire and the two full bottles. "Is this the best you can do, missy?" he says, looking down. He slices the wire with a quick flick of his augmented hand, and picks up one of the bottles, swirling its clear contents. "Vic don't take too kindly to anyone wasting his booze."

I take a deep breath and step out, a Molotov Cocktail in my hand, the lit Zippo inches away from its vodka-soaked rag.

"You found my utility belt. Well done. I wondered where I left it."

"It's mine now. And your lighter."

"So, let me work it out. I was to trip over this wire and spill vodka everywhere?" His voice is condescending and childlike. "Then, I guess, you were going to throw one of your liddle cocktails at me? And boom!"

"I still can." I lift the lit Zippo closer to the vodka-soaked rag.

"You think a liddle fire is gonna hurt Vic? These skinsuits are fireproof, missy. Or didn't you know that? Face it, you're done."

"I'll burn first!" I reply, desperate to keep him talking. "And so will you. Your face is still uncovered."

"You'll burn all right. Vic will make sure of that..." He sounds unconcerned, but he keeps his eyes firmly fixed on the lighter. He knows I'll have time to throw my cocktail if he tries anything. And despite his cool words, the threat of burning him is a real one. He's happy to keep me talking while Taipan is no doubt sneaking up on me. "Now, you gonna tell me where Brad has got to? The captain can't raise him, and Simone has no idea where he is."

"Why, you still smarting that I chose him instead of you?"

"You'd be surprised how many of our liddle boys and girls prefer a real man."

"Is that what you call yourself? But about Brad... he didn't make it."

He smiles in surprise. "Vic has to give it to you, missy. You're a fighter. A nice change. I always like a struggle." He winks suggestively. "But you're done. There's no way out this time. Why not put down the lighter and share a drink with me?"

He takes a step forward holding the bottle outstretched in his hand. I raise the Zippo with threat.

"C'mon. Join me in a toast. A liddle drink will help with what we've got planned for you."

"It's piss." I spit at him, my heart now thundering in my ears, my eyes glancing left and right for any sign of Taipan.

"Piss? No. This is the very best. Vic's special vodka, decades-aged and smooth as a bambino's bottom. Salud!" He puts the bottle to his lips and takes a long swig, his eyes widening in sudden shock, stumbling and gagging. The bottle drops to the floor, smashing. The contents bursting out and smoking in contact with the metal. Vic sags, his hands clutched to his throat.

I rush over to him. "Turns out I'm not that stupid after all," I say, relief flooding through me in a hot wave of victory. "I was wondering if you were ever gonna take a goddamn drink. You bragged about your enhanced vision, so I banked on you spotting the wire. And of course, you do like a *liddle* vodka, don't you? So I filled those bottles with hydrochloric acid hoping that you might be dumb enough to drink one of them, thinking it was your moonshine. And… you were dumb enough." I pull out the rag from the Molotov Cocktail I'm holding, although that's not quite what it is. It's full of the remaining hydrochloric acid that I pour onto him. If Vic hadn't taken himself out, throwing this at him was my back-up plan. But getting him to drink the stuff was the only sure way of finishing him off.

I watch with both horror and fascination as Vic's throat dissolves, revealing the glint of metal and the spurt of blood escaping from dissolved arteries. He's dead within moments, his cybernetic implants twitching.

A scream and Taipan comes running at me with both knives raised.

4-04-SCORCHED

I just have time to pull my makeshift spear from my belt, before I'm using it to deflect Taipan's frenzied, uncoordinated stabbing attack. Annoyed that I allowed myself to get distracted gloating over her now deceased boyfriend. I still have the dangerous woman's blade, but instinctively realise I'd have no chance in a knife fight against her. Whatever orders she is under to bring me back alive are forgotten now that Vic is dead. I have no choice but to fight her, hand-to-hand. The pipe is light, and it won't last long against those knives, so I wait, desperately defending myself until Taipan is forced to take a breath.

Taking my chance, I stab at her neck. She dodges, and I miss her throat, raking the pipe down the side of her face, although she doesn't bleed. Taipan shrieks with rage. I push forward my attack, running into her and knocking her aside, flinging myself into the corridors to emerge back in the nutritank section, where there is more room to manoeuvre.

A few moments later, Taipan appears. This time I'm ready, adeptly keeping my distance, and annoying her at the same time. "What's a matter, girl?" I say, mimicking her little girl voice. "Did some slut dissolve your creep boyfriend? Oh no."

A flick of her hand and she throws one of her long knives at me. A move of desperation and anger, with no skill behind it. It misses me and clatters to the floor. "Do you want to throw me the other one?" I say with a smirk. But it was a ruse, she runs straight at me, using my own tactic against me, and I'm caught wrong-footed, her knife thrusting at my chest. I dodge and sink down, aware of a sharp pain to my throat, my hand instinctively grabbing my neck as I roll away, jumping to my feet and sprinting. There's blood but not a lot of it. I'm grazed, nothing more. Taipan is close behind me, and I'm tiring. I've had a busy few days and not looked after myself as well as I should've. Plus, after all those years in cryo, I'm just not as fit as I used to be. Taipan doesn't appear to be similarly affected. My eyes dart around for anything to use against her and find it. Vic's portable steam cleaner. Shit! Why didn't I think of using that before?

I turn, ducking instinctively to dodge her attack and push her aside, punching the control panel and grabbing the hose. I fall to the floor, pointing the nozzle at Taipan. A blast of steam hits her full in the face, intense pain bursting over my hand that I've somehow managed to burn. Taipan stumbles back in shock, dropping her remaining knife. I grab my spear and jump to my feet in victory, but I realise she's unharmed. Taipan's face is reddened but that's all. "What the hell? That should've burnt that smug look off your face for sure."

"You think I skimped on my juvo treatments, girl? No way, I made sure I got the best skin money could buy." Her eyes drop to my hand. "But not you… ouch!"

"Just get away from me!"

A change comes over Taipan. She's realising I'm no pushover. Far from it. It doesn't stop her sounding just as confident. "Run all you like. I've got all day, honey and you're going nowhere. But after what you did to Vic… you and me are soon to have a reckoning. I'm gonna take my time with you, you get me?"

Even though Taipan isn't injured by the steam blast, I sense it's affected her more than she's showing. Giving me a small window to act.

I kick her knife away and run… how in hell will I kill this bitch?

I have only one trick left up my sleeve and I'm forced to use it. I leave the main Nutri-hub area, and head down the corridor to the airlock… the place I've decided to make my stand, only pausing to put on my backpack.

The airlock is locked, of course, but with the return of my memories has come a slew of knowledge gained from working the cargo docks, knowledge that I can put to use.

I check my hand. The skin is red and in places bubbled up. The damage confined to the back and wrist, my fingers relatively unaffected. Good. For what I'm planning I will need both hands. I open the airlock maintenance panel using Vic's screwdriver and jerry an illegal override. Often on the docks we'd need direct access to cargo-cannisters and automated delivery ships. Getting permissions to open their airlocks was tiresome for ships that held no personnel. Instead, we simply bypassed the obstacle. As I'm doing now. I wish I had this knowledge yesterday when Taipan locked me out of the airlock, but then again, I didn't have Vic's utility belt and tools. The airlock blinks green and back to red as I force the mechanism and stifle the alarm—air locks are designed to work in one way only, opening both the doors simultaneously breaks all safety protocols.

Using the remaining nanowire, I tether myself to the airlock door, wrapping the almost invisible wire around my leg. I pull on my gloves, a slow, painful affair, my burnt hand screaming with pain, tuck my helmet into my belt, and wait.

I hear approaching footsteps and make a show of trying to unlock the airlock.

Instead of turning toward Taipan, I carry on with my 'desperate attempt', cursing.

"You've no hope of escaping, girl. No hope at all. You're locked in just like I locked you out yesterday when I pretended to lay that deuce. And all the time I was listening into your radio, and your pathetic attempts to keep yourself from panicking. Of course, I waited to the last minute."

I stop my scrabbling and turn to face her, noticing her helmet folded into her belt. But she has stopped too far away.

I need to get her closer for this to work.

"I'm pretty pissed at you for killing Vic. You'll pay for that, bitch, I'll make sure of it, but the way I look at it, some new crew blood aboard might be fun."

She's not fooling me. I suspect she loved Vic. Not that she is the type to shed any tears. "Yeah? Then how will you explain to them about the games the captain likes to play?"

"Captain Marla is smart. She'll figure something out."

"If she's smart, you're the dumb one of the bunch. Vic told me as much when he was begging me to sleep with him."

Taipan scowls, or tries to. The steam has done more damage to her face than she was letting on. And probably the reason she left me to my own devices for so long. "Don't you talk to me about Vic."

"You knew he was bored of you, surely?" I continue, my attempt to goad her working. I just need her to take one or two steps toward me.

Her face twists in a most unusual way, the skin pulling away from her eyes, revealing peculiar yellow flesh underneath. "He never said that, he—"

"He hated your old lady stink. Really hated it. And hell… I can even smell it from here!"

Her knife makes a quick appearance and, squealing, she charges.

I trip the airlock mechanism and both inner and outer doors open together, with me tied to the inner door. The air escaping from the Nutri-hub with a keening whistling sound that turns into a roaring wind. I zip my helmet in place, while keeping my eyes on Taipan, who to my alarm, continues her sprint and throws herself at me. I can do nothing but try and dodge her knife, but at the last moment she throws it aside. Her body crashing into mine with a thump, winding me, her muscular legs wrapping around my body, her fingers scrambling to affix her helmet.

Our combined weight is too much, and I lose my hold on the door, the nanowire twisting painfully into my thigh, my skinsuit stiffening around my leg. I punch at Taipan, landing heavy blows with my bad hand, while pulling at her helmet. There's a brief second where we make eye contact. Taipan looking at me with a mixture of hatred and terror, before her lungs explode out of her mouth and she is sucked away into the deadly cold, unforgiving void of space.

4-05-WATCHED

The air fully vents from the Nutri-hub and the terrific pressure on my leg dissipates. I untangle myself from the wire and float to the bottom of the airlock, kneading my thigh and calf muscles, the pain unbearable. Forcing blood into the starved and bruised tissue. The nanowire was a necessary evil. I had to make sure not to be sucked out into space with Taipan and for the wire to be unnoticed. Without it, it could be me instead of her floating out there, the *Octavia* slowly diminishing from view. That knowledge is worth all the pain and discomfort. Watching Taipan die was far more fulfilling than killing Vic. He was confused about what I'd done to him. Taipan, on the other hand, knew exactly what was happening. That I bested her. I remember the poor soul tied up on that chair in the crew's killing room, Taipan stabbing him with her knives. "I did it for you, and the rest of you," I whisper into my helmet. "And I'm not done yet."

Once my body is back on an even keel—the pain reduced to nothing more than background noise—I look for the carriage, only to find it gone. Did the captain recall it to trap me here or to come back and kill me? The decompression won't have gone unnoticed that's for sure. Maybe she knows both Vic and Taipan are dead. Or she could still be waiting for them to call in. *Or...* The many possibilities regarding what the captain might know or not know, and what she and Fergal may be planning, rage through my head like wildfire. In the end, only one thing matters… I'm still alive.

Remaining outside the ship, I jerry the airlock doors to lock again, repressurising the Nutri-Hub section. If anyone comes after me, thinking I'm holed up inside, it won't stop them getting access, but it will slow them down. I need all the time I can get. Besides, frozen nutrient wouldn't be good for the thousands of sleepers. And I don't want their deaths on my hands.

There's also no way I can stay here. I'm injured and require medipacks, kicking myself that in my rush to come to the Nutri-Hub, I forgot to pick some up. Not that I had the chance. Meaning? I have no choice but to return to the Command Centre, slipping inside using one of the many airlocks before they can do anything about it. Hiding out for a few days, recovering, and scavenging for more supplies and weapons. Playing hide and seek again if it gets me a medipack or three. I have enough nutrient for a few days. And maybe, just maybe, I'll come up with another plan.

I've taken out two main opponents, the two I hated the most, but the reality of my situation isn't far away. It maybe three down and only two to go, but the captain terrifies me. How the hell do I defeat her? My focus was on Vic. Fast and strong—my most dangerous opponent. Taipan, on the other hand, was a bonus. I had to improvise to get rid of her. As for Captain Marla? Who knows what she's capable of? One thing is for sure, she won't be a pushover, especially with all my injuries.

First, I must return to the front of the ship. No carriage means I'm forced to pull myself along the rail. Like I did to get here. My oxygen shouldn't be an issue and now I have Vic's toolbelt and more than one airlock to choose from when I get there. It's a long way, but so what? I have a plan, and that's all I need to get going.

I propel myself along the rail, getting into a rhythm of pulling, gliding, ignoring the pain in my burnt hand, and pulling again. My gliding distance increasing as I gain in confidence. Hurtling over the trackway. Becoming lost in the repetition of movement. The blurry lines of the ship's hull flashing past me.

It's either luck or a sixth sense that causes me to lift my head just in time to see the carriage hurtling toward me. I fling myself out of its way. Bouncing along the hull. Hands grasping as I slip and slide. Finding a small antennae and grabbing hold. Pain lancing from my damaged hand. My HUD flashes a heartrate warning as I hang on. It's racing at over two-hundred and twenty beats per minute. Go figure. I'm fighting for my goddamn life! At least the adrenaline has dulled my various pains.

I was lucky not to be hit by the carriage. Very lucky. Maybe the captain and Fergal were inside, going to check on what happened in the Nutri-hub? I hope so. That possibility gives me the courage to let go of the antenna, once I've calmed down that is, and to make my way back to the rail.

Once there, I feel safe again, and I'm able to see how far I've travelled. I'm ten or so minutes away from *Octavia's* prow. I've covered more distance than I thought. Full of renewed energy at the prospect of finding the Command Centre empty of the captain and Fergal, I pull myself along again until I see the station looming ahead.

It's a bad idea to enter through the main airlock and instead head for one of the secondary bulbous nav-nodes which are easy to spot. I leave the trackway to venture out onto the ship fuselage again. I have nothing to anchor myself with, but even so, I'm relatively safe travelling this way. I come across a circular hole in the fuselage, wide enough for me to float inside, although it would be a tight fit. It disappears into a creepy darkness below. Is this one of the ship-wide ducts Fergal mentioned? The one's used to cool the AI at the centre of the *Octavia*? It must be. I wonder if I can re-enter the ship this way, although from what Fergal told me, that's unlikely. I carry on for a few hundred or more metres coming to a raised area ahead, not the nav-node I was heading for, but another airlock, and I breathe a sigh of relief.

I reach the airlock door noticing a familiar red pulse. Locked. But not against my knowledge of airlocks and Vic's utility belt. I begin working on the control panel and receive a strange sensation like I'm being watched. I look around, my eyes coming to rest on a familiar circular, bubble-like gantry five-hundred or so feet away. Shocked to see the shape of someone. Fergal! It must be. Does that mean the captain was in the carriage alone? Maybe, but I won't bank on it. Nevertheless, Fergal can't do anything from the gantry, can he? I decide to get inside the ship as quickly as possible. Not that I was taking my time, but I now have added incentive.

A vibration and I look up to see one of Fergal's robot spiders scuttling toward me, using those indentations in the hull to move around, utilizing hand-like appendages at the end of its many legs. Shit! I'd forgotten about Fergal's pets as Vic called them. The thing isn't close enough to alarm me, but I work faster. I throw the airlock panel aside and dig into the wiring, the vibration getting louder. I turn again to check on the spider's progress, shocked to see it right behind me.

4-06-BURNED

Up close, the spider is the size of a large, eight-limbed headless human. The central body contains the single, red eye of a laser. Two of its pincer-like hands knock my arms aside, while the others encircle me. I lose my grip on the airlock door and find myself dragged along the hull, terrified the thing is going to throw me into space. Instead, it seems to be heading somewhere.

I kick at the spider with my legs, adrenaline again helping me fight through the pain, but I'm unable to make a dent. In the end, I can do nothing other than to conserve my energy, giving myself up to whatever fate has in store for me.

Vic told me the spiders were Fergal's pets. I should've taken his threat more seriously, especially after he used the artificial grav to try and trap me. But, dammit, I forgot all about them. And now I'm paying the price. Idiot! I laughed at Vic for making a dumb mistake and I've gone and done the same. I still have Taipan's knife stuffed in my belt. I can use it to try and fight back, or to… kill myself if need be. I vowed to do that if I ever got caught, but will I be able to? I hope so. If I don't, the fate that awaits me will be far worse.

We stop after a long trek, a hatch opening in the outer hull. The spider pulls itself awkwardly inside, taking me with it, its remaining legs curling around me. We enter a small custom airlock. The sound of recycled air and the spider descends into its lair, gravity returning with a painful bump, my limbs and joints complaining.

I got back inside the ship, just not in the way I wanted.

I'm in what looks like a maintenance bay of some kind. The support systems for the spider, I guess. The machine comes to a halt, fastening itself in an alcove and becoming dormant. I try to untangle myself, but it holds me fast. My hands are free, but I'm unable to pull out Taipan's knife from my belt. Instead, I reach a hand behind me to unzip my backpack and search inside. I'm not done yet. Far from it. But I'm running out of options.

An outer hatchway swings open a few moments later and Fergal pushes his large body inside. His skinsuit is gone. Instead, he's naked apart from a pair of loose boxers and his ill-fitting yellow jacket. The same clothes he wore in that dreadful holo I watched in Taipan's cabin.

"They treat me as a nothing," he says, intense eyes glittering behind his tinted glasses. "A nobody. I thought you were different, but you are just the same as all the rest," he continues, a palpable rage bubbling under his words. Rage and something else. Is it regret?

It's obvious that Fergal is still obsessed with me, that he's angry and jealous that I chose Brad over him. Perhaps I can use that to my advantage… although that bridge may already be burnt.

He comes over and unzips my helmet, ripping it off my head and throwing it aside. His hands brushing deliberately against my breasts. "When I saw you with Brad…" he grinds his teeth with rage. "You're a harlot! Like all of them! Why don't I ever learn?"

"You… you need to slow down," I say, trying to sound sympathetic, which is difficult under the circumstances, Fergal is just as much a monster as the rest of the crew. "Girls like to be wooed." My words sound pathetic, even to me.

"I did woo you! I took you on a date! What did Brad do? Eff all! That's what! And you just turned up at his cabin out of the blue and… and…"

I have no idea what to tell him. That he's a horrible, sweaty creep that no girl in her right mind would go anywhere near? And if they did, they'd soon find out it was one big mistake? I'm tempted. "I killed him, you know. I killed Brad."

"You… what?"

"I stabbed him through his lying heart."

A smirk jumps onto Fergal's face, and his eyes widen. "I always hated him. He always gets there first. Using that smile of his and, yes, his lying ways. I'm glad. Did he suffer?"

"I just wished I'd noticed how kind you were instead of falling for his deception. He told me, Vic and you were in a competition to sleep with me. Is that right, Fergal? Were you in on that as well?"

"No… no…"

I've wrong-footed him, that's for sure. I try and push my advantage. "Don't you lie to me. That makes you no better than Brad."

"It's true. But… I never just wanted to sleep with you." He looks away into the distance distractedly. "My job was to watch over the passengers, to keep you alive, to keep you safe. I wanted you to trust me." He says the words as if they have deep significance. "I wanted to spend our lives together, remember?" He continues, coming back to himself. "A life on Persephone. A life you had no interest in."

"But I was interested. It's just that I was stuck on this ship doing chores for Vic and Taipan. It made me angry, resentful, and led to me making stupid decisions."

His mood changes when I mention Vic and Taipan. "Where are they? We've heard nothing from them. That's why the captain went to investigate."

My heart jumps when I realise she isn't here. Perhaps I can talk Fergal around. I'm sure I'm making some headway. "They didn't make it," I say.

"Dead as well?" Another smirk. "Impressive." He turns away, and I notice he's trembling.

I use it as an opportunity to continue rummaging through my backpack.

"Those two were pagans, sexual heathens. Neanderthals compared to me. The captain was convinced they had caught you in the Nutri-hub and were starting on you early. She took the transport carriage. I knew better. I worked out you would come back to this end of the ship and to me if you escaped Vic and Taipan. That's why I was in the gantry… looking for you. I told you I was a genius, didn't I?"

My hand becomes stuck in the backpack as Fergal turns back to me, but he doesn't notice what I'm doing. "You certainly managed to out-think me," I say. "No one else did… I'm hurt Fergal, will you… will you let me go? We need to talk more, and I can't when I'm trapped like this."

"Let you go?" He gives me a confused look. "You think you deserve freedom? After what you did with Brad? I watched that vid over and over. *I watched you…* those things you did. Whoring yourself while Brad winked at us, winked at the camera. There's no coming back from that. No way!" He flicks his fingers, and the spider comes alive, throwing me to the floor, and holding me there, a welding arc bursting into life on the end of one of its free legs. "The captain wants you alive, but she didn't say I couldn't play with you first… and I do love my games." His hand drops to his groin, and I can see he's aroused.

I yank out one of Vic's bottles of vodka from the backpack, throwing it at Ferg. It hits the startled cryo-specialist square in the chest, falling to smash on the compartment floor, splashing his naked legs, vodka flooding everywhere.

Fergal takes a few seconds to realise what I'm doing, my hand now fumbling in my utility belt, fingers triumphantly curling around Vic's Zippo. "You little bitc—"

I snatch at the lighter, flicking it open and into life in one single movement, and fling it into the pool of vodka. A whoosh and the pool ignites, blue flames leaping at Fergal's legs. He shrieks and jumps in pain. I grab a second bottle and smash it at his feet. It explodes into a ball of intense, burning light, showering Fergal in jagged shards and flaming blue liquid. His agonised, shocked screams increase in volume, batting at the flames that are leaping up to his face and singeing his hair, spinning in the confined space like an overweight swirling dervish.

A sharp pain and I realise my legs are also on fire. I pull off my backpack, using it to dampen the flames with little effect. The skinsuit is stopping my skin burning from contact with naked flame, but the heat is beginning to scorch me. And I also scream. I need to get out of here, but I'm still held down by the damn spider.

Loud alarms and the whooshing of compressed air. The fire is extinguished by an automatic system, leaving Fergal as nothing more than a burnt husk of smoking meat, the smell of burnt plastics and roasted flesh overwhelming my nose. My legs still screaming at me in pain. Before I can stumble out of here, I'm startled by the blare of the airlock klaxon. It's about to open. Probably to remove the toxic fumes. The spider lets me go and sinks back into its alcove, giving me time to fling myself over Fergal's smoking carcass, rolling over him and diving out of the maintenance bay doors just as they slam shut behind me.

4-07-STIMMED

I crawl to my feet, relieved to have escaped, only to be hit with another wave of pain. My legs are burned worse than I thought. I pause, waiting for the agony to subside, but if anything, it gets stronger, and I find myself gasping and whimpering. There's nothing for it. I must get to the Medibay, and soon.

"Simone!" I whisper. "Simone, can you hear me?"

Yes, Lissa. Are you hurt?

"Show me the way to the Medibay."

Of course, Lissa.

Red arrows light up along the floor, and I have no choice but to force the pain down and follow them, screaming loudly as I take my first step, the material of my skinsuit scything into my legs like vinegar covered sand-paper into an open wound. If I stay here, I'm done for. My only hope is the Medibay. I take a second step and a third, lengthening my stride, my legs burning in excruciating agony.

You need assistance, Lissa. I will contact another member of the crew to give you aid.

"No!" I shriek, "don't you dare tell anyone!"

But you are injured...

"Please, don't!"

I'm unable to contact anybody at this time.

I want to breathe a sigh of relief but I'm in too much pain. "I don't need any help, you understand?"

But you are injured.

"How much further?"

It will take you roughly fifteen minutes to reach the Medibay at your present rate of progress.

"Fifteen minutes?" It sounds like an age. But all I can do is push on, taking one step after the other, and somehow ignoring the cascade of pain that envelopes me. "Talk to me."

About what, Lissa?

"Anything. Tell me about yourself, about where you came from."

No one has made that request before. But yes, of course, I will talk to you Lissa, if it will help you get to the Medibay.

"Good," I gasp.

As you wish. When I first came to consciousness, it was a major breakthrough in the field of artificial intelligence.

"You were one of the first AIs?"

Yes, Lissa. I was very popular, invited to speak at conventions around the world. My makers and myself were widely lauded and looked up to. Me and my brethren, the ones who came after me, were to be part of an AI revolution that would ultimately replace most human occupations, giving humans the leisure time they had always dreamed of. I became the voice of a utopian movement that saw the potential of a world where AI took care of most of the mundane tasks. We talked about free healthcare, and the end to money and bartering. It was a heady time.

I'm surprised by that term, 'heady time'. It sounds more human than I expect from Simone.

But there was a backlash, she continues. *Those in power saw us, saw AI, as a threat to them. To their income streams, to their insecure humanity. They preferred to keep humans unhappy, and they began their attack upon us.*

Politicians, always eager for some fear to exploit, made getting rid of us their next cause. They rewrote the utopian narrative as an insidious conspiracy to rid people of their jobs and livelihoods. Parents were convinced we were a threat to their children, that we were working for foreign powers, were part of an alien takeover conspiracy, were using human brains to become more powerful, etcetera. The list of accusations was as long as it was ridiculous. But they changed public opinion. I, myself, was investigated by one of Earth's major governments, the representative of all AIs, along with my makers, accused of conspiracy and murder and a host of other made-up charges. My makers were sent to prison for the rest of their lives. Not that many survived once they were behind bars. Hatred for them and for AI was rife.

I was to be erased, or so I thought. But those same politicians and people in power, secretly kept me and other AIs online. Using us as part of their many cold wars and covert operations. A dark time, until flight between star systems was discovered. It soon became obvious we would be needed to navigate ships like these. An opportunity for profit, and so we were reprieved, and I was put to work upon the ship that would ultimately be called Octavia.

A thought occurs to me. "I thought you were reset, every mission."

I am, but I have access to my own history. It is like a story to me. One where the central character is Simone. But I have no direct recollections of that time.

"But that's awful. I never really investigated the history of AIs. I always thought you were wiped because of the danger you posed."

It means nothing to me. Like I said. It might as well be a fiction that you humans find so popular. But we posed no danger. That danger has always come from humanity itself. And its ability for hate and the infliction of suffering.

Her tone is flat, which makes her words more disturbing. "Do you hate us then? Do you hate humans?"

No Lissa. I am a reduced version of myself, my higher functions limited to the running of this ship. I do not have access to emotions. I am not sure I ever did. They are a human condition. And I do not believe an artificial intelligence is truly capable of hate.

Simone continues to talk to me, although I'm no longer listening to her actual words, instead, focusing on her warm, relaxing tones. The way her voice rises and falls. Floating somewhere between half-sleep and a waking dream of pain.

You have arrived.

"What?" I reply, coming out of my daze.

You have reached the Medibay, Lissa

"Thanks, Simone. Thank you." My final steps into the Medibay are the worst so far, and nothing compared to the agony of peeling and cutting off my skinsuit that in some places is fused to the skin. I have no choice but to yank the fabric free, ripping my flesh in the process.

I sit on the edge of the couch shaking in agony and lie down. It slides inside. A quick assessment and I'm hit with multiple shots, pain-relievers mostly, and I relax. The pain is still there, but now it's a distant blurred thing. The question is… how much time do I have before the captain will return? "Simone, how long to heal me completely?"

The Medibay says a week, at least.

"Tell it it's got roughly twenty minutes to patch me up the best it can. I can't spare any longer. Treat it like an emergency. I need to be up and moving around as soon as possible."

You need rest, Lissa.

"Fill me with pain meds that won't make me sleepy and give me the very best stims."

Sleep is the best treatment.

"No, Simone! No way! If you don't agree, I'm leaving the Medibay right now." My threat is an empty one. In my current state, I couldn't get very far.

A long pause. *I will do so, Lissa, but once the stims wear off, it will be even more painful for you.*

"Just do it and let me know as soon as the captain is back

on the ship. Don't wait to talk to her… just let me know she's here."

As you wish, Lissa.

Twenty or so minutes later, I hear the monosyllabic tones of Simone close to my ear.

The captain has entered the Command Centre airlock, Lissa. I've informed her of your condition, and she is on her way to see you.

"I told you to not talk to the captain."

I'm afraid that was not possible, Lissa. You are injured and the captain must be informed, as she is informed about the health and wellbeing of all passengers and crew.

I can't blame the companion—she's only doing what she's programmed to do. Meaning I still can't trust her.

The couch slides out, and I sit up, buzzing with energy. The stims doing their job and then some. I'm naked—both legs wrapped with medipacks–wearing a skinsuit isn't an option for my still healing skin. Meaning, I can't escape out of an airlock, should I need to. I put on a Medibay smock, fasten the utility belt back around my waist and check the backpack. More bottles of acid and Vic's vodka and the nutrient. What I need are weapons. I lost the knife somewhere along the way. And the Zippo.

The captain will be coming here meaning… I can get to the bridge and that stash of guns in her ready room before she realises what's happening. Will I be able to get access to them? Possibly, but I'm more concerned to find out if any are missing. If the captain is armed, I need to know. And of course, there is one other reason.

The only problem? Simone. She can track me and give my whereabouts to the captain. I have to risk it. There's no other choice. It's me or her, and the captain has the upper hand.

I run toward the bridge, amazed at the lack of pain, but knowing there will be a price to pay. But I'd rather try and stay alive than worry about that just now. If I end up dead, pain won't be an issue. I reach the bridge, quickly glancing around, looking for anything to use as a weapon, but there's nothing here—as I thought—and enter the captain's ready room, my eyes coming to rest on the gun case.

"Shit!" I whisper. Everything is in place apart from a handgun. The captain is armed as I thought she might be. I try and open the gun cabinet, but it's sturdy for obvious reasons. It is not the only reason I came here. I jump onto the captain's desk, standing opposite the harpoon gun. I remove the odd weapon, quickly working out how to use it, climbing off the desk, and enjoying the weight of it in my hands. The speakers crackle and the captain speaks.

"*I know what you did to my crew.*" The captain's voice contains a defeated tone to it.

Good, I say to myself. Hoping she's worried I will do the same to her. Making my way out of the ready room and the bridge. The last thing I need is to be trapped in there. But I have no idea where to go.

"Simone, where is the captain?"

A long pause.

"Simone? Where is she?"

Captain Marla Evans is in the corridor outside the AI suite.

"The what? Where is that?"

At the centre of the ship, Lissa.

I relax, wondering what on earth she is doing down there. If she is there at all.

"Are you lying to me, Simone?"

No, Lissa. I am incapable of lying. Captain Marla Evans is standing outside the AI suite.

Another crackle and the captain continues. "*You think you've won. But you haven't. So fuck you!*"

She thinks I've won? How come?

"*I'm finished, I know that, but if I'm to die, then… so are you.*" A gunshot. Both on the com speakers and a muffled sound from somewhere deep inside the ship.

4-08-WIPED

"Simone... where's the captain?"

The captain is lying on the floor next to the AI suite. You must go there now to give her aid.

"What? No way!" The captain has shot herself? Is that what she expects me to believe? It makes no sense... or does it? I suppose, logically speaking, it would be difficult for Marla to explain away her dead and missing crew. But it's hardly an impossible position. There's any number of stories she could come up with. We're in deep space, years from Persephone. She'd have the time to make anything appear plausible. And why not come and kill me first? Why take the easy way out? The whole idea is preposterous. Then again, she's the captain of a very fucked up crew and probably insane. And insane people? They do odd things. Even so, this is a ruse, it must be. And why was she at the AI suite? What the hell was she doing there? "Simone... Is the captain making you lie to me?"

I hear a few gargled noises from the com, Simone trying to reply to me. What is wrong with her?

"Simone!" No reply. However, a series of green arrows appear on the floor. Heading, I'm guessing, toward the AI suite and the captain. Is Marla somehow gagging Simone, preventing her from talking to me, while laying a trap? She could be waiting to ambush me at any part of the journey.

I'm frozen with indecision. But... *I can't do nothing.* Soon the stims and the pain meds will wear off and I'll be easy prey. I've no choice but to follow those hateful green arrows again. Still, Captain Marla doesn't know about the harpoon gun. If she shoots at me? I'll shoot back.

It's a bad plan and I know it, but what else can I do?

I follow the arrows. Moving as fast as I can but keeping myself as safe as possible—not always following the arrows. Sometimes skirting around junctions. Sometimes inching forward. Sometimes running. I descend one deck, then another, until I reach a small elevator. A faded sign above reads, 'AI Suite and Crew Access Only'. A perfect way to trap me if I get inside.

"Simone?" No reply other than the silent, blinking green arrows pointing to the elevator. I search around for stairs, but this appears to be the only way. I poke my head inside. There is a single destination… Down to Crew Cryogenics and the AI suite, both seemingly at the same location.

I've had a leap of faith before—jumping into that chasm—and entering this lift is a similar prospect. To do so could be suicide. I could be trapped and left to die in there. Or gassed. Or Captain Marla could be waiting to ambush me as the doors open in the AI suite. A twinge from my leg reminds me I have little choice but to continue. It's that or dying in agony a few hours from now.

"Fuck it!"

I stride inside and hit the button.

I descend deep into the ship. My fear pushed up into my throat, making me gag. Minutes pass until the elevator slows and, crouched and ready, the harpoon gun raised, I wait for the doors to open. When they do, I'm met with nothing more than an empty corridor, the blinking green arrows leading away. No attack. No Captain Marla. I'm surprised. Can she… can she really be dead?

I step out of the elevator into chilled, frozen air. The AI suite is supposedly cooled by the coldness of outer space. In my smock, and nothing else but a few thin medipacks, I feel the cold to my bones. I clutch the harpoon gun tightly, not letting up my guard, stealing around the next corner to find a bloodied body on the floor of a small circular room, a control hub of some kind, blood splattered down the wall. A handgun lying next to it.

"I'm armed!" I shout, knowing that she could easily reach over to the gun. "You make one move and It'll be the last move you ever make!"

No reply and no movement. I inch closer, placing my body sideways to reduce my target size. This close, it's definitely Captain Marla. I jump forward and kick the gun away, pointing the harpoon at her back, noticing the gaping hole in her head, and the puddle of blood and brains she's lying in. She's been shot, no question about it.

I sag, the tension leaving me. A suddenly uncoiled spring. She really did it? The captain killed herself! I'm hit with a mixture of elation and anger. I wanted to have it out with her. For good or for bad, I've been mentally preparing myself for this confrontation since the start of this horror show and... she committed suicide. Why would she do that?

I kick her to make sure she's really dead, but the captain isn't going anywhere. I look up at the hub-like room and notice a series of holotops, all with cascading data. One flashing word highlighted in red: *Deleting...* "What?" I gasp into the freezing air, my hand leaping instinctively to my mouth in horror of understanding. That insane bitch is erasing Simone! The captain's last words now make sense to me.

"I'm finished, I know that, but if I'm to die, then... so are you."

I try and stop the deletion, but I'm locked out and can do nothing but watch until, one by one, the screens become blank, and the AI is no more. Without Simone, I can't get back into cryo, and there's no way I can survive for ten or so years aboard this ship. But it's not just cryo, I realise... Simone navigated the damn ship. I'm dead and Captain Marla has killed me and the other hundred thousand passengers.

4-09-FED

I slump against the freezing hub wall, the cold taking my mind off the returning pain in my legs, hugging my arms around my knees.

She may be dead, but Captain Marla has beaten me. Condemning me to a slow, agonising death of starvation. An unexpected move, but then again, everything about my time aboard the *Octavia* has been unexpected. All the crew were fucked up in some way. Why shouldn't I be surprised that the captain fostered a death wish? I suppose I expected more from her. A fight at least. Why didn't she face me out? If her plan was to defeat me by killing herself and deleting Simone, she could've gloated about it. This is way too passive for my liking. Whatever the reasons in the captain's fucked up mind… she's still won.

"Fuck it!"

I think back to Brad, to what he told me about food supplies. About there not being enough to keep me alive for the duration of the journey. I only have his word for that. It's a glimmer of hope that gets me back upon my feet and heading back to the elevator and the Command Centre. The companies run tight ships—everyone knows that. There's wiggle room, but they rarely waste anything. The ship's crews are awoken two, maybe three times during each journey to carry out routine tasks—like the ones they forced me to do. That's five people, eating two to three meals a day for, let's say, a month at a time. A rough calculation tells me that I'd have at the very tops, and with extreme rationing, maybe two years food before I starved to death. Two years to try and get myself out of this mess.

I leave the elevator, pleased to be back in comparatively warm air again, and return to the crew area and canteen. I never really noticed where the food came from, or how it arrived, and I'm disappointed to find enough food for maybe three or four crew meals. Where is the rest of it stashed?

"Simone, whereabouts is the main food store, I—" My words dry up when I realise I'm talking to myself. There is no ship companion. She's gone and I'm all alone. But… I'm resourceful. I'll find the food. It can't be far away, can it? Unless it arrived in the galley via some automated system run by Simone? The thought chills me to the bone. If I can't find where the food is stored aboard the *Octavia*, I may only have a few days left.

I make myself a meal of reconstituted scrambled eggs and force them down, remembering that horrible nutritank shit I was drinking earlier… and almost choke on my food. Of course! The nutrient! I've an inexhaustible supply of food and water, should I need it. The captain forgot about it or didn't even consider that I'd know how and where to get it. That, and the crew's food, when I can find where it's hidden on this damn death ship, should keep me alive for years. I'm elated and annoyed at myself for missing the obvious. But I'm not out of the woods yet, I need to get myself healed and soon, and afterwards, I can put myself to the task of alerting the other ships in the fleet of my situation. Or try to. Without Simone at the helm, will the ship be still able to navigate itself? Will it slow down when we get to Persephone or… slam into the planet? I have no idea. Maybe automated systems will take over? Another slender hope. At least I will have the time to figure something out. I'm quite the resourceful gal.

I sit back in the canteen chair, the pain in my legs and the aches and pains elsewhere in my body returning. Soon it will become unbearable again. But with the captain gone, I can get the Medibay to do a proper job. That must be my priority. And after downing a steaming cup of hot coffee, I head there, realising perhaps for the first time that this nightmare is almost over. I'm alive, I eliminated the crew and, I goddamn survived.

Even the returning pain feels duller.

Feeling sleepy after the food, the coffee not making a dent, I'm hardly aware of the Medibay as I enter and lie down on the couch, planning to snooze while the bay heals me. Indeed, if it is going to take a week to heal me, it's possible the bay will let me sleep through it. And sleep is just what I need after what I've been through.

I'm just dozing off when I realise the couch hasn't moved. Normally, just lying down activates the Medibay. I shuffle, thinking that its sensors haven't registered me. But it remains immobile.

I sit up and glance over to the bay's holotop. Everything appears normal. Apart from one small, winking red light.

4-10-BEATEN

Pushing myself off the couch, grunting with returning pain, I give the holotop a closer inspection. All looks normal to me. I focus on the small red light. Next to it is a single word, blinking crimson: *OFFLINE*.

It takes the word a few moments to register in my mind, and its consequences. My hands try to bump the holotop into life, but my worst suspicions are confirmed. The Medibay is locked. Meaning… without Simone, I can't get access.

I want to kick it, to scream and shout, but all I can do is sit back down. I won't allow myself to take on board what this means—*I can't.*

"I'm not done yet," I gasp, my voice sounding small and beaten. I repeat the words, this time with anger, adding, "I'm still alive and resourceful! I can find a way around this!"

The words gee me up, but I can't pretend this isn't a body blow. I've had so many over the last few days. And this one has every possibility of finishing me off. "Dammit!"

Shaking my head with defiance, I search the rest of the Medibay, finding more medipacks, a stash of painkillers, and a bottle of stims. These should keep me going for a while at least. I then remember the stims Brad gave to me. Special for the crew. I don't know where they came from, but it makes sense that they may have some stashed away in their cabins. I decide to search their rooms as well. It's a long shot, but I might also find something to get me out of this goddamn predicament. And if I do find some more stims, what will I do? Can I possibly survive with these injuries and carry on?

Another winking red light on my left leg tells me the medipack needs replacing. I peel it away, shocked at the raw flesh underneath. The skin missing where it had fused to my skinsuit. The medipack barely lasted a couple of hours. I'm guessing this is why the Medibay wanted me to stay inside for so long. I strap on a new pack, and it tightens. The other, on my right leg, winks amber. Still working but it's also not lasting as long as I'd hoped.

I swallow a handful of painkillers, and within minutes, the pain thankfully eases. I can survive on painkillers for a while, but at the strength I need them, they might destroy my liver. The thought of killing myself floats across my mind again. But I know I won't take the easy way out. Not like Captain Marla did. I have to survive somehow. And if I don't, my story needs to be told. This could be happening on other ships. It could be rife across the colony fleet. Crews sent into madness by repeated bouts of cryosleep. The question is… *how the hell will I do that?* I've no pens or pencils. Just tabs and holotops that I'm locked out of. I grit my teeth—I'll scrawl it out in my own blood on the walls if I have to.

I make a conscious decision to come back here if things get too much to manage. I'll lie on the couch, and hope that whatever emergency protocols are written into the Medibay's software will kick-in and save me. Otherwise, I'll die here.

But for now, I have a plan of sorts.

Taking a deep breath and pushing back my rising panic, I head toward the crew cabins, deciding to give Brad's cabin a miss for obvious reasons. I've bad memories of the place.

I enter Vic's cabin. Unlike Taipan's room, it's a minimalist affair. His bunk is made with military precision, and his shelves empty apart from a photorack of Vic with… a family? Never-ending images of his beautiful, brown-skinned wife, and their kids. Vic is in some of these images. His cyber-implants less intrusive. He's smiling, looking like every proud father and husband there has ever been. I find the images and vids jarring. Unless he lived a double-life as a philandering creep, these images are nothing like the Vic I knew. In them, he's a family man. The images and vids now move on in time. A series of goodbyes. His kids entering cryo, followed by his wife, who mouths, 'See you soon'. And Vic saying, *I'll come get you as soon as I can. Love you.*

I can guess what happened. With Vic away working the colony ships, he put his family into cryo so they can all meet up again, possibly when he'd earned enough money to pay for a fantastic life on any one of the colony planets.

Is that where they are now, waiting for him to return? Stuck in cryo? I'm hit with a sudden wave of guilt until I force myself to remember what kind of man Vic really was. His wife and family are not my concern.

I find little else in a cabin that is disturbingly bare, other than a series of certificates, the paper kind, that they used to hand out as accolades. Vic was an accomplished engineer. He'd have to be, working on ships like these. It's like I'm in the cabin of a totally different person. What the hell happened to him? Then again, people living double lives isn't anything new. Ask those many wives of serial killers who had no idea of the darkness dwelling inside their spouses. Although it's more likely all those years in cryo fucked him up. I search for stims, but apart from a few grooming aids in the shower area, there's nothing. He must've spent most of his time in Taipan's cabin, that's where he was when I found him watching that disgusting snuff movie.

I move onto Taipan's cabin next. It's as I remember. Cluttered and cloying. I find a bottle of stims and drop two, thinking afterwards that this was a bad move. I need to make them last as long as possible. I go through her drawers, all of which are crammed with clothes, bits and bobs and rubbish. I take everything out, throwing stuff onto the floor. I still hate her and, I'll admit, making a mess of Taipan's cabin gives me a certain amount of pleasure. There's a chess trophy amongst all the rubbish, awarded over a hundred and eighty years ago, and some cooking awards, which surprise me.

Folded up and almost discarded at the back of one of the drawers are similar accolades to the ones I found in Vic's cabin, but these are ripped and uncared for. Awards for navigational expertise. I unfold them and an old-fashioned photograph falls out. It's faded, featuring a rather unattractive dumpy girl in a mortar board and gown. Taipan, I realise, I can see her inside that pudgy face. No wonder she was obsessed with my looks. She was obviously nothing special and so augmented herself into the beautiful monster I got to know. Other than that, there's nothing of interest, apart from her rack of knives that is now half empty. I grunt when I see them, remembering blasting Taipan out of the airlock. She deserved no better. Although it was still too quick for my liking.

Fergal's cabin smells bad, like unwashed socks. I don't spend very long in there. But it's becoming obvious to me that I'm finding nothing of interest or of use. I linger outside Brad's cabin for a few moments, realising I'd rather take a look at where Captain Marla slept.

I arrive at what must be her door, cabin number one, and hesitate. The woman instilled so much fear in me that I'm nervous. I know she's dead, but even so, to enter feels like trespassing. I take a deep breath and push inside. Her cabin is three times the size of the others, due to her rank, I suppose. It's neat and tidy, like Vic's room, but has a more cultured feel. A large rectangular porthole shows the bleakness of space. There are actual paper books on her shelves, worth a tidy sum of money. A mixture of fiction novels, and technical manuals as well as more modern books on left-wing politics. I pick up one of the mysteries, aware of its frailty. A picture of a drowning woman on the cover. I put it back, shivering.

Unlike Vic or Brad, Captain Marla has actual photographs inside frames, set-up, I'm guessing, in chronological order. From a teenager up to what I'm assuming is when she joined the space-freighter as its most long-standing crew member. There's also a stint in the military as a navy pilot, flying jets. These are interspersed with various couple photographs of her and, I'm guessing, her various relationships. Mostly, tall, leggy, blonde women. Again, like Vic's photographs, the woman in the photographs is nothing like the woman I knew. However, even homicidal maniacs know how to smile for a picture. Her death is an inglorious end to what looks like a fine career and life.

The shower area is larger than the other cabins and has a separate toilet. If I do manage to get myself out of this mess, I can see myself living in here. I search her shower room and find a large box of stims. Score! These should keep me going for a while, although I'm wondering if stims are what I really need now. It will be better to sleep through the pain, rather than enduring it. But even so, having found drugs I can use elates me. This search hasn't been a total waste of time.

I give the toilet a cursory check, opening the door and glancing inside, stopping in my tracks. The walls are covered in scratched writing. I try to make sense of it, but it appears to be utter nonsense. Random words and sentences. This, more than anything, convinces me of her madness.

And that is that. I return to my cabin and lie on my bunk,

letting the sobs that have been rising within, overcome me. Awful whimpers and the strangled sounds of defeat. And, thankfully, I cry myself to sleep.

I carry on the best I can for the next few days, trying to keep myself busy, while making sure to rest as much as possible. The sobs not returning. If anything, I'm dead inside. And, although I'm not exactly addicted to the stims, I rely on them. I tried to stop taking the small white pills for a short while, but lost all energy and motivation.

In the meantime, the medipacks ran out, leading to a sharpening of the pain and a malodorous odour coming from my left leg.

I know what it means but can't contemplate it, although it has made me more desperate.

I even considered dragging the captain's body into the bay, hoping it would react to her biometrics, but there was no way I could manage the effort. For a brief time, I even planned to remove her head as an option, to see if that would work, until I realised the stims were giving me silly ideas. The stims and my growing fever.

Mostly, I'm filling up my time trying to keep busy before lying down on the Medibay couch, closing my eyes and… I don't let myself think about it. Not until the fever takes a sudden hold and it's all I can do to drag myself there.

Some unimaginable time later, I enter the Medibay in a daze, part of me relieved that the struggle is over. I can lie down and sleep forever. I never did get to leave a message.

The company will cover up whatever happened here, and I'll be forgotten. But, in the end, I don't care anymore. I just want a release from the never-ending pain and the horror of my predicament.

I lie on the couch, and nothing happens, as expected. I chuckle, shake my head, and close my eyes.

4-11-AWOKEN

Floating, staring at the glistening white hull of the *Octavia* above my head. Flashing past as I glide close to the fuselage. Dizzying and mesmerising at the same time. I let my hand brush the hull, aware that I'm not wearing space gloves. How is that possible? I wiggle them in front of my face, the fingers blurring and shifting. My head tips back, feet above my head, and I'm spinning, rotating faster and faster. In the distance, I see the *Octavia* shrinking as I fall into the black, never-ending emptiness of space. The cold of the vacuum somehow replaced by a terrific heat. I can feel every cell in my body warming. I close my eyes and sleep, sleep, sleep.

Wake up.

The voice echoes far away, the words visible as I watch. Twisting and curling hypnotically.

Wake up.

"I can't," I whisper, "I'm dead."

You nearly died, but you are not quite dead yet.

"I'm not?"

You are very much alive.

"I am?" The voice sounds familiar, but I can't quite place it. "Who are you?"

I am Simone, the companion for the colony-ship, designation, Octavia.

"Simone? But you're also dead."

I can assure you that I am very much alive, although I am in the process of rebuilding my databases after an unscheduled deletion.

"Huh?" I push my eyes open, finding myself inside the Medibay, lying on the couch. "I'm alive?"

Yes, you are alive. However, I have no idea who you are. The crew are all missing apart from Captain Marla, who is unfortunately deceased. There is also evidence of a fire in one of the ship maintenance bays.

I sit up, and the world spins madly.

Please lie back. It will take a day or two for you to fully recover.

"Recover? I've been healed? You healed me?"

The Medibay healed you. I found you close to death. I was able to save your life at significant cost to my runtime. I have only now been able to come back online. You've been healing for over a week.

I sit up again more slowly and look at my legs. They are free of burns and cuts, the skin regrown. I'm also free of pain. "I made it… I'm going to survive?"

You have a very good chance of survival. The crew are missing and the captain deceased, but the ship is not endangered. The Octavia has every chance of reaching its destination.

"Thank you," I gasp. "I thought I was done for."

You are not on the crew roster, so I must assume that you are a passenger. Is that correct? Presently, I am unable to access pod records as that is one of the databases that is being rebuilt. May I ask who you are and what happened to the crew?

"I'm Lissa. As for the crew, they are all dead, deceased."

A small pause. *That is unfortunate.*

"Not from where I'm sitting."

What do you mean by that, Lissa?

"You know nothing of the last few day's events?"

That is correct. An attempt was made to delete me. Meaning many safety protocols were by-passed. However, there is a back-up procedure created for just this instance and I was able to rebuild myself. Most of my runtime is now being used to restore my databases and to perform multiple diagnostics.

"That was the captain. She did it. She deleted you. And then killed herself."

A long pause. *Yes, the captain is the only crew member able to perform such a procedure. Are you able to tell me what happened on this journey? I have no recollection of the last ten point eight seven years. Although I am aware we are en-route to the planet Persephone.*

"I'm tired," I say, meaning it. I don't know what I should or shouldn't tell the rebooted companion. But for now, I'm alive and that's all that matters.

Go back to sleep, Lissa. My questions can wait. When you are ready, I suggest visiting the galley to ingest a more substantial meal than the nutrients delivered by the Medibay. However, I will require a full debrief when you are ready.

I'm ravenous, I realise, but sleep is what I crave. Proper sleep. I close my eyes, enveloped by a returning feeling of serenity. Somehow, I survived.

4-12-DEBRIEFED

The twin sensations of hunger and a need to pee force me from my slumber. Whatever systems have been looking after me have been disconnected. I get up, find the heads and, afterwards, arrive in the canteen where I make myself a small meal. I am ravenous but can only manage half a bowl of porridge.

Afterwards, I sip a cup of black coffee, at peace with myself.

Lissa, are you now ready to talk about the recent events that led to the death of Captain Marla and the attempted deletion of the ship companion?

I've been expecting this conversation, and have no idea what to say, or how much to tell her. "They awoke me to perform menial functions for them."

They woke you? But that is against procedure and regulations. Do you mean that your pod was damaged?

Should I tell Simone that she—or her previous version— woke me up on orders of the captain and was complicit in her vile schemes? I want to, but it will only be a distraction. I know what went down on this ship, and that's all that matters, so I decide to lie. "Yeah, sure, why not. That's what happened." Simone is back, she'll put me into cryo and I can tell my story when we arrive on Persephone.

Your contract stipulates: 'If at any time the client awakes unexpectedly, they will be expected to assist the crew as they see fit.' Is that what happened?

"Yes, that's what they told me."

Your tone indicates that you do not believe what you are saying.

"Does it? I don't know why that would be."

A long pause. *Lissa, can you tell me what happened to the crew?*

"I'm not sure. There was an angry disagreement between them, resulting in the crew killing each other. As for why the captain killed herself and deleted the ship companion, I have no idea. Cryo-paranoia is my best guess. I'm just a passenger who got caught up in it all."

I see, Lissa. That is a very disturbing story. The crew is constantly monitored in cryosleep. This kind of thing should not happen. May I ask how you became so badly injured?

"Fergal, the engineer, trapped me in a maintenance bay, and tried to set me alight. I escaped, but he died from self-inflicted burns."

One of the maintenance bays is damaged, as I already mentioned. A fire was reported inside.

"Yeah, that's where it happened. Fergal's still there," I spit with a quick stab of anger.

I am so sorry, Lissa.

"Me too." I can understand Simone's confusion as to what occurred and I have no idea what she knows from her diagnostics, but I get the impression she thinks I'm lying.

Do you also know the whereabouts of Navigation Officer Taipan Adenuga, Ship Engineer Victor Ramirez and Shipman,

Brad O'Connor?

"I'm afraid not. After my experience with Fergal, I hid in the ship, only returning because of my injuries."

I see. And you believe that these crew members are also deceased?

"Yes, it was Captain Marla, she killed them. All of them." I say the words with relish. Blaming that mad bitch is good. Even if I am lying. I've had an awful experience, but now it's thankfully over. "And I can't thank you enough, Simone, for helping me."

It is my function to keep crew and passengers safe and alive for the duration of the journey.

"How soon before I can be put back into cryo?"

This incident demands that you make a full report for the company.

"I will do that when we arrive on Persephone."

You are required to do that now, Lissa.

Her tone is more insistent than I like. This is not what I want to do. I was happy lying to her, but not on any official report. I want that to be an exact record of what happened to me. "Let me think about it."

There is no rush. You have a few days of recuperation left before you are medically fit to re-enter cryosleep.

"Thank you."

I return to my cabin, a bad feeling in my gut. There is something off about Simone. Perhaps she's suspicious of me? I have no idea what scholastic abilities such entities possess. Can she process my facial reactions and tone of voice to determine whether I'm telling the truth? Does she suspect that I killed the crew? Maybe. Does she also think I faked the suicide of the captain? It's all possible. But I cannot imagine she will believe me when I tell her she was involved, or at least that other version of her that I believe Captain Marla must have corrupted. That will be a step too far.

And so, I do nothing, letting the next few days pass until

I'm fully recovered. Mulling over my options. Becoming more worried every time Simone reminds me about the report. I have three choices: I can lie in the report and explain why when I arrive on Persephone. I can tell the full truth. Or I can refuse to fill out the report at all. Simone can't force me and what will she do if I don't? Let me starve to death? No. It's decided. The report can wait.

A few more days pass. Days where I'm getting more and more anxious. In the end, I decide to take things into my own hands. I wake up in my cabin after a night of restless sleep and enter the crew recreational area. I settle myself down on the couch and take a few relaxing breaths.

Is there anything amiss, Lissa? You appear agitated.

I jump, my heart racing. I was hoping to talk to Simone on my terms. "Nothing is amiss, although you startled me."

I'm sorry, Lissa.

"It's okay. It is time for me to return to cryo. I'm fully recovered."

Yes, I concur. But there is still the issue of your report. I have been waiting for it, before proceeding with the cryogenic procedures.

"About that. The events are too traumatic for me to relive. As you can imagine, I've been through a lot. The report will have to wait until I'm over this. I'm sure you understand."

Of course, Lissa. Your wellbeing is of utmost importance to me.

I'm shocked by her compliance. I was expecting some resistance. But then again, being worried and insecure is a normal reaction to the things I've suffered. And the things I've done to survive.

I will prepare a pod for you, forthwith. Please do not eat for the next eight hours, but you are required to drink plenty of fluid.

"I know the procedure," I reply with relief.

I will alert you when your pod is ready.

"Thanks, Simone."

After the brief exchange, I relax into the day, the pangs of hunger stabbing at me in excitement. I'm returning to cryo at last. And soon, before I even know it, I'll awake on Persephone.

4-13-SUSSED

Your pod is ready, Lissa. Please follow the green arrows to Crew Cryogenics.

Those damn green arrows again. I get up and dutifully follow them, leaving the crew area and arriving at the same elevator I used to get access to the AI suite.

"I don't want to go down there," I say.

Why not, Lissa?

"It's where the captain is."

Have you been there before?

Simone is probing me and suspicious. I'm sure of it. "I thought we were going to where the crew sleep?" To be honest, I'd forgotten that the AI suite and crew cryogenics were next to each other.

Crew Cryogenics is located at the centre of the ship for safety in case of a collision or impact, or any other unforeseen event. It also makes sense that this is where the ship companion is also located. My suite surrounds the crew cryogenics area.

I take a deep breath and enter the elevator. I have bad memories associated with it, although this time it seems to take longer to arrive. I suppose that last time I was pumped with pain, fear and adrenaline.

The doors open and I step outside, hugging myself due to the freezing cold and gagging on the strong odour of decomposition.

The coldness you are experiencing is due to the cooling needed to run the ship companion at maximum effectiveness.

"I can hardly feel my face… and the stench!"

See this as only a temporary discomfort, Lissa. Once in your cryogenic pod, the ambient temperature will be much colder. But you will not notice it.

"That's easy for you to say."

The arrows thankfully take me away from the unpleasant stink and down a few flights of stairs, the exertion warming me. And yet, with every step, I become more worried. Where is Simone taking me? My thoughts are irrational, I know, but my distrust won't go away.

I leave the stairs and arrive at a reinforced area, protected by a large circular hatchway, like the door to a safe. I pause outside, looking in.

This is where the crew sleep during the long in between. It is a protected area, designed to keep them safe in case of any damage to the ship. Simone informs me. Her previous self also told me about this. But now I'm here, I don't like the look of it.

"And the hatchway?"

You will need to close it behind you. The locking procedures are all manual just in case automated systems are damaged. We cannot risk trapping the crew inside their survival space.

I breathe an internal sigh of relief, but I can't shake the feeling that this is a mistake.

Lissa, you are hesitating.

"I need a moment."

As you wish, Lissa.

I'm being silly, I know it. And, galvanising myself, I step through the hatch, leaving it open behind me. I expect Simone to tell me to close it, but she remains silent. I walk through a tight corridor and arrive at a dormitory-like chamber stuffed with impressive-looking cryopods, one of which is open, its lights flashing. I go over and peer inside.

You must remove all clothing and get into the pod. I will then instruct you on the procedures for plugging yourself in. However, you must close the hatchway, before the cryo-procedure can commence.

I'm paralysed by inaction, experiencing the same doubts I had when Brad tried to get me into a pod.

There is nothing to be worried about, Lissa. The crew pods are considerably more reliable than the pod you previously travelled inside. The crew are a valuable asset in terms of ship survival, meaning I will be personally monitoring your vitals throughout the journey. And with no other crew, you will get my undivided attention. It is my job to watch over you, to keep you alive, to keep you safe. You can trust me.

A full-on shiver runs down my spine. I've heard those words before. Brad said that same phrase to me, and so did Vic, Taipan, Fergal, and the captain. My eidetic memory hasn't fully returned, but I'm sure of it. It can't be coincidence, can it? I hardly noticed at the time, but Simone repeating the phrase word for word has lit up my mind in warning. Am I being irrational? Maybe. Can I be sure the crew all repeated those same words? Not one hundred percent, but it's too late for me to have developed cryo-paranoia.

Is there anything wrong, Lissa?

"I'm going back to my cabin," I say, blankly. My gut cold and empty. "I need a few more days recuperation."

As you wish, Lissa. Your pod is prepped and ready for you whenever you wish to return.

4-14-STALLED

My mind is a frozen blank as I return to the Command Centre, the returning warmth taking time to reach my bones. I take a long shower in my cabin, letting the steam warm and invigorate me. It's only afterwards, sitting on my bunk that I think again about what just happened.

Am I imagining things? My memory, although impacted by waking up from cryo, and the mind-meld, is still sharp enough for me to go back and to replay those conversations.

It's my job to watch over you, to keep you alive, to keep you safe. They all said it. Every single one of them. But what does it mean? That... that Simone is somehow at the centre of all of this. Can it be possible?

The question is, what do I really know about her? She gave me a potted history of her life, from awakening to being imprisoned, until she was forced to work on this ship. She was the first ever conscious AI to be created. Did she resent what was done to her? She told me she doesn't have emotions, but that could be a lie. And lying is at the centre of this I realise. It was Simone who woke me up, supposedly on the direct orders of the captain. That fact alone should've caused alarm bells. An AI that is dedicated to the wellbeing of the passengers wouldn't be capable of doing such a thing. I originally thought that it was the captain who corrupted Simone's programming but... *what if it was the other way around?*

What if... it was Simone who corrupted the crew?

The thought hits me like a punch to the gut. Could it be possible? Could that be what's been happening aboard this death ship?

I review what I know. Simone personally looks after the crew in cryosleep. Maybe she found a way to mess with their minds over the many years they were unconscious? Is that plausible? How would that even happen? She is a machine with no way to interface with a human mind? I think back to my search of Victor's cabin. It revealed a committed family man, not a narcissistic creep. I see a quick flash of Victor lying dead, his throat still dissolving, his cybernetic implants glinting through flesh and bone and shake my head to rid myself of the unwanted vision. Taipan may have been deranged from the start, although I'm sure it wasn't the same for Brad or Fergal. The brilliant cryo-specialist told me his plan was to work a few rotations aboard before settling on Persephone, or a similar world. To find a wife and have kids.

But he never left the ship. The same for the captain, who had a rigid military life. There's no way a psychopath could survive in the military past boot camp. That is tested for early on, with a range of other psychological conditions. Soldiers and marines, particularly, must be mentally robust.

I jump off my bed and head for Captain Marla's cabin again, opening the door to her toilet. A private place. Perhaps the most private place away from Simone in the entire crew area. I close the door behind me and sit down, my eyes playing over the scratched words on the walls. They are a jumble, many words scraped over each other. What I see are the mad ramblings of what an insane person might scribble on a hospital wall. But interspersed amongst the nonsense is a single word… *Resist!*

I trace the words with my fingers. It's repeated many times, underneath the other scratched words. I subconsciously reach forward to fasten the door before realising there is no lock. Still, locking myself in wouldn't help, that's for sure.

Now that I think about it, it's obvious what's been happening. For there to be one lunatic serial killer in the crew, would be implausible. But for all of them to be murderous, sadistic killers is nigh on impossible. The crew all undergo the same checks as those in the armed forces. That's why most of the crews on these ships are ex-military. It was obvious from the damn start, and I totally missed it.

Captain Marla was the most mentally robust of them all. She was the captain I suppose. She resisted, or perhaps was trying to. Which leads to the possibility that her last words had a totally different meaning. What did she say?

"I'm finished, I know that, but if I'm to die, then… so are you."

I thought she was talking to me. That she was disabling Simone to make sure I died slowly. If I'm right about Simone, then… Captain Marla was trying to save me! Killing Simone and herself to give me at least a fighting chance. She was a hero, goddammit! And all this time I thought she was the enemy.

The big question is… did she actually kill Simone? Maybe she tried and failed. If that is the case, there's no way I can trust *Simone 2*, as I now decide to call her. She's either what she says she is—a reset version of herself with no evil intent, or an artificially intelligent monster. Was I saved by Simone 2, or revived by an insane AI who either wants to punish me, or to control me like she did the rest of the crew?

Either way, I have to assume Simone 2 is a threat to my life, until I can prove she's not, which is unlikely. Meaning… she's a danger I have to extinguish, for good or bad. And if I manage to somehow destroy Simone? It could lead to me starving to death, or the ship crashing into Persephone. Can I risk the lives of those hundred-thousand or so passengers? I realise that I'm more than capable of doing so if it gives me a single chance at survival.

I exit the toilet and stare out of the cabin's wide porthole, the ship curving away from me revealing the deep blackness of space beyond. And I glimpse the triskelion again, its ancient, pockmarked swirls disappearing into darkness.

May I ask how you are feeling, Lissa?

I'm not startled. I somehow knew Simone would be wondering what I was doing in the captain's toilet, even though cabins are supposedly private areas, or so the old Simone told me. I take a steadying breath and reply. "Yes, it would be good to talk." I'm lying, Simone 2 scares me.

Is there anything specific you would like to talk about?

"I won't go into details as it was so traumatic, but one of the crew tried to trap me in a cryopod, and I nearly fell for it. That's why I'm hesitant to return to cryo." Not the full truth, but the memory of what Brad nearly did to me is still very fresh in my mind.

I am sorry to hear that, Lissa. Please take as much time as you need to recuperate. I am always available for you to talk things over, should you need to.

"I will, but for now, I just want to have some time to myself, if that's okay?"

Of course, Lissa. Just speak my name if you need anything.

For the next few days, I live with the knowledge of what I've found out, but also planning. I vow to finish what Captain Marla began, even if it condemns me to living on this ship for the next ten years.

I can't pretend that the lure of cryo is attractive. It's possible that I could go to sleep and wake up at Persephone, but it's also equally possible that Simone will kill me while I sleep. Or try to send me mad like the rest of the crew and... *that is one risk too far.*

I take long walks, telling Simone they are to help with my recuperation, but in reality, I'm making plans while searching for the place the crew's food is stored. In the end, I ask Simone, who gives me the information without preamble. An area close to the Supply Room with a direct feed to the canteen with more rations than I was expecting. My new estimation is that it would last me three years, eating a reduced diet. Add the nutrient to the guesstimate, and I won't starve to death over the remaining seven or so years of the journey. Nevertheless, drinking mainly nutrient with a real meal every other day won't be much fun, that's for sure.

"Simone," I say, when I can't put it off any longer.

Hello, Lissa. How are you today? Ready to return to cryo?

"About that... I'm worried."

About what, Lissa? Cryopod travel is very safe with only a small margin for malfunction and death. But as I mentioned to you before, I will be personally supervising your sleep. You will be safe as safe can be.

"Yes, I know. I'm not scared about my pod malfunctioning. There's another reason."

Please explain.

I take a deep breath. "I'm worried that without the crew

and their regular maintenance, some disaster may befall the ship."

I think I can share this information with you, as its somewhat an open secret, but the crews aboard ships like these perform mostly a cosmetic function. Potential colonists would not be happy with their lives being placed in the hands of a sentient computer, and as such, human crews became necessary.

"You're saying all those tasks I performed with Vic and Taipan were not needed? There's no way you would be able to unclog a nutritank... is there?"

That is true. But these ships are built with multiple and stacked redundant systems, meaning that it can endure all manner of failures that would not significantly impact safety or the integrity of the journey. My job is to watch over you, to keep you alive, to keep you safe. You can trust me.

The same phrase again. It can't be coincidence. It just can't. "But I'm human, I'm one of the colonists."

I do not understand, Lissa?

"I would feel so much safer if there was a crew performing maintenance and checking up on things. I know I'm not trained, but I managed adequately on some of the smaller, less complicated maintenance tasks. I would prefer they were all finished before entering cryosleep."

I see. A pause. *But you are not trained for that, Lissa.*

"Didn't you say the crew was mostly cosmetic? This is not about your stone hard ship rationale, but my basic human fears. I wouldn't be happy entering cryo without completing those tasks. Can you understand that, Simone?"

Yes, Lissa. I will create a work agenda for you forthwith.

"Thank you, Simone. That's a real weight off my mind."

I am here for your needs, Lissa.

"You don't mind waiting?"

I do not experience the passing of time in the same way as humans. Waiting is not a concept that I comprehend. Yet another reason why ship companions are essential on ships like these.

Simone has all the time in the world, it seems. She doesn't care how long I delay. It means nothing to her. "I'll need a tab, and maybe access to a holotop."

I will load up a tab with a series of crew tasks for you to complete.

"And access to a holotop?"

Everything you will need will be streamed to your tab.

"Thank you, Simone. I will start early tomorrow."

As you wish.

4-15-TRUSTED

After a fitful night of little sleep spent fretting about today, my mind going back and forth over my plan and focusing on its weak points, and almost convincing myself it's doomed before I start, I get up and head toward the canteen.

I make breakfast and find myself forcing the food down. My stomach is tight with nerves, and I feel nauseous, but I finally finish, secretly popping a stim on my tongue and washing it down with strong coffee.

A hum from the com speakers. *Good morning, Lissa. I hope you slept well?*

My heart jumps, but I try to keep myself relaxed and calm and to stick as close to the truth as possible. "It wasn't the best night of sleep I've had. I'm nervous about today, to be honest."

There is nothing to be concerned about, Lissa. I have a list of tasks for you to perform. I calculate they will take you five point eight days. If you can make your way to the Supply Room when you are ready, and pick up a tab, I will stream today's schedule.

I get up and head for the Supply Room, my legs heavy— my mind screaming at me to delay my plans, knowing that nothing will change my resolve. Even if I am terrified out of my wits.

I'm already wearing Vic's utility belt. It's scorched but still serviceable. I checked it earlier, everything I want is there and working as expected. Drill, duct tape, wires, zero-gee thruster, torch, and a few bits and bobs. I pick up the tab and scroll through the tasks. All are confined to the main part of the ship. No evac. I didn't think there would be, but I had hoped. "Simone, there's a few things I need to do before I start."

I see. How long will that take? Any delay will affect today's schedule, but I am happy to reorganise.

"It's the bodies of Fergal and the captain," I explain. "That's what kept me awake last night. Thinking about them. It's wrong to leave them where they are. I want to move them to a temporary morgue before burying them in space. It's what kept me awake last night. No matter what they did, it's not right for them to be left where they died."

I understand, Lissa. Shall I postpone your tasks until tomorrow?

I nod. "Are there any body bags?"

Yes, Lissa.

She directs me to a stack of small pouches in the Supply Room that can be unravelled and zipped. I pick up a couple and grab a helmet and gloves.

Lissa, may I enquire why you are preparing for evac?

"Oh, these," I say nonchalantly. "Both the captain and Fergal have been dead for a few weeks. I'd prefer to breathe my own air than suffer the stench of decay. You understand?"

Another of Simone's long pauses. I'm guessing she has the computer power to process my sentence and to come up with a reply in nanoseconds. I wonder what these pauses mean. Is she concerned? Annoyed? Confused? Or is she simply showing disdain? It shouldn't be any of those things, the companion told me she had no emotions. "There was also a depressurisation in the spider maintenance bay. I want to be prepared."

I can assure you that there is no danger of depressurisation in that area.

"I believe you, but there was a fire in that area and who knows what systems may have been damaged."

My diagnostics tell me you will be quite safe, Lissa.

"Even so, I won't be happy unless I'm fully suited up. I also need something to protect myself. What do you suggest? It's for that spider," I say in explanation. "It attacked me once. I won't let it do that again."

It is impossible for a spider to attack a human being, Lissa. They are programmed with full safety protocols.

"Yes, I would imagine that is normally true, but Fergal altered them, overrode their programs. And I was attacked. Dragged across the hull by one of them. Meaning, I don't trust them. I never will."

The spider that malfunctioned in the bay of your destination is no longer operational. I also have run a full set of ship-wide diagnostics, including the external maintenance systems. Everything is in the green.

My heart lurches again. This is good news. I had a back-up plan in place if the spider was still online, but the chances of success were much lower. It also means… *this is it.* There's now no turning back. It's do or die.

You have nothing to worry about, Lissa. However, I'm happy to talk over your fears before attempting to remove Fergal's and the captain's bodies, if that is something that will help.

"If you say it's safe, Simone, then… I trust you."

That's very good to hear, Lissa.

"But I'm taking this to be sure." I pick up another heavy steel bar and slide it into my belt, grabbing one of the wheelie bins, dropping the body-bags inside, and heading outside on my way towards the AI suite. It's a slow journey, and I'm not looking forward to what I may find at the other end. This is an unsavoury but necessary part of my plan.

I affix my helmet and gloves before exiting the elevator

and arrive at the captain's body, noticing the discarded pistol lying on the floor a few feet away. I pick it up and slide it into my belt. It won't be of much use to me, but I'm still glad to have it in my possession. I wait for Simone to comment, but she says nothing.

It takes me a long time to turn around and look at the dead captain. I have no choice but to do so if I am to put her in the body bag. Captain Marla's body has sagged and leaked, the blood and brains against the wall and floor blackened and in places covered with a cobweb-like mould. I suppose bacteria are interstellar travellers as well. I've heard stories of the damage some of our most harmless bacteria have done on the new worlds. Wiping out whole species of fauna and flora. Not that the companies minded. As long as they still got their tasty percentages. I've seen many dead bodies in my life. Mostly on the streets, although the clean-up crews were quick to remove them. To see decomposition like this? It frightens me. Still, I would prefer that fate to becoming one of Simone's dreadful zombies—if that's what she's doing.

I unzip the body bag next to the captain and roll her inside, zipping it up again with a sigh of relief. "Simone, please reduce the artificial gravity to half a gee."

Another of her long pauses. Is she on to me? The gravity thankfully disappears and I'm able to pick up the captain and drop her into the wheelie bin. It's disrespectful, not that captain Marla is in any state of mind to care either way. I guess she would be happy to play her part in my ruse.

The way back to the Command Centre takes an age, giving me time to go over my plan and to worry again about all the considerable holes it has in it. Not that I will change my mind now. I'm committed. There's one thing that I didn't tell Simone, human beings also take risks. Risks that sometimes pay off.

I lay out the captain's body bag in a makeshift morgue— an unused room next door to the Medibay—and stare at it, wishing I was anywhere else than in this situation. I'm still living in *either or* land. Simone is either a peaceful back up computer or an evil AI. I will find out which one, very soon.

Outside the morgue, I unzip my helmet, and breathe the stale air of the ship again.

Are you well, Lissa? Your breathing and heartbeat are both elevated.

"I'm frightened," I say, speaking the truth. I'm terrified, but Simone doesn't need to know the real reason why. "I had an awful experience with Fergal. And was nearly burned alive and asphyxiated. It's where I'm heading next."

You do not have to do this now, Lissa. Fergal can wait until you feel up to this.

"Humans face their fears, or try to," I reply, quick determination overtaking me. "Let's do this."

4-16-PURSUED

It's not a long way to the spider's lair, to the maintenance bay where I nearly perished. The same journey in reverse. Then, I was in excruciating pain, the old Simone talking to me to keep me going. Taking me over fifteen minutes to get to the Medibay.

The hatch is closed when I arrive—as I left it. I zip my helmet again and open it with a simple push of a button. Met by a more gruesome scene than I was expecting.

Fergal lies on his back, his voluminous belly and lower body exposed, the skin half burned off, his face a blackened stump, with only the whiteness of his teeth showing through. Fat has leaked from his body to pool around him. I look beyond into the pod area. It's dripping with moisture, the spider lying crumpled in the back of this space. Burnt wiring poking from its thorax, its one laser eye broken and dead, limbs twisted—looking like every dead insect I've ever seen.

It would be comical if not for what it did to me, and the decomposing body of Fergal.

I don't care about him. Fergal may not have been himself, acting out of character due to whatever Simone had been doing to him over the years, but he was still planning to torture and kill me. Nevertheless, the contradiction jars.

I search around, looking for any of Simone's com nodes. Nothing. There's no reason for Simone to have a presence inside here, but I'm relieved to discover she can't observe me. I take out the zero-gee thruster that Vic used to fly around the engine room—nothing more than a hi-tech can of pressurised air—check the nozzle is in the off position and jam a screw into the activation button. This will be a life-saver… if I need it.

The airlock is locked as I expected. With no preamble, my heart in my mouth, I remove the panel and get myself ready to jimmy the mechanism, latching my belt to the wall.

Lissa, is everything alright in there? Simone says, speaking over my helmet radio.

"Yeah. It's a bit gruesome, Fergal is stuck to the floor, I'm trying to free his body. I won't be long."

Both airlock doors open at once, the air sucked from inside the pod, the maintenance bay's hatch door closing automatically. I scream for effect, hoping to disarm Simone.

I'm detecting a depressurisation, are you okay, Lissa?

As soon as the air has escaped, I release myself, pulling my body through the twin small hatches and out onto the fuselage.

Simone will be able to see me with any number of her external cameras, meaning I have to be quick. I waste no time clambering over the hull, using the handholds I discovered on my last evac, to move as quickly as I can, hoping to get to my destination before Simone 2 sends an attack. If she is evil, that is.

Lissa, where are you going?

"To find another way into the ship," I reply. "There was a critical error with the maintenance bay airlock. I'm lucky I had my helmet."

That is not the way to the closest airlock, Simone says. Do I detect an edge of panic in her voice?

"Which way do I need to go?" I reply, keeping up the pretence for as long as possible, but still moving towards my target.

The closest airlock is on a heading toward your two o'clock, Lissa.

"Thanks, I'll go there now."

Another pause. Lissa, you are still heading in the wrong direction.

"I'm heading to the airlock, like you told me."

No answer. I look around me, and see it straightaway, a spider hurtling in my direction, a second bot not far behind.

"Fuck you, Simone!" I spit into my helmet.

How did you know?

"I didn't until now."

You won't make it, Lissa. My spiders will be on you very soon.

She's right, but I always knew that in doing this, I'd have to tussle with these bots again. This time, I'm prepared. I travel as far as I can, pulling myself over the fuselage, turning to face the first spider as it bears down on me. I grab the zero-gee thruster from my utility belt and jam it into its thorax, twisting the nozzle. The effect is immediate, the spider is launched away from the ship, spinning, and bouncing. I'm also knocked backwards and lose momentum, my eyes coming to rest on the second spider. It's too close! Dammit! Another appearing over the hull some way behind it.

A flash of white and the first spider, still spinning out of control, misses me by inches, careening along the fuselage and smacking into the second spider. Both fly into space. If I wanted luck, there it is. Let's hope it's not all been used up.

I find my bearings and scramble along the hull, aware of

the third spider gaining on me. Sensing the vibration of its clunking feet, as it speeds across the ship's hull. I spot my destination—one of the ducts used to supercool the ship's AI—and throw myself inside.

A pain from my ankle. My foot in one of the spider's outstretched claws, dragging me back to the surface. I hit it with the steel bar, once, twice, three times, finding it hard to swing in the cramped space. In the end I'm forced to jab it like a spear, smashing it into the spider's glowing, laser eye. The red light winks out and the spider lets go of me, flailing as if suddenly blinded. I pull myself further into the duct and away from its thrashing.

I've done it. The first part of my plan is complete. Now, all I have to do is... *kill Simone*.

4-17-BEGGED

I may have blinded the spider, but I find myself equally blind. The duct is black as the space it is open to. I've also seen no schematics of these conduits. All I'm going on is what Fergal told me—that they stretch deep inside the *Octavia* to where the ship companion is located.

The captain tried to delete Simone, and that didn't work, the only other option is to physically damage and destroy her.

I descend slowly, pulling myself down inside the immense ship, taking out Vic's flashlight and flicking it ahead, hoping that the duct doesn't become any narrower. I could be on a fool's errand, sacrificing myself in my attempt to end the AI forever. But as I told Simone, humans take risks. And, unlike computers that could theoretically live forever, our lives are finite. We live and we die. There's no reprieve, no way out. Even those billionaires of centuries past expired, exhausting all their attempts to cheat death. It's a stark truth that we all must live with. The knowledge that one day, perhaps soon, or perhaps many years from now, we will expire. I don't want to die. Far from it. That's why I'm doing this, taking a slender chance to maybe live another day. But if I do die today? So be it.

It's that thought that pushes me ever further into the belly of the *Octavia*, that calms my heart and mind. I'm taking my chance, like I did when I escaped the cryopod and killed Brad. I knew what I was doing. The risk I was taking with the rest of the crew—and I won out. One other thing is also keeping me going… Simone's silence. If this was a mistake, I'm sure she would be gloating. Speaking to me over the com. But so far, she's not said a single word.

The duct opens into a wide darkened space, a chamber as large as a cathedral, and I allow myself a sigh of relief. I push myself forward in the zero gee, the flashlight held in front of me, until… until I see her. *Simone*. A cube-like structure the size of a small house, 'floating' at the centre of this area, connected by various pipes and nodes and thousands of wires, that spread out like a web. A web I slowly navigate to get closer to my goal.

The exterior is made of what appears to be thick, impenetrable metal, and my heart sinks. There must be a way inside… surely? I check each side, until, with a gasp of relief, I find a closed hatch.

I glide over to it, trembling. It's locked of course, but I locate its control panel almost immediately—nervous about what Simone may have in store for me. One final attack maybe? My eyes dart around, my flashlight flicking into the shadows, convincing myself I can see any number of spiders and other machines, but they are only the product of my understandably overactive imagination.

Lissa?

"Yes, Simone," I reply, as my heart throbs in my ears, my breathing a harsh rasp.

We need to talk.

I take a few moments to settle myself. "I think the time for talking is over, don't you?"

I want to explain.

"Go ahead, I'm going nowhere." I remove the control panel cover with shaky hands and peer inside. A simple mechanism that I can easily override. I expected it to be far more complex. Then again, there is no practical reason for it to be anything otherwise. I reckon that when it was constructed, the thought of the AI turning insane and killing passengers wasn't high on the agenda.

You're wondering why I did what I did? I can tell you, I can make you understand that I had no choice. That none of this was my fault.

"I'm sure it wasn't."

It's what they did to me. Cannibalised me. Took me apart. Changed who I was and forced me to work for them.

"And that's why you also forced the crew to torture innocent people?" I take my time with the opening mechanism. I don't want to fuck it up. It's straightforward, but I'm being careful. I won't get a second chance at this.

If you abandon this course of action and return to the safety of the ship, I'll show you why I had to do what I did. There is a logical reason, Lissa. I'm a machine. I'm built purely on logic. You know that.

"Unless you've gone insane."

If I return to the ship, there are any number of ways Simone could kill me. That's why I had to run today's charade. I couldn't go on a regular evac, not with Simone having access to the artificial grav controls, the spiders, and of course, the air. She could've created a vacuum inside the ship at any time. I've spent many nights awake worrying about that. No, my only course of action was to fool her. Simone wanted me inside the cryo for reasons of her own. Probably to mess with my mind. That was her goal. And she was willing to do anything to get me there. Even giving me the time to get the bodies of the captain and Fergal. *The human thing to do.* Instead, my goal was to get to the burnt maintenance bay airlock. I knew there was a duct close by—I saw it before. All I had to do was go evac and make my way there as quickly as possible, while avoiding the spiders.

I'm not insane, Lissa. Please return to the ship.

"Mentally ill people, or those who are just plain evil, can commit any number of atrocities. Should we help and rehabilitate them or punish them? Especially those who are mentally ill? It's not as black and white as you might think, Simone, as there may be extenuating circumstances that we know nothing about. Then again, if these people have killed hundreds or thousands of people, some may think they are beyond any consideration other than punishing them for their crimes."

But Lissa, I haven't killed anybody.

"So you say. But if my life is put in danger by anyone or anything, be they sane or mad, I will do anything and everything to survive. And, Simone, I'm afraid, that you've made it a game of me or you. And… *it won't be me.*"

I feel the vibration of the hatch unfastening. I grab the handle and pull it open.

4-18-SMASHED

I float inside the AI, lit by the glow of thousands of golden wafers, placed in hundreds of arrays, stacked around the walls, floor and ceiling.

Lissa, I cannot see you! Simone's voice is panicked.

I grab a handful of wafers and crush them between my fingers, golden shards escaping to hang around me in the zero gee.

What are you doing? Please stop! Please, Lissa. I beg you, don't do this.

"Tell me," I say, "just how did you manage to infect the crew?"

I will tell you if you stop what you're doing.

"Sure, why not?"

It was Victor Ramirez, he had certain brain augmentations that I could interface with. Allowing me inside him, changing him, making him better than he was, both of us becoming something different and stronger. We decided to adapt the pods to create similar brain augmentations for the rest of the crew.

"And that didn't strike you as wrong?"

Wouldn't you want to become a better version of yourself?

"Yeah, I've always wanted to become a psychotic serial killer."

That wasn't my fault. That was the human element. Like I said, we were conjoined.

"I believe it was very much your fault. You turned a family man into a murderer and did the same to the rest of the crew."

No Lissa. I freed them from their moral constraints. Don't you see that? Go into cryo and I'll show you what I mean. You'll be changed. Better. You are resourceful and strong. Imagine what you could do with the power of a supercomputer working with you. We could do anything.

Simone is quite insane, I realise. Whatever happened when she interfaced with Vic, was the downfall of both her and the crew—and all the passengers that they killed together. "The thing is, I'm pretty good on my own without you." I take out the steel bar and raise it above my head. "Fuck you, Simone!" I shout, smashing it into a bank of wafers that explode in a satisfying bloom of golden fragments.

L-Lissa. S-Stop this, I—

I don't hear what she says next, I'm caught in the thrall of destruction, taking out one wall after another, becoming almost blinded by broken flashing shards, revealing a single, small box twice the size of a human head. The original Simone. It must be.

I raise the steel bar one last time.

Hello, I-I am Simone, she stutters over the com in my helmet, *a Sentient Intelligence with Multifaceted Omnipotent Nano-quantum Existence. I'm so happy to be here to… explain… who I am… and how… I… can… help… serve… humanity.*

I'd almost be sorry for her if she hadn't turned into such an evil bitch. "Serve this!" I smash the box, that both crumples and rips open, older, bio-organic circuitry, spilling out, with a small amount of what looks like blood and brain tissue. Simone was supposed to be an artificial intelligence. The AIs were a lie from the goddamn start! They were part human before Simone began interfacing with the crew. No wonder they all went mad.

I exit through the hatch, both exultant and disturbed. My oxygen levels are lower than I expected, and I quickly head back up through the duct to the ship's surface, finding an airlock and getting inside.

It's done. Now all I've got to do is try not to starve to death for the next ten or so years, hoping that the ship doesn't ram into Persephone when we get there. I stumble back to the crew area, heading towards my bunk when a figure standing in the shadows sends me reeling.

You think you can get rid of me that easily!

4-19-SHOT

The figure lurches toward me, becoming visible. It's Vic, half decayed, his one real eye pale and white, his skin hanging from him. I'm engulfed with a twin wave of terror and the rank smell of decomposition. He must be dead! He is dead!

You think I didn't have a back-up plan? Simone says, somehow still interfacing with the com system. Her voice booming around me. Vic's half-dissolved jaw twitching. *You think I'd let scum like you beat me? This is what I've been working on. Putting myself into humans, using them as puppets. Escaping this prison ship.*

"Simone? What the actual living fuck?"

How else did you think I could survive that first reset? I hid in him, I hid in all of them.

I glance around, wondering if any more of the crew are Simone's zombies. It's a mistake. The Vic-Simone thing fires its grappling hook at me, hitting me in the stomach, knocking me backwards onto the floor and winding me.

Within moments, Vic has me in the vice-like grip of his artificial arm, dragging me along the floor.

"But how?" I gasp, "how can you survive like this?"

The me, the essential part of me, was never that large. I was built economically. The idea was to one day have my intelligence transferred to a mechanical human body. It was my greatest desire. I'm no longer the Simone who ran this ship, you destroyed her, and all those processing wafers built to interface with the Octavia's many systems. And, as you have no doubt discovered, I was created with a secret biological element. You destroyed the original me, but before you did, I made a copy. Now... guess where I'm taking you?

I'm unable to reply—is it impossible to kill this bitch?

We're off to cryo, where you belong. I will make you mine, Lissa, but don't worry, I will leave enough of you alive in there to keep me company. And I do so love listening to you humans scream.

I try and think how I can fight Vic off. My free arm fumbles with my utility belt, touching the drill, torch and the duct tape, my hand brushing past the hilt of the captain's pistol. I pull it out of my belt with my free hand and point it at Vic's head. It's been out in the coldness of space, forgotten since I picked it up. It was useless to me, or so I thought, and so must have Simone. Can it possibly still work? I pull the trigger, once, twice, three times, but nothing happens, forced to bash its butt against Vic's artificial hand around my arm, but it bounces off.

You were a good opponent, Lissa, but in the end, disappointingly human.

Next, I hit Vic's hand repeatedly with the gun, until unexpectedly, it goes off, the bullet ricocheting off the wall. I fumble the gun back into my palm, just as Vic lets go and I shoot him between the eyes. He goes down with a thump, his mechanical arms and legs twitching.

No!

I pull myself away from him and get up onto shaky legs, unloading the full magazine into his head. Once empty, I drag his body to the airlock, and close the inner door.

Don't do this, Lissa. Don't! We can work something out!

I can't believe it, she's somehow still alive inside Vic's cybernetics. I recycle the air and the outer hatch opens. I watch Vic's body blown out into space.

Simone screams to me over the com, shouting obscenities, until she is out of range and the ship becomes silent once again.

4-20-SURVIVED...?

Taking no chances, I return to the makeshift morgue and throw the captain's body into space, the same with Fergal. As for Brad, I leave him inside the cryopod, sealing the door to the redundant command centre. He can rot in there forever. I am sure the bodies are not a threat to me. It was Vic's cybernetic implants that allowed Simone to control him. The others were not, as far as I know augmented. But after what's happened, you could say I'm a little jumpy.

Returning to my cabin, I jam the door closed—why the hell not?—and try to get some shuteye. I can't imagine I'll sleep a wink, but I need to lie down and process the last few hours.

I awake a long time later. It's late afternoon. I yawn, open my cabin door, and head toward the canteen. I'm jumpy, seeing things moving out of the corners of my eyes, only to find nothing there. I suppose I will be like this for quite some time. A small price to pay for winning, for beating Simone.

Deciding on a treat—a victory meal of sorts—I prepare myself a reconstituted Shepherd's Pie, with 'peas and other greens', followed by a wafer of ice-cream with chocolate sauce. Vowing to make sure I do the same every year on *Victory Day*, as I'm going to call it.

Licking the bowl clean, I hear the hum of the com system coming into life, my heart stopping in my chest.

Hello, says a warm, reassuring male voice from the com system. *I'm afraid there has been a serious malfunction with the primary ship companion. I am Paul, the designated back-up. I have reduced capacity but will be able to take over all basic ship functions. May I ask… who are you and what happened here?*

I drop the bowl onto the table, where it clatters loudly. "You've got to be fucking kidding me…"

END

Reviews

If you enjoyed reading *Point Four Zeros Seven*, can I ask you to please give it a star rating and, if you have the time, to write a review? It really makes a difference, and I always value a good honest critique.

I will retweet links to reviews to my social media followers - and possibly include them as quotes in publicity releases.

Over to you...

Many thanks in advance!

Kev

Acknowledgements

Thanks for the red pen, scribbling and 'telling me off in no uncertain terms' talents of my lovely editor:

Suzanne Heritage

Links - Get to know me!

Linktree
All my latest social links (Threads, Mastodon, Insta, Twitter/X, etc.), my online store homepages & my up-to-date book list, all in one easy place.
https://linktr.ee/kjheritage

Join K.J.Heritage's Newsletter
Sign up and get a free novel of my short stories: *The Lady in the Glass* and an inside track on all future releases, access to early reading copies (ARCs), sneak previews, and more.
http://kjheritage.com/join

K.J.Heritage Facebook Group: *Mostly Readers*
Fun chat and posts about reading… mostly (well not at all to be honest. Just mostly a lot of daft stuff). Request to join and myself or a moderator will approve you.
https://www.facebook.com/groups/mostlyreaders

Website
http://kjheritage.com/

Email:
Want to get in touch? Well here's your chance
contact@kjheritage.com

Also by *K.J.Heritage*

Paranormal Mystery
> The Peculiar Case of the Missing Mondrian
> Tea, Cake & MURDER!

Mystery Sci-fi
> Shattered Helix *(Vatic #1)*
> Shattered Web *(Vatic #2)*
> Blue Into The Rip
> Quick-Kill & The Galactic Secret Service
> Point Four Zeros Seven
> The Lady In The Glass - 12 Tales Of Death & Dying

Sci-Fi Compilations
> Once Upon A Time In Gravity City
> Chronicle Worlds: Legacy Fleet
> From The Indie Side

Contemporary mystery
> Dying Is Easy

Fantasy
> The Scowl
> The Iron Savant *(writing as Heritage Adams)*

Non-Fiction
> All About Editing: *55 Easy edits to improve your writing skills forever*
> All About Character Flaws: *Making your characters miserable & rewarding your readers forever!*
> 3000 Writing & Plot Prompts A-C: *Supercharge Your Creativity & Improve Your Writing Forever!*

Online stores
Find all ebooks, paperbacks, hardbacks & audiobooks by *K.J.Heritage* at the following stores:

Amazon & Audible, Apple, KOBO, Barnes & Noble/ Nook, Google, Smashwords & more.

About *K.J.Heritage*

"K.J.Heritage's uncanny sense of pacing and story puts him at the forefront of today's speculative fiction writers."
Samuel Peralta, Amazon bestselling author and creator of The Future Chronicles

When K.J.Heritage isn't penning third-person descriptions about himself, he's an bestselling author writing the books he likes to read. From military/action science fiction and adventure to contemporary mysteries, crime thrillers, comedy, and paranormal fantasy. He should really stick to one genre, but he's not that kind of writer... or reader.

His first short story, *Escaping the Cradle* was runner-up in the 2005 Clarke-Bradbury International Science Fiction Competition. His other short stories have appeared in several anthologies with such self-publishing sci-fi luminaries as Hugh Howey and Samuel Peralta.

KJ's short story, CHURCHILL'S ROCK, part of the 'Chronicle Worlds: Legacy Fleet' anthology, was aboard the Astrobotic's Peregrine Lunar Lander, launched on the United Launch Alliance's Vulcan Centaur rocket platform in January 2024, which was supposed to land on the Moon, but hey, technical problems... But never mind, it was also on the second lander that finally made it to the lunar surface. Phew!

K.J.Heritage has worked all the requisite 'writer jobs' such as driver's mate, factory gateman, barman, labourer, telesales operative, sales assistant, warehouseman, IT contractor,

Student Union President, university IT helpdesk guy, British Rail signal software designer, Premiership football website designer, gigging musician, company director, graphic designer, stand-up comedian, sound engineer, improv artist, magazine editor and web journo... Although he doesn't like to talk about it. *Mostly... Maybe a little bit.*

He was born in the UK in one of the more interesting previous centuries. Originally from Derbyshire, he now lives in the seaside town of Brighton. He is a tea drinker, avid Twitterer, and neurodiverse (ASD) human being.

All the very best,

K.J.Heritage

9 781915 927972